Hickory Flat Public Library
2740 East Cherokee Drive
Canton, Georgia 30115

From Scratch

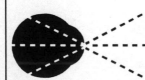

This Large Print Book carries the
Seal of Approval of N.A.V.H.

From Scratch

C.E. Hilbert

THORNDIKE PRESS
A part of Gale, Cengage Learning

GALE
CENGAGE Learning·

Farmington Hills, Mich • San Francisco • New York • Waterville, Maine
Meriden, Conn • Mason, Ohio • Chicago

LIBRARY OF CONGRESS CATALOGING-IN-PUBLICATION DATA

Names: Hilbert, C. E. author.
Title: From scratch / by C. E. Hilbert.
Description: Large print edition. | Waterville, Maine : Thorndike Press, 2016
|Thorndike press large print clean reads
Identifiers: LCCN 2016012164| ISBN 9781410490667 (hardcover) | ISBN 1410490661
(hardcover)
Subjects: LCSH: Single women—Fiction. | Man-woman relationships—Fiction. |
Secrets—Fiction. | Large type books.
Classification: LCC PS3608.I4173 F76 2016 | DDC 813/.6—dc23
LC record available at https://lccn.loc.gov/2016012164

Published in 2016 by arrangement with White Rose Publishing, a division of Pelican Ventures, LLC

Printed in Mexico
1 2 3 4 5 6 7 20 19 18 17 16

To my family of friends . . . God
blesses me each day
through you.

1

The aroma of chocolate, intermingled with caramel, melted into Sean's senses as he crossed the threshold of Only the Basics Bakery. The scents of the little shop enveloped him like a warm sweater in the middle of winter and he suspected any of the dozens of cookies, cakes, and pies on display would vanish as soon as they found their way onto a plate in front of him. He wished he could make the shop's owner, Maggie McKitrick, disappear as quickly.

"Have a look around. I'll be right with you."

Echoing from the backroom, the voice was faceless, but Sean would know its lilt in his deepest sleep. It sent chills up his spine each time he pressed play on his answering machine. He was certain said voice, and the petite body housing it, had nagged nearly an inch off his over six foot frame in the last few months with complaints, threats veiled as needs, and ridiculous upgrade suggestions for the building the voice's owner rented from him.

"I'm so sorry you had to wait," she said as she pushed her way through the swinging door that separated the cozy café from the cramped kitchen. Her eyes focused on the floor as if she needed to measure each step. Wiping hands on her flour-covered apron, she lifted her head — lips stretched wide with a smile, and stopped just behind the counter.

Only the glass display case separated them.

Her eyes locked on his face, sliding her bright grin into a tight-lipped frown. "Oh, it's you."

"It's me." Sean couldn't stop his lips from lifting at the corners.

Maggie might be an annoying tenant, but she was picture-postcard pretty. With her long mass of curly, dark brown hair tied in a messy mound on the top of her head, she appeared nearly an inch taller than her petite five foot three. The only flaws on her face were a few small smudges of what looked like a mix of flour and chocolate on her left cheek. She crossed her arms and leaned against the back counter. "Did you come to fix the back door, or are you just looking for more money, Scrooge?"

Matching her stance, Sean propped his hip against a small café table. The table legs squeaked against the floor with his added weight. "Ms. McKitrick, I must remind you that you haven't paid your rent for the last two months. If you don't pay, I'll be forced to evict you and take you to court. I'm sure you don't want to lose your little business."

She shoved away from the counter. Her hands landed on top of the display case with a thud; her knuckles whitened. The fire shooting from her gaze made Sean thankful for the small barrier the refrigerated case provided. "Don't patronize me, you big bully. I haven't paid my rent because you haven't fixed one thing on my list. In my lease agreement, it clearly states that if the owner, that's you and your never-seen brothers, refuses to keep said property in good condition then the tenant, that's me, has the right to refuse payment. Nothing that needs fixing has been fixed." In one seamless motion, she pushed off of the case and began counting on her fingers. "I have a leaky toilet. The ventilation in the kitchen is spotty, at best. And, you agreed to put an additional deadbolt on the back door when I signed the lease six months ago. I believe the door is still deadbolt free, using the toilet might officially be a medal event in surfing, and I am contemplating seeing the doctor about an inhaler. So, I refuse payment."

Sean raked his hand through his short, blond hair, sucking in a deep breath to soothe the two-headed beast of anger and annoyance rising from his belly. "I've sent handymen over several times in the last two months to fix all of your requests."

"And yet," her arm swung in the direction of the kitchen as her voice shifted from annoyance to what Sean could only classify as exasperation. He recognized the tone. Most of the conversations with his mother during his teen years and after sounded remarkably like Maggie at the moment. "I still have a leaky toilet, bad ventilation, and a lack of proper security. How do you explain that?"

"Perhaps, it's because each time I send someone over to fix your problems, you smile at him, hand him a muffin, a cup of coffee, and offer him a seat in your café." He stepped to the counter, resting his palms on the smooth, cool surface.

She resumed her position against the glass case, mere inches from his face. Releasing a slow breath, her voice lowered an octave. "Well, I was only being hospitable. And it wasn't as if you sent dozens over. Each time, you've sent over Mr. Thompson, who is on the near side of ninety. Aren't you worried he might break a hip or something? Is he the cheapest guy you could find, Scrooge?"

"Taylor." Silently he prayed for calm.

Her head tilted slightly to the right, freeing a piece of her crazy hair. "What?"

"My name is Taylor. Not Scrooge or Big Bully or Meany. It's Taylor. Sean Taylor."

"I know."

"Then I'd appreciate you using my name."

"Whatever," Maggie muttered. Turning from the display case, she began wiping an undetectable mess on the back prep counter.

Scrubbing a hand over his face, he let out a long sigh. "And, I sent over Mr. Thompson, because he goes to my church and I know he can use the money. He would be too proud to simply take a gift, so I gave him the opportunity to earn some of the money he needs doing something he's done most of his life."

Her hand slowed and her shoulders slumped. With the towel stretched taut between her hands she swiveled to face him. "I didn't know."

Gone was the anger and fierce Irish temper. Instead, her face held true compassion, her heart reflecting in her eyes. "I gave him coffee and a muffin every time he came because he looked so worn out." A slight smile touched her lips. "The last time he was here, he told me about his wife, Martha, and how she used to make a homemade pie for dinner every night. He was wiping his eyes with his bandana and I just didn't have the heart to ask him to crawl around on the floor to fix the toilet."

"Martha was great. She gave me and my brothers piano lessons, but we had a hard time staying still long enough to learn anything more than 'Heart and Soul.'" Their gazes met and for the first time in over two months, he saw Maggie. Not his frustrating tenant. Just Maggie. *Focus, Taylor. Rent. Business. Landlord. Any of these ringing a bell?* He took a step back from the counter, shook his head and laced his arms. "Ahem," he cleared his throat. "Ms. McKitrick . . ."

The entry bell jangled announcing a new customer.

Sean shelved the speech he was preparing in his head. No need to have the whole town gossiping about his landlord-tenant issues.

Maggie's expression sparkled as she looked past him and greeted the new distraction. "Hello, Mr. Mayor." She skirted around Sean. Reaching the mayor, she shook his hand.

He was surprised she didn't tug the good ole' boy politician into a bear hug, spreading flour across the crooked tie and rounded belly of Gibson's Run, Ohio's fearless leader.

Sean tightened his arms across his chest as he watched her exuberant greeting. She seemed to love everyone. Everyone but her landlord.

"Good morning, Miss Maggie. How're you today?" The mayor said with a nod of his head and a chuckle in his voice.

"Oh, I'm OK, Mike, except for some . . . umm . . . difficult customers." She rolled her eyes toward Sean. "How'd you like a blueberry-lemon muffin? They're cooling in the back. I made them with organic sugar, unbleached flour, and substituted butter with Greek yogurt. So Beth should be all right with you having a little treat for breakfast." Without waiting for his answer, Maggie scurried to the back kitchen leaving Sean and the mayor alone.

"Chief . . ." the mayor said with a slight tip of his head to Sean.

"Mayor Donaldson, how're you this morning?"

"I'm just fine, Sean." He took a step toward the display case. Rubbing his belly,

13

he perused the decadent contents. "I hope you aren't harassing our sweet Maggie. Seems as if that might be against the law and a conflict of interest." He turned his head and winked a single eye toward the badge Sean wore on his work belt.

"I think it's the other way around, Mayor." Sean leaned against the small café table. This was business. He wasn't leaving without his rent.

Mayor Donaldson twisted away from the display counter and gave Sean a politician's placating grin. "Give her a break, Sean. She's a new business owner. A little lady out on her own without any family support. We here, in Gibson's Run, we need to be her family."

"I appreciate supporting small businesses, mayor. But, it's a business, not a non-profit. She needs to keep up her end of our contract."

Before the mayor could respond, Maggie breezed through the connecting doorway with a small brown box tied with raffia ribbon. "Here you go. I threw in a couple mini-carrot muffins for the assistants at the office. Ask them to stop by and tell me what they think."

"Thank you, Maggie. I'm sure the ladies will love them." He lifted the box from her hands. "I'll take a black coffee, as well, and then leave you and the chief to . . ." He looked from Maggie to Sean and back to Maggie. "Chat." He handed her a few dollars to pay for his muffin and coffee.

Maggie worked quickly, retrieving the mayor's coffee and his change from the register. "Thank you for supporting the bakery. Have a great day."

Taking the coffee, he smiled. "I'll see you tomorrow, Maggie." He gave a slight nod of his head. "Chief, would you mind opening the door for me? My hands are a little full."

"Certainly," Sean pushed off the table. "Have a good day, mayor." The tiny bell jingled as he shoved the glass door open.

"You can follow him," Maggie said over her shoulder as she fiddled with the mugs on the shelf above the back counter.

"Ms. McKitrick, we haven't finished our conversation," he spoke to her back. "I don't want to be tough on you, but you aren't giving me much of a choice."

Waiting for a pithy retort, he took in the full length of her for the first time in weeks. From her slightly gaunt frame to the frayed hem of her chef's coat, Maggie would never be confused with a carefree socialite. Concern bubbled in his chest. *We are her family.* The mayor's words rolled through his mind

15

as a vision of his mother, twenty years earlier wiping down the tables in this very space, superimposed over Maggie. He took a slight step closer. "Are you having money problems? Is that why you haven't paid your rent?"

She spun toward him, the color rising from the base of her neck to her hairline. "I am not having money problems." She tossed the dirty rag in a bucket. "I just don't think I should have to pay when you aren't fulfilling your part of our contract."

He felt heat burn at his collar and his stomach twisted.

She was right.

Sean hadn't been following through with his responsibilities. His brothers trusted him to manage the properties they shared. The other stores and apartments in the strip of buildings the Taylor brothers owned were self-sufficient. Except for the occasional water leak or furnace filter, all he needed to do was collect the checks each month. But Maggie's building was the oldest in their holdings and often needed the most attention. Her complaints were valid. He hated that she was right.

He released a slow sigh. "OK." He raised his hands in surrender. "I give. I'll make you a deal. You close at seven and I'm off duty at eight. I'll meet you here tonight, I'll fix the toilet and the lock, and then you'll give me two months' rent. I promise I will find someone in Columbus with exhaust experience to come in to give an estimate in the next week or two. Deal?"

"Deal," Maggie said with a twinge of a smile in her eyes.

He must have been mistaken. She shared smiles with everyone except him.

"See you tonight." Sean nodded his head in what he hoped was an authoritative manner. Shoving open the front door to exit, he prayed that the woman never committed a crime. He would likely allow her to convince him that he had forced her into the felony.

Maggie hoped the warmth of the shop hid the flush spreading across her cheeks as she watched all six foot three inches of rugged masculinity, with a dimple-cheeked smile and dark brown eyes the color of pure cocoa, walk with purpose toward the police station. How could one man make her angry in one breath and with the next inhale turn her heart into a puddle with his kindness towards an aging friend?

After six months, she would hope her reactions, good or bad, to be simple and straight forward; like nice, sweet vanilla. But when it came to the good chief she was all Rocky Road. "Ugh," she moaned a grunt of frustration.

She slammed open the swinging door connecting the bakery with the kitchen and retrieved the cup of coffee she'd been sipping earlier. Setting amidst the cooling racks of her Better-Than-Your-Momma's Chocolate Chip cookies, her fourth morning jolt had been interrupted by the jingle announcing the chief. Now the coffee cup was cold to her touch. She poured the stale contents into the stainless steel sink as she flipped the switch to start her personal coffee maker. The machine popped and spurted as she rinsed out her mug. No reason to dirty another dish. She would have plenty by late afternoon when various groups from the high school huddled around her café tables.

Out of the corner of her eye, she spotted the stack of mail she'd abandoned with the arrival of the chief. Placing her cup on the long prep table, she sorted through advertisements, offers to win a million dollars, a notice from her bank, and a small sample of shampoo promising to make her hair gleam like diamonds.

The fragrance of the nutty Colombian blend filled the cramped kitchen and drew her attention. She filled her mug, lifted it to her lips for a tentative sip and glanced at the clock. Her interns wouldn't arrive for at least another hour. The time for a leisurely coffee had exited with the chief.

Grabbing the mail, she pushed the door open with her hip as she swallowed another deep drink. She slid onto the tall stool behind the register, continuing to sift through the various sizes of envelopes, throwing junk in the recycling bin and what she needed to review later in a stack on the back counter.

At the bottom of the pile was a wide envelope with a Florida postmark. Her mug slipped from her hand and crashed to the floor. She ripped open the package with a single tear and peered inside. A folded strip of paper slithered from the opening. With shaking hands, she unfolded the note. Her vision blurred as tears pooled, but the scrawled letters across the middle of the page were clear as crystal.

HE'S OUT.

2

An hour after closing, Maggie was lifting one of the last cakes from the display case when she caught sight of Sean crossing the street toward the bakery. Her palms began to sweat. Steady girl.

The note had her jumping at her shadow most of the day. If she wasn't careful, her worries and her inexplicable attraction to him would be a neon sign of confession glowing all over her face, and her landlord would switch into cop mode.

Cop mode translated into attention. Attention meant that her game of hide-and-not-quite-seek would end with her as the loser. *Focus on all of the reasons why you don't like him. Why you can't even think about a relationship with him or anyone else.*

A chill slammed through her body as the image of a pair of thick, black glasses flashed in her mind's eye. Swallowing deeply, she shook her head. She hip-checked the swinging door and set the cake on the stainless surface of the prep counter with a soft clink. Yanking off her splattered apron and well-worn chef's coat, she dusted her hands down the front of her sweater and jeans, sweeping off any stray flour or powdered sugar. She tossed the apron and coat into a plastic clothes basket on top of the day's used towels. With a quick scan of her reflection in a drying cookie sheet, she shrugged her shoulders with a sigh. *Guess it'll have to do.*

She lifted one hand to the door and the other hand to her head, releasing her heavy curls from the makeshift bun she'd erected earlier in the morning. As she walked through the doorway, a soft sigh melted through her body with the wave of tingles rolling over her scalp. For sheer mass, her hair deserved its own zip code. She wasn't always the prettiest girl in the room, but her hair definitely made a statement: Beware Trespassers.

She wasn't too concerned that her curls would frighten the good chief. Despite what she was loathe to call a "moment" earlier today, Sean barely noticed her beyond her rent check, or lack thereof, and she was fairly certain he'd never think of mixing business with pleasure. Not the perfect police chief.

Shaking the weighty bulk with her fingers, she took one additional step into the café to avoid the door tweaking her in the back, and gave herself a pep talk. *Remember, he's your landlord. Not your friend. He's . . . come on! Think of a reason. There were a thousand this morning. He's mean. Well, except for his kindness to sweet Mr. Thompson. And, renting this building to someone with cash, but no credit history. No. No. No. He's mean. He's a bully. He's the landlord. Tonight is business. Stay on the offensive. He's a cop. You can't trust anyone — not even cops.*

The chief walked into the café and her heart dropped to her stomach, crushing all of her arguments with a thud.

Sean pushed open the front door. The jingling bell announced his arrival. His gaze shifted to the connecting door and he froze. Reflexively, he tightened his grip on the handle of his toolbox. The vision of Maggie, hair down and no apron, hit him like a prize fighter in an opening round. Swiping the back of his hand across his mouth, he couldn't tear his gaze from her.

She was catch-your-breath stunning, but her saucy mouth usually curbed her appeal. In the six months he'd known her, he had

22

not experienced the full force of the water-fall of tresses framing her gorgeous face. Seeing her hair flowing around her shoulders made him yearn to tangle his fingers in her curls. He said a silent prayer for God's strength and willpower. Tonight would be a challenge.

A sweet twist of her lips matched the twinkle of welcome in her eyes. She stopped just inside the narrow walkway connecting the dining area and the sales counter. The smile seemed genuine, free from her typical nasty bite.

Maybe they'd made a breakthrough this morning as they'd bonded over Mr. Thompson?

"I really appreciate you coming," she said.

"Well, I'd like to pay the mortgage on the building . . ."

Her smile bent to a snarl. Pivoting on her heel, she said, "Oh, yes . . . the rent." She rammed open the door and let it swing back, nearly slamming into his face.

He sucked in a deep breath and then released air slowly through tight lips. He slid his hand up the smooth wood and pushed the door forward with the barest touch of his fingers. *Thanks, Lord. That helps.*

She waited for him by the first of three prep tables, her arms crossed. Her foot tapped to an impatient rhythm. "I have my checkbook handy. As soon as you finish up, I'll write you a check for three months' rent. How'll that be?"

"No need to give me more than the two months' rent."

She turned toward the back of the kitchen.

He followed as she expertly wove through a delicate obstacle course laid out in the shoebox-sized kitchen, stopping just to the left of the back door. Memories of running through the door to sneak a warm cookie off of one of his mom's trays floated across his mind and squeezed his heart. Closing the final two steps to the rear entrance, he set his tool box on a wooden crate and crouched down next to the door to inspect the existing lock. He risked a quick glance over his shoulder.

With her arms hugging her middle and her brows lowered in a questioning glare, she exuded the intimidation intensity rivaling his former partner.

He suppressed a chuckle. "I can take it from here. You don't need to supervise, unless you don't trust me?"

"Of course, I trust you." A tiny sigh slipped through her lips and her arms dropped to her sides. "I guess if you don't need my help, I'll wrap up the kitchen."

Glancing back towards the bathroom, "Please, don't forget the toilet. One of the interns nearly wiped out on the growing lake in there today."

He nodded. He caught the shimmer of water pooling around the base of the toilet. If he wasn't careful, he could be replacing an entire floor rather than tightening a few nuts. "Gotcha. Lock, then toilet."

She opened her mouth as if she wanted to add a comment. But silently, her lips slammed shut as she twisted away from him and scooted back toward the kitchen. A silent Maggie was definitely more attractive than the speaking version. When she stepped out of his view, he rose and shifted back to project number one, replacing the dead bolt. Staring at the door, he struggled to concentrate on the simple steps he learned from Mr. Thompson when he and his brothers first inherited the building. *Come on Taylor. Get with the program.* Running his hand down the outside edge of the wood, he zeroed in on the existing lock. The facing was severely damaged. He wouldn't be adding an extra lock tonight. He would be replacing one.

He unhooked the latch on the toolbox. Metal clanging against metal echoed off the walls of the tight space as he shuffled various tools. Shoving aside loose nails, tiny screwdrivers and two pocket knives, he found a pew pencil hidden under a receipt for the paint he'd purchased to spruce up the building three doors down from the bakery. He lifted it from the cubby, marked a few spots where he would drill the cylinder for the deadbolt, and then dropped the pencil back into the tray.

Pulling the tiny metal rack from the box, he released a soft sigh at the sight of his coveted and very expensive drill. God definitely wasn't in favor of a love affair with inanimate objects, but this drill was high on his "like" list. He turned the drill in his hand and fit it with the best bit for the job.

In two swift moves, he yanked the old lock from the casing. He scrutinized the damage. The deadbolt was a mess. Someone had broken into the bakery. He glanced over his shoulder.

Maggie was scrubbing a cookie sheet and swaying to the soft sounds of jazz floating in the air. Why hadn't she reported the break-in? Was she unaware? Or maybe she was reluctant.

Telling the police meant telling him and that may have been enough deterrent.

Break-ins were rare in Gibson's Run. A few B and E's from time to time, often by local high schoolers looking for a thrill in a town with only two traffic lights — one of which was always blinking. The police division only employed four full-time cops. As chief, he was one of them.

He stared at the mangled face and shaft. Whoever had taken a fancy at getting into the bakery either really liked Maggie's cakes or had some anger management issues.

He lifted the new deadbolt out of the box and slid it into the opening. The drill whirred, tightening the screws in place. Sliding his hand against the fresh lock and slightly damaged door frame, he scanned the back entrance and parking lot.

A single light, perched on a warped electrical pole, flickered and hummed against the chill of mid-October. Security definitely needed to be upgraded.

He glanced through the framed passthrough window, and his eyes locked on the gentle movement of Maggie's hips as she swayed with the beat. She had an unconscious grace he hadn't noticed before, or rather, he hadn't let himself notice.

From the first moment she walked through the door with his childhood friend, Jane, to enquire about renting the empty building, Sean was struck with her unique beauty and presence. Her smile and unabashed enthusiasm for her new business kindled a desire he could not fan to flame. Instead, he quickly shoved his instant attraction to her onto the back shelf of one of the many cubicles in his brain and plopped her into a folder marked business associate. He was her landlord. He wasn't her friend. He couldn't be her boyfriend.

They were in a business relationship and that was all it should ever be. His brothers trusted him to run their joint properties with professionalism. They would not appreciate him making nice with the pretty baker. Actually, they wouldn't care about the landlord-tenant issue and would probably love for him to make nice with the pretty baker. Then they would have something to hold over his head. One could not underestimate the power of a good burn amongst brothers regardless that two out of three were in their thirties. That's what brothers did. Hassle. Tease. Burn. They might be too old for noogies behind the barn, but they would never be too old for sibling harassment.

Sean wasn't about to give the two yahoos he shared DNA with any softballs to pummel over the back fence of his ego. And yet, at this particular moment, watching Maggie clean up the kitchen, he was having a hard time remembering all of his sound reasons for his not-mixing-business-with-pleasure rule.

But whether or not he should date Ms. McKitrick wasn't why he was here tonight.

He shifted his focus to the parking lot. He needed to talk to Maggie about upping the security, maybe putting in a couple cameras or motion detectors that would be directly tied to the station. He began mentally making a list of the necessary improvements to ensure her safety. It wasn't just because she was renting his place. He'd feel the same need to protect any of his residents. He was the police chief. This was his town. The safety and security of all of the residents was paramount. Sure, that was it.

Maggie lifted a soapy hand and reached for a scrub pad. The faint whirring sound of the drill laid over the woeful tones of a trumpet solo. Jazz warmed her soul. The woeful tunes were an outward voice to her inward pain and nothing she had musically experienced before or since rivaled the peace she found in the melodies. She squeezed the scrub pad to eliminate some of the excess water before attacking the burned caramel coating a large cookie sheet. She was thankful to have the culinary interns, but they were both still learning her ovens and their timing was not quite right.

Today, Anna-Beth, a perky twenty-two-year-old from Portsmouth, Ohio, tried to make a new recipe she was developing for caramel apple cookies. She misjudged the temperature in the convection oven and the cookies ended up as a giant, charred slab of caramel without a speck of recognizable apple to be found. Nothing had been salvageable. Instead of the chewy, apple goodness Anna-Beth promised, Maggie was left with pruned fingers as she attempted to rescue the sheet, scrubbing the pan back to shiny.

The sound of steel wool against metal scraped at her ears, but she released a dreamy sigh. She was living her dream. She owned her own business in a town that was starting to feel like home. Life was peaceful and calm with the exceptions of a certain landlord and unexpected envelopes.

When she opened the package from Florida that morning, her mind had skittered through various exit strategies. She always had a plan. She had multiple. Today's message sent her from high level future concepts into deep dive tactics. She'd run dozens of scenarios through her mind before noon, all while playing happy hostess to her unaware patrons. She shouldn't need any of the plans, her initial design was nearly flawless, but one could never be too cautious.

She hoped she was right; that she was untraceable. Maybe she could finally stop running.

She liked this new dream; this new life.

Maggie's life.

Pruned fingers and burned cookie sheets were a small price to pay. For the first time, in more years than she cared to think, she felt settled and safe, almost unafraid. She wasn't about to let today's little note rob her of stability. She needed to stay calm and alert. If she didn't, the monster would not only haunt her dreams, but she would give him the power to leap into her hours among the living.

She flipped on the faucet, lifting the heavy metal pan under a stream of water to rinse, and then settled it on the large drying rack. She released the stopper and the dirty water swirled down the drain. The popping sound of the water from the expandable sprayer against the metal sink mixed with the whirring of the drill, drowning out the jazz and sucking Maggie's thoughts back to her landlord.

Not that she should have thoughts about her landlord. Well, at least not beyond when the rent was due and maintenance issues, but she couldn't seem to stop. He was like the last brownie in the pan, too tempting to resist.

Sean Taylor. The middle child of Lorraine and Frank Taylor was the only Taylor boy still living in Gibson's Run, not that his status made the family's presence any less tangible. Even though their parents had passed, everyone in town still talked about Frank and Lorraine and their boys as if they were going to walk into her shop any day. There was something all-American, real and sprawling about the Taylor family.

Something Maggie always wanted but never had. She wanted a slice of Americana, simple, sweet, and quietly uncomplicated. And thanks to her little shop and the man fixing her back door she could sense it nearly in her grasp. Maybe Sean was more than just the holder of the key to her building? Maybe he was part of her dream, too? "Well, that's just silly," she muttered as she wiped down the inside of the stainless steel sink.

"What's silly?"

Maggie whirled around at the deep timbre of his voice, flopping soap from her hands onto the floor.

He wore a Henley T-shirt that had seen

better days and equally well-traveled jeans slung low on his hips. He leaned against the tall metal shelf that held various cake pans, cookie sheets, and mixing bowls, and crossed his arms. He looked annoyed. "What's silly?" he asked again.

Heat rose from Maggie's belly, flaming up her neck. "Oh, nothing. I tend to talk to myself."

He stepped away from the shelf, closing the gap between them.

Maggie's stomach dropped. When was the last time she had been this close to a man?

Him.

A shot of ice through her veins slowed her heart to its normal pace. She turned her back. The slow burn of bile replaced the flutter of nerves. A healthy reminder of how quickly butterflies twisted into a swarm of hornets ready to sting. "Are you all finished?" she asked over her shoulder.

"Yep. I'll have to come back later this week to fix the toilet or I'll send someone. It needs a new wax ring and Bauserman's closes at 6:00 PM. I should be able to pick up what I need tomorrow. If you don't mind, I can send Mr. Thompson over first thing in the morning. Just don't distract him, OK?" His voice cracked as he spoke.

"That'll be fine."

He could have suggested that Sissy Jenkins, the town busybody, whom Maggie avoided like a root canal, would be her new barista and she would have agreed. She would agree to anything to give her the space she needed to return to neutral. Nice, happy neutral. "Do you want me to walk you out?" she asked without turning from the sink. She happily would carry him firefighter style back to the police station if he would grant her the space she craved.

The jazz trumpeter's trademark trill seeped through the crowded space as she waited for his response. Gritting her teeth, she turned with the final cookie sheet in her hand. With a sigh, she stretched around him to stack the pan on the rack. Her back against the sink, she looked him in the eye. She always made eye contact. She refused to be frightened of anyone. Not ever again.

He smelled like the outdoors, the kind of aftershave that made her think of men chopping wood, strong men who rescued damsels in distress.

Her heart started fluttering again. *Get it together, girl.*

His eyebrows scrunched as if he was trying to solve a problem.

She didn't think it was the wax ring on her leaky toilet.

"Umm, so . . . umm . . . have you noticed anything missing recently?" he asked.

HE'S OUT.

The bold scrawl of the morning's note flashed through her mind. She sucked in a deep breath as the two ton weight of her past crashed down on her. Scrubbing a hand over her face, she tried to keep her voice light and unconcerned. But she wanted to run.

"I'm sorry. My mind's distracted. What did you say?" She misjudged the space as she moved and her foot landed on the bottom shelf of the baker's rack next to a stack of metal mixing bowls. Instinctively, she lifted her foot to save the bowls from clattering to the ground and tumbled forward into Sean.

He reached out his hands, gently touching her arms to steady her. "Whoa. Are you OK?"

She broke away quickly. Heat bulleted from her toes through her body, flooding her cheeks with color–exploding the butterflies permanently housed in her stomach into a riot. "I'm good. Just a bit clumsy," she mumbled, biting her bottom lip.

He shoved his right hand through his hair and tucked his left in his front pocket, letting out a sigh.

Swallowing, she sidled around him until she stood behind the stainless steel prep table and wrapped her arms around her middle. "Now what were you saying? Am I missing stuff?"

His brows drew closer together, deepening the crease in the middle of his forehead. "Huh?"

"You said something about missing stuff. Why would I be missing stuff?" She released her arms and rested her hands on the smooth metal surface.

"Oh, yeah. Umm . . . it looks like someone tried to tweak your backdoor."

Every hair on the back of her neck stood at attention. Shallow spurts of breath thrust past the knot fighting to rise in her throat. Her hands gripped the edge of the table. She willed her stomach not to reject the chocolate chip cookie she'd eaten just before Sean came. She swallowed, forcing the lump back down her throat. "What do you mean, tweak?"

"The backdoor lock was pretty messed up. Why didn't you mention that earlier?"

A wave of frustration engulfed the fear growing in her belly. "I believe, Chief Taylor, that I've requested a new door lock for the last two months. Wouldn't that qualify as 'mentioning' it to you?"

Sean lifted his hand to his neck and methodically kneaded the space just above his collar bone. "Sorry. But why didn't you tell me that someone tried to break in?"

Lacing her arms, she slowly turned from the table. With a soft push of her shoulder, she opened the door and walked into the café. "Because I didn't know," she said. She dropped onto the nearest chair. The heavy thud of male footsteps stopped to her right. She twisted in her seat, rested her chin in her hand, and lifted her focus to him. His gaze locked with hers and the concern reflected in them tilted her balance. *He's a cop. Don't forget. Sharing isn't always caring. Keep your troubles to yourself.*

He slid a chair away from the table and slowly lowered his long body onto the seat. Leaning back, his arms casually draped across his legs, he waited.

She dropped her focus to the mosaic table top and traced the tiny lines of grout holding the intricate picture together. Her mind raced as she tried to develop a story. Something to appease the questions she could feel brewing behind his focused, police-worthy stare. She should be better at it now, creating new stories. She had been telling stories for most of her adult life. Her finger stopped following the pattern, and she leaned back in her chair, matching his pose.

Shifting forward in his seat, he rested his elbows on the table. "Do you have any idea who would want to break in to the bakery?"

A flash of thick glasses and a twisted grin shot through her mind. She hugged herself tight, shook her head in the negative, while her heart screamed, "Yes!" She shrugged her shoulders. "Maybe someone was super hungry and couldn't wait until I opened?"

A grin lifted Sean's lips and deepened his left cheek dimple. "I haven't had much of your baking, not being your favorite person and all, but I can't imagine committing a crime for a loaf of bread or a muffin."

"Jean Valjean did."

"Who?"

"Jean Valjean, *Les Miserables,* the Hugo novel? They turned it into a musical and a movie and it won all kinds of awards?"

"Not much of a musical theater guy." He shook his head and winked.

"Oh." Biting her lip, she tried to think of a reason to kick him out. She needed time alone. Time to review her plan. Strategizing and scenarios would grant her the peace she required. "Guess you have a busy day tomorrow?"

He nodded and again with the furrowed brow. She was tempted to offer him advice on an anti-wrinkle cream she just discovered. At this rate, he would need a vat of the stuff before he reached his next birthday.

"I don't want to keep you." She moved to stand.

He reached out his hand to stop her. "Maggie, I would like to clear the air."

A bubble of panic seemed to expand to dome-size, causing her breaths to shift from slow and steady to a short staccato rhythm. Clear the air? She relied heavily on her air being just a bit foggy. "What do you mean?"

"You and me."

At warp speed, her panic bubble burst as her resident swarm of butterflies dive bombed her stomach. "You and me?"

Releasing her wrist, he lifted his hand to his neck, kneading it as if he was trying to press the air out of a batch of twelve grain bread. "Well . . . what I mean is that you and I, we don't seem to get along very well."

A subtle, soft mist of sweet calm washed over her.

He wanted to talk about their business relationship.

She relaxed against the back of her chair. "You could say we don't always see eye-to-eye. Sometimes you make me a little, what's the right word, angry?"

"Just a little bit." His smile stretched into

his eyes, again deepening the dimple in his cheek. "How about we start from scratch? Truce?" He extended his hand to her and waited.

She fought against the tremor of delight that shimmered through her as his strong fingers wrapped around her hand. In his warm grasp, her hand felt tiny, as if he could crush every bone with the slightest squeeze. And yet, with the simple touch, she felt his protective strength race through her. This was a man who protected women. She had almost forgotten about his species.

"Truce," she said, lifting her gaze to meet his. Those chocolate brown eyes melted the last block of the wall of ice she raised around her heart, a makeshift fortress against her attraction to him. She was in trouble.

His grin deepened. He released her hand and stretched his long legs under the table, linking his fingers at his waist. "It'll be nice not to have to drive to a fast food joint every morning to get my coffee."

She stood and moved to the display case, breathing deeply, thankful for the separation a few steps gave. "You go to a drive-through every morning instead of buying a cup of coffee from me? Now I am offended." She slid open the door to retrieve the plate of salted caramel brownies, the last dessert standing in the refrigerator case, forgotten with his arrival an hour earlier.

With her free hand, she shifted a French press under the hot water tap attached to an elaborate coffee and espresso machine, and flipped the lever to a slow stream. With a plop, the ground coffee settled on top of the water and she stirred. She placed a brownie on each of two small plates. Balancing the plates and forks in one hand and the French press and mugs in the other, she crossed the half-dozen steps to the table and set the coffee in the center.

"The coffee will take a couple more minutes to brew, but then it will go perfectly with these."

Placing one brownie in front of Sean, she slid onto her seat, the other decadent dessert wooing her. She pressed the tines of her fork into the soft gooey texture. With the small bite of brownie, her eyes closed as the symphony of sweet and salty flavor melted over her tongue and reminded her of why she selected pastry arts over savory cuisine. "Mmmm." Everything was better with a little chocolate and caramel. She opened her eyes and stared straight into wide, dark brown ones. She could feel her cheeks grow warm. "Sorry. I really like brownies."

"I guess."

She reached for the French press and swallowed against the thickness in her throat that had little to do with the brownie. With a hiss of air, she lowered the plunger filling the small area with the delicate aroma of the dark roast. Pouring coffee into each of the cups, she handed one to Sean, before picking up her own and leaning back in her chair.

He lifted the mug to his mouth, taking a tentative sip. A deep sigh escaped his lips. "Amazing."

"No more drive-through coffee, agreed?"

"Agreed." He took another deep drink, and then set the cup beside his plate. Grabbing his fork, he drove it into the brownie and shoved a bit into his mouth. A slow smile stretched across his lips. "Awesome," he said. "Simply, awesome." He pointed to the brownie with his fork. "What do you put in these things?"

She shrugged her shoulders. "Just chocolate and some caramel."

"That's a straightforward lie. You must get some special ingredient from heaven because this is the best thing I've ever eaten. And that's saying something, since my mom used to own this place."

"Your mom owned this place? I thought this was just a building you and your brothers owned together."

"She was the last one to have a bakery here. I'm surprised someone in town hasn't mentioned it to you."

"They may have tried, but I usually change the subject or find another room to be in when you or your family becomes the topic of conversation." She lifted her coffee cup and drank deeply, averting her gaze.

He chuckled, "That bad, huh?"

Flush burned her cheeks. "Sorry. I know it's a sin to be angry, so I just tried to avoid sinning too much."

"Well, I'm glad we called a truce then. I wouldn't want to be the source of your daily confession to Jesus."

"Me, too."

"Well, you are sitting in what used to be Taylor's. Just one word. My mom wasn't big on fancy. She always said if people in this town didn't know who the Taylor was or that she baked, then they weren't from Gibson's Run. When my dad died, Mom was all alone with three boys. I was twelve and Joey was only five. We were both too young to do much. Mac was sixteen and tried to keep the farm going, but she knew it was a futile battle. She tried to sell the

43

farm land to Henry Grey, your friend Jane's dad, but he refused. He didn't want us to lose our 'legacy'. Instead, he leased the land from my mom.

That money was enough for her to buy this building and a small house in town. She rented out the upstairs apartment and went to work doing the only thing she ever truly loved doing, besides being a mother. She worked six days a week in the bakery, from the time I was thirteen years old, until the cancer made it impossible. Closing the store was the hardest thing my brothers and I had to do after her death. It was like losing her and Dad all over again."

Maggie stretched across the table and brushed her fingers across his hand. "I am so sorry, Sean. I had no idea." She glanced around the shop. "This was your mom's bakery? Huh. I figured it was a little café or coffee shop or something. I just thought I was super blessed to have the industrial mixer and dishwasher already in place."

"We've had a few cafés try to start up in the space over the last ten years, but nothing has lasted more than a few months. We've never had any problems renting out the other spaces, but then again, we were more flexible with what we would let go into them. Mac, Joey and I always said this needed to be a bakery. That's what mom would've wanted. But it's kind of hard to find bakers who want to locate in Gibson's Run." The corners drew up on his mouth. "Then you came along."

She sighed and withdrew her hand. "Then I came along."

Through the high-performance wide-angle zoom he could see her stuff a curl behind her ear. The rapid-fire click-click-click of the camera was the only sound in the tiny car. Her hair was different, but he would fix it. Once he had her back where she belonged, he would fix everything. The hair, though irritating, was a minor inconvenience. He lowered the camera from his face and could almost hear her laugh. The musical quality of it had transfixed him when he first met her nearly a decade earlier.

That stupid cop was laughing through whatever mundane story she was feeding to him.

His hands tightened against the lens. He would teach her that she couldn't talk to other men like that, igniting their lust. But he would be fair.

She would have her lessons, and if she resisted she would have to suffer the pain of her sin. There were always consequences when one sinned. She would eventually bend to his will. Women were supposed to submit to their mates, God ordained it. Once she learned how to be obedient, they would be happy together. God sent her to him. She was meant for him.

He set the camera on the console and twisted, lifting a three-ring binder from the passenger seat of his rented car. He gently turned the plastic covered pages filled with pictures of her, his Mary Margaret.

He hated that she called herself Maggie now, such a common name.

Who was Maggie? Did Maggie sing like an angel or listen to him as if his words came directly from God? No. No, Maggie lived in this backward town, in a backward state in the Midwest. Maggie dressed in a tent and looked as if she belonged in a refugee camp. His Mary Margaret was a lady. She was a beautiful vision from God. She belonged to him. He would just have to remind her. God had given her to him, until parted by death. She would learn that they were forever; he just had to teach her the proper lesson.

Patience. Good things come to those who wait.

And Mary Margaret was a very good thing.

3

The following morning, Sean walked into the station and found the other officer on duty already at his post; with his feet propped up on his desk, he snored like a bear in hibernation.

Alvin Murray was an OK guy, but he was the kind of cop that required Sean to be on duty simultaneously. Alvin had been counting down the days until he could cash in his retirement benefit check and move to his houseboat on Buckeye Lake since a week after graduating the academy. On Alvin's best days, protecting and serving the residents of Gibson's Run was an afterthought. Thankfully, the town didn't require any real police work beyond the occasional traffic ticket.

The door clicked closed behind Sean. Crossing the four steps from the main entrance to Alvin's desk in two seconds, he set two cups of coffee and a bag of muffins from Only the Basics on the paper-strewn surface.

Alvin's response was a snort and a soft whistle through his lips.

Should I wake him? He looks awfully peaceful.

The ring of the main phone line interrupted his thoughts. He glanced at his deputy.

Alvin didn't budge.

Sean reached across the desk to answer the phone. "Police."

"Hello. Chief, it's Sissy Jenkins."

Sean knocked Alvin's feet off the desk with a thump and rested his hip against the now open space.

The deputy rubbed his face with the back of his sausage-fingered hand and scratched his belly as he looked at Sean.

Sean rolled his eyes, focusing his attention on the caller. "How's it going, Sissy?"

"Well, Chief, I'm a little worried." Of course, Sissy was worried. She was born worried. At least once a day she called to inform him of her latest worry. He always felt as if Sissy should have business cards created: World's Biggest Worrier — will worry for you, about you, with you, and because of you — free of charge.

"What is it that's got you worried?" Today.

"Well, there's been a strange car parked down the street all morning."

"All morning, you say?" Sean looked over the stack of reports sitting in Alvin's in-box and found two on top that had little more than the date typed. He slid the reports across the desk to Alvin, who was sipping from one of the cups of coffee, and lifted an eyebrow.

Alvin rubbed his hair and sniffed at the coffee's lid.

Sissy chattered in his ear. "Why yes, Chief. There's been a gold foreign sedan with Maryland plates parked a block up the street for over an hour."

Sean closed his eyes and pinched the bridge of his nose. "I'm not sure that an hour is really something to get worried about, Sis." Opening his eyes, he glanced at the disarray of papers. He shuffled them and spied a complaint filed by Sissy a week earlier. He yanked the paper from the pile, snatched a pen out of the Merry Christmas Dad mug, drew a large question mark on the top of the page, and shoved it in front of his deputy.

Alvin sucked in a mouthful of coffee with a shrug of his shoulders and turned to boot up his computer.

Dropping the report back into the pile,

Sean rubbed the base of his neck. He could feel a headache building. Maybe he was allergic to Sissy Jenkins. He seemed to get a headache every time she filed a citizen's complaint. Listening to Sissy was similar to sitting through his high school World History class — he knew the words coming from her mouth were important, but every last one of them ran in one ear and out the other.

She prattled on for countless minutes. And then there was a pause, just the sound of her breath coming through the phone.

Aww, man. She's waiting for me to say something. What was she even talking about?

He cleared his throat. "I'm sorry. What did you just say?"

Sean could almost feel the heat of Sissy's sigh before she rewound her soliloquy. "What I was saying, Chief Taylor, is that I filed a complaint last week about the very same automobile. It was parked across the street all night last Sunday evening and I saw it two weeks ago for two days straight just sitting in the parking lot of the bank."

Sean shifted on the desk and looked out the large picture window overlooking Main Street toward the bank. "Did you ever think that someone may have moved to Gibson's

Run from Maryland?"

"Well, I would know if someone moved to town."

"Yeah, I guess you would." He puffed out a breath. "Maybe this person is on an extended visit with someone who lives on your street?"

"Chief, I am not an alarmist, but I do keep track of what is going on in my neighborhood. Trust me, if someone was visiting from out of state I would know about it."

Sean thought he heard the faint tinkle of drapery hooks in the background. "I'm sure you would."

"Chief, I do not like your tone of voice. You forget I was friends with your mother. She would be very disappointed knowing you are treating me like this."

The mother card always worked on Sean. "Sissy, I'll send Officer Murray over as soon as we get off the phone. He can take your statement and check out the car. How'll that be?"

"Well, I guess it's better than nothing. Sean, I am not crazy. There is something not right about that car. If you have a pen and paper I can give you the license number right now."

"Alvin will be over in fifteen minutes. He can get all of the details then. We'll keep all of the important information together that way. OK?"

"I guess that'll do. I just know something is amiss."

He drew in a long breath. "I believe you. We'll look into it. Have a good day." Sean hung up the phone before Sissy could discover something else she wanted to share.

Sissy Jenkins was a kind enough woman, but she accounted for nearly fifty percent of the paperwork at the police station.

"Alvin. Sissy Jenkins is seeing some suspicious behavior in her neighborhood. I need you to go over and take her statement."

Alvin swiveled his chair and faced Sean. "Seriously? I have a stack of paperwork to get through. Can't you go take her statement?"

"Nope. You volunteered yourself when you were taking a nap this morning."

Alvin released a long sigh and thrust himself away from his computer, the wheels of his chair wobbled as they spun. He yanked his city-issued, deep blue windbreaker off the hook. He thrust his arms in the sleeves, and the GRPD embroidered above the chest pocket threatened to pop threads as he tried to zip up the front. Failing, he glared at Sean. "If I didn't know better, I'd say you just like giving me stupid work."

"If you didn't fall asleep at the office, you wouldn't volunteer yourself so often. Have fun."

Alvin jerked open the door and stomped away without a word.

Sean couldn't suppress the pull of his lips as he watched Alvin wriggle behind the wheel of one of two GRPD police cruisers. Turning his back to the window, he nudged open his office door with his foot, and quickly scanned the tidy contents of his desk. The inbox was empty. His pen holder held seven black ink pens and a mono-grammed coffee cup rested on a cork coaster. Dropping the bag of muffins in the center of his desk, he gulped a quarter of his coffee before swapping the ceramic mug with his to-go cup from the bakery.

He slid into the high-back office chair and tugged at the bag. He could smell the blueberries and lemon before he opened the sack. Maggie sure could bake. Thank God for the truce. He shoved his mouse to wake the computer from hibernation, and the office hummed with the soft buzz of the motor. As the screen flickered from black to blue to a security warning, he sank his teeth into his muffin, followed by another quick sip of coffee.

The coffee was now more room temperature than hot, but the flavor was better than one hundred cups of fast food's best. It must be the brewer. Maybe she put something extra in the water? Or the beans? He took another sip and sighed. Fast food joints could do fries . . . coffee was Maggie's domain.

Despite the two months of back-rent now paid and near constant nagging, Maggie was an excellent tenant. Her business was growing daily. She had loyal customers, the mayor included. Both his brothers would be home in a little over a month for Thanksgiving, and he thought they'd be pleased with the woman trying to fill their mother's shoes. No one would ever fully take the place of Lorraine Taylor in this town. But Maggie McKitrick was definitely bringing a wonderful bakery to life in little Gibson's Run. Shifting his attention from the bakery to his computer, he tore off another piece of the muffin and popped it into his mouth. And now he was enjoying the benefits.

Hours later, Sean was elbow deep into filing reports with the County Sheriff and the City of Columbus concerning a string of petty thefts in the area, likely the explanation for Maggie's break-in, when Alvin returned to the office with the stealth of an elephant being attacked.

Lifting his head, Sean peered through the glass wall that separated his office from the rest of the station.

Alvin plopped into his chair before laying his forehead on his crossed arms.

Sean had to hear this story. He dropped his pen and closed the short distance. Leaning his hip on the edge of the desk, he casually laced his arms. "So, how was Sissy?"

Alvin raised his head. His eyes held the misery of a man who had been sentenced to life in prison or one who had spent two hours with Sissy Jenkins. For some, two hours with Sissy might be worse than life in prison.

"That bad, huh?"

"She had pictures and a detailed log. Whoever the owner of the car is could probably file stalker charges against her. She wouldn't let me leave until I promised to do a full background check on it and the owner."

"Pictures and a log?" Sean asked.

"Take a look for yourself." Alvin slid a small drawstring satchel across his desk.

Lifting the bag, Sean unknotted the string, stretching the top to reveal the contents: a small spiral notebook, a packet of pictures sealed in a Ziploc bag, and a thumb drive. He drew each of the items out of the bag and laid them on the desk between him and Alvin. He flipped open the notebook to the first page.

'Thursday, October 4th, 10:15 AM.'

Sissy's writing often slipped from straight English to the shorthand she'd used as her husband's secretary. He hoped that she'd written enough in the good old-fashioned alphabet for him to translate. The detailed record cataloging Sissy's suspect's day-one movements spanned the first four pages of the notebook. Mrs. Jenkins had been a busy lady.

Sean quickly scanned the remainder of the pages; noted times and dates for the movements of the questionable vehicle. Two solid weeks of detective worked logged with methodical precision.

Alvin was right.

Mrs. Jenkins was a stalker posed as a concerned citizen. Definitely a dangerous combination. *Maybe I should hire her.* A shudder ran through his body at the thought.

"So, what do you want me to do, Chief?" Alvin asked.

Sean stood up and unsealed the Ziploc bag with a rip, tossing a dozen pictures onto

Alvin's desk. Casually fingering the photos, he lifted his gaze to the deputy. "Run the plates, and then give her the guy's clean report."

"Do you want to talk to her about boundaries?"

"Naw. She's just lonely since Mickey died last year. Keeping tabs on everyone in the neighborhood makes her feel useful. We may want to omit her activities, when and if the owner of the car comes in to complain. She doesn't mean any harm." Sean stacked the photos and laid them on top of the journal. He fingered a grainy photo on top of the pile of a man walking from the car wearing a hoodie, jeans, a ball cap and what he thought could be thick glasses — likely the owner of the car. He hoped he didn't have to meet him in person. He would be forced to explain Sissy. And explaining Sissy took finesse he didn't always possess.

"Whatever you say," Alvin said and turned to his computer.

Sean walked back to his desk, hollering over his shoulder. "Don't forget to check out the license plate. It's probably nothing, but Sissy's bound to be right sometime, statistically speaking."

4

The subtle sounds of soulful, New Orleans jazz filled the café bakery as Maggie rang up a coffee to-go and half a dozen cupcakes for Jenna Arnold. "Let me know what Tyler thinks of the strawberry shortcake cupcakes. I'm not sure I love the consistency, but I wanted the surprise of the strawberry to be inside." She handed the kindergarten teacher her coffee and a square craft-paper, brown box filled with her newest cupcake variety.

"I'm sure he'll love them, Maggie. He loves everything you make. He wishes I could bake like you." She lifted her shoulders in a shrug. "This'll be a wonderful treat for him. He has the Bar coming up and he's been studying like crazy."

"I'm sure he'll do great. Enjoy the cupcakes. When he passes the Bar, tell him I will make him any treat he wants. His choice . . . on the house."

Jenna's face shone. "That's so nice." She gave a quick wink. "And, it will be excellent motivation. He'll be sure to pass on the first try. See you later."

Maggie waved as Jenna pushed open the door, balancing the coffee cup on her box of treats. She dragged her gaze back to the shop and noticed Mr. Hopper's empty coffee cup. She grabbed the coffee pot. "Mr. Hopper, can I top you off?"

He looked up from his copy of the *Dispatch,* shook his head, and smiled. He was near eighty and had a fondness for long, sweater cardigans, bow-ties, and newsboy hats.

Maggie's own grandfather had passed away when she was only six years old, but she liked to think he would have been just like Mr. Hopper. "You let me know if that cup gets cold. We'll get you some fresh. OK?"

"You're too kind to me," he said with a pat on her hand.

"Anything interesting in the news, today?" She asked.

"Just the same crime and exploits. Makes me glad that my Annie and I moved to Gibson's Run fifty years ago."

"No crime in Gibson's Run, Mr. Hopper?"

His head tilted to the side. His caterpillar-like eyebrows drew together. "Well, now that you mention it. I ran into Sissy Jenkins at the bank the other day and she couldn't stop chattering about a strange car parked up the street from her house, but I don't think it's anything for you to worry about, Miss Maggie. That woman could find a nefarious character in her bowl of oatmeal."

Her stomach twisted at the mention of a strange car.

Sissy was irritating, but she was observant.

"Did Sissy happen to say why she thought the car was suspicious?" Maggie's body tightened with wariness.

He shook his head. "She might have, but when Sissy talks my ears tend to hear white noise." He patted her hand. "Don't you worry. Gibson's Run is too small for anyone to get away with much of anything. If there are degenerates running around town, that Taylor boy will find them. Won't be too hard, neither. Why, they'll stick out like a corn stalk in the middle of a soy bean field."

She nodded in affirmation as she turned from his table. Sucking in a deep breath, she lifted a silent prayer that his words were true. She cleared another table and placed the remnants in a gray bus tub with dishes and flatware accumulated over the last few hours. She was grateful for the frustrating task. It kept her hands busy and shoved her consuming worries blissfully to the back of her mind.

Business was steady. Only a few months into her little adventure, she felt good about where she was headed. She replaced the coffee pot on the warmer and hoisted the bus tub against her hip. Slamming through the swinging door with her shoulder, she called out to her intern. "Anna-Beth. Hey, do you mind running the dishwasher?"

"No problem," Anna-Beth shouted from the back pantry.

Hitching the bin higher on her hip, Maggie continued. "Have you seen Steve? He's supposed to be working on the dough for the bagel order in the morning." She dropped the tub into the sink and continued toward the back room, wiping her hands against her apron. "Anna-Beth, are you in the pantry?" She yanked open the door.

As if they'd been splashed with cold water, her two interns jumped apart so quickly they banged the metal shelves, crashing boxes of baking soda and cans of baking powder to the floor in a puff of white.

Anna-Beth tugged at her chef's coat.

Steve began wiping his mouth in rhythmic circles.

"What are you two doing?" Maggie was so stunned her voice barely raised an octave.

Steve shoved his hands in his pockets. "Well . . . um . . . I came in here to get some dry yeast because, you know, we used up all of the cake yeast this morning. And then, Anna-Beth came in to get some flour and . . ."

Maggie closed her eyes and scrubbed her face with her hands. "I don't need a play-by-play, Steve. How long has this been going on?"

The two interns had only been working in her shop for a couple weeks. That couldn't be enough time to start a make-out-in-my-boss's-pantry relationship, could it? Of course it was.

She'd fallen that fast once.

Steve's eyes drew tight into a squint. "Umm . . . what do you mean by this?"

"This," Maggie's hands started to wave in giant circles. "Faces-suctioned-together-in-the-pantry, that this. What other this did you think I meant?"

"Oh, well, I guess about two weeks or so?" Steve asked, with a shrug toward Anna-Beth, whose face was growing dangerously red.

"Two weeks?" Maggie spun back toward the sink. Slamming dishes from the bin into the industrial dishwasher, she mumbled. "Two weeks? Two weeks? I can't even tell the chief I think he's got a nice smile and I've known him for six months." Two weeks? How did I not notice? She stopped, wiped her hand on a towel and twisted back toward the pantry. "You're fired. I am sorry. I hope you are happy together, but I won't — can't — have employees fraternizing during business hours. We discussed what acceptable behavior looked like when you both started. Between this and some of the kitchen mess ups, I just can't have you here anymore. Understand?"

Both interns' heads bobbed up and down as they shuffled out of the small room.

Maggie's shoulders sagged. What just happened? She'd just fired her only help; that's what happened. She sighed. No use whining over spilled baking powder. She needed to start the dishwasher and get busy with dough prep. The mess in the pantry would have to wait.

Several hours later, Maggie was wiping down the largest table in the café after the "cool-girl clique" left. During the week, the table was inhabited by nearly every teenage posse and senior ladies group in town, but not at the same time. They always seemed to time their visits so that when one group vacated another was waiting to pounce. Business was business, regardless of how annoying some of the clientele might be.

Not that she was complaining. One cup of coffee per group member was better than zero cups of coffee, even if they did split one piece of cake between eight forks.

She shifted her fifth bus-tub of the day to balance on her hip, wiping the spot where it had rested with her rag. Tossing the damp cloth in the bin, she glanced at the clock mounted above the entrance to the kitchen, ten till seven. She could survive.

What could possibly happen in ten minutes?

She carried the tub back to the dishwashing area and lowered it into the deep stainless steel sink. Separating the dishes, she tried not to think about the fact that she was officially intern-less. She was on her own for the bagel order of twenty-dozen in the morning. And, for the Fosters' anniversary cake that weekend. And, the Saturday doughnut rush. And, for every other day until a new class of students started in the winter.

The winter quarter started in January. January was nearly four months away. In four months she would likely be in the crazy house and out of business. She needed to get help. Cheap help. And, she needed it two hours ago. *Dear Father, what am I going to do?* She hauled down the top of the dishwasher and started the machine.

At least you don't have to wash the dishes by hand.

She felt a twinge at her lips. Leave it to Jesus to bring her crumbling life into perspective. He was good at gently whispering reminders of how blessed she was. Looking heavenward, she sighed. "Thanks. I just needed a little, friendly reminder."

The bell announcing a customer chimed through the store and Maggie's aching shoulders dropped. "One more to go," she muttered. She wiped her hands on the towel resting on the sink, plastered a smile on her face, and shoved the swinging door open into the café.

Standing barely inside the door, bathed in the setting sun, was Sean Taylor.

Maggie smiled with genuine warmth. "Well, Chief, twice in one day. How'd I get so lucky?"

His left dimple deepened as he spoke. "Well, Miss McKitrick, I was hoping you could help me with a couple things." He closed the gap between the front door and the service counter in two long strides. The man was tall and all that height seemed to be in his legs. He rested his palms on the counter and locked his gaze with hers.

The café suddenly seemed to rise twenty degrees in temperature. Maybe the dishwasher was overheating?

"So the things I need help with . . ."

"Huh?" Maggie's head tilted to the side and she thought she could feel her brain oozing out of her ears.

"The reason I came in," he reminded her.

She stood taller and straightened. Maybe if she stood super straight she would retain a small portion of her brain. "Right. The reason. What was the reason again?"

"I haven't told you yet."

"Oh." She turned her back to the display case as she felt heat burn at her cheeks. Could she not go a single conversation without blushing in front of this man? "So what can I do for you?"

"Well, first . . . you can turn around. We called a truce yesterday, remember?"

She pivoted toward him. Her eyes locked their focus on the top of the case. Maybe if she didn't look at him she wouldn't feel like a melting ice cream cone. "How's that?" she asked.

"Better . . . but do you mind if we sit?" He gestured toward the table where they'd eaten brownies the night before.

Her stomach's cadre of butterflies fluttered awake. *Get a hold of yourself. He's being polite. He's your landlord, remember? It's only business. Not cop related at all. I'm sure. Well, nearly sure. And, remember, you've sworn off men.* The man-fast must stay intact. No men, not even men who look like they walked off the cover of a magazine. She glanced at his back as she followed him to the table. Nope. Not even them. *Just say no to men. Stay strong, girl, stay strong.*

He slid a chair away from the table and gestured for her to sit.

She glided into her seat, while he lowered his long body onto the chair opposite. She willed the wings of the butterflies to still as she waited for him to begin.

Sean bridged his fingers, resting his chin on them. "Did Mr. Thompson make it over this morning?"

A smile tugged at her lips. "Yes, he did. And I showed him the leak and then left him alone."

"All fixed, then?"

"No more surfing."

"Good. Good."

They sat in silence, the daily soundtrack of music punctuating the quiet.

Maggie cleared her throat. "You wanted to ask me something. Was it about Mr.

Thompson? I promise I didn't bug him at all. He was out of here in under an hour."

He shook his head. "I believe you. That really isn't why I came over."

"OK. Why did you come over?"

"I don't know if you are aware, but I used to work for the Columbus Police."

Maggie had no idea he had worked or lived anywhere but Gibson's Run, but she couldn't understand why that was important. He didn't think they needed to know each other's life stories now that they were playing nice, did he? She swallowed against the lump thickening in her throat.

He dropped his hands, flattening them against the ceramic tile table top. "Well, I was on the force for several years and I am still pretty close with a lot of the guys."

"So . . . you were a Columbus cop?"

"I was a Columbus cop."

"And?" Point, Taylor?

"Oh yeah, there's this fundraiser, it's a dance really, and somehow I ended up on the organizing committee, so I have to go and I was wondering . . ."

Is he asking me on a date?

"We are looking for someone to cater the desserts, and since we are now in a truce, I figured, who better to ask than you."

The burn of embarrassment rolled

through her stomach. *He isn't asking me on a date. He's giving me a job.* Great. Just great. She stood. "Who better to ask? Yep. Sure no problem. I can make your desserts."

"What's wrong?"

"Nothing. Nothing. The job will be great." She snatched her rag from the table and darted back behind the counter. *How could you even imagine he was thinking anything other than a catering gig? Didn't you swear off all men, anyway? Why do you care?* Man-fast, remember? Man-fast.

He followed her behind the counter. "What's wrong? I thought we were good. Why are you going all . . . all Maggie on me?"

She turned and thrust her finger in his chest. "You can't be back here. This is for employees only, and as of today that includes me and me alone." She knew she was being ridiculous. Why was she mad? Maybe she was tired? She definitely wasn't disappointed he wasn't asking her on a date, was she?

"I'm confused? I thought you'd appreciate the business. And now . . . now you're yelling at me?" He jabbed her in the shoulder with his forefinger. "And, poking me. What's your problem, McKitrick?" He rocked back on his heels, lacing his arms.

"And, what do you mean 'it's only you, now'? What happened to those two kids?"

She sighed. She did appreciate the business. He was being helpful and she was a loon. She rubbed her hand over her face. "I'm sorry. It's been a weird day." She leaned her back against the counter and matched his casual stance. "I fired the interns today after I caught them making out in the pantry. I could handle suffering through their repeated culinary mistakes, but I explicitly told them I had a zero-tolerance policy for fraternization. And then, after just two weeks, they are in the pantry like they were seventeen and under the bleachers at a high school football game. I spent the rest of the afternoon running between the front to ring up customers, and the back prepping dough for this big bagel order in the morning. And, I guess I didn't really understand when you said you had to ask me for something."

He rested his hands on her shoulders, giving them a soft squeeze.

His gentle touch washed a wave of shivers over her body. She raised her gaze and saw genuine concern reflected in the depths of his eyes. She bit her lip, hoping she masked the gentle warmth that bloomed from the core of her soul. "I'm sorry."

He dropped his hands. "You're forgiven." He took a slight step backward. "Not to tread on a sensitive subject, but are you interested in the catering job?"

"I think so. Who's the party planner?"

"Jane Barrett."

She felt her world steady at the mention of her friend who had led her to Gibson's Run. "Why didn't she just ask me?"

"She took over the ball last minute. Our original coordinator went into early labor. Jane and I were on the phone discussing the arrangements and realized the desserts hadn't been finalized. When your name came up, I said I would ask you. I told her I was coming over anyway, so it would save her a call."

"You were coming over, anyway?"

Sean shoved his fingers through his hair. "Well, sure."

She lifted a single eyebrow and waited for him to continue.

"Well, I thought you might have some more of those brownies. Maybe you were going to throw them out." He shook his head and sighed. "That would be a tragedy."

She giggled. "You came over for a brownie?"

He shrugged his shoulders. "Well they're good brownies. Who knew you were going

71

to umm . . . release your frustration on me."

"I guess you deserve a brownie on the house. Have a seat and I'll bring it out for you."

She turned to the display counter and slid open the door.

He walked to the bakery entrance, flipped the open sign to closed, and then slid back into his seat.

She dragged her attention from the delicious cop to her delectable brownies. Lifting the oblong plate from the case, she spied the metal dispenser that held the homemade whipped cream. She plucked the dispenser from the cooler and rested it in the crook of her arm. She set the platter of brownies and whipped cream in the center of the table.

Sean eyed the desserts. He shifted his focus back to her, his dimple deepening in his cheek. "What, no coffee?"

"Give me a second, Chief. I was only born with two hands." She waved her hands in the air as she walked back to the counter. Yanking forks from the silverware jar, she simultaneously picked up coffee mugs with two fingers and then swiped the half-full coffee pot with her free hand and made her way back. She filled each cup, before placing the nearly empty pot on the table, and slid onto the seat across from Sean. She offered him one of the two forks still in her hand.

"You make that seem like a ballet. Perfectly choreographed. I would have dropped the forks, at least."

"Years of restaurant service. Trust me. You have to be able to balance a stock pot on your nose in some of the kitchen spaces I've worked. You get used to having as much in your hands as you do on the prep counter." She depressed the nozzle and a mound of frothy, white cream dressed her brownie. She took a bite allowing the chocolate to soothe the rough edges of the day.

Sean leaned back in his chair with his coffee cup in hand. His watchful gaze rested upon her as he tilted the mug for a deep drink.

The butterflies, long quiet, began to flutter their wings and she felt the sudden rise of heat to her face. She shifted the lukewarm cup of coffee in her hand. She couldn't blame pink cheeks on the mug.

Stupid blushing. She was never quite comfortable being the focus of someone's undivided attention.

He set his cup down and leaned back in his chair. "So, what's this about firing your interns?"

She sighed and traced the rim of her cup.

"They went to find the extra sugar in the pantry, but found it between each other instead."

Sean's face lit up with a grin worthy of a sixth-grade boy. "You're kidding?"

"Nope. Pretty much firing the interns was the low point of the day, but it never really rebounded from there." She stopped her tracing and looked him in the eye. "And it started out so well."

He reached out and gently touched her hand. "Why don't you tell me about it?"

A wave of tingles swam over her body with his touch. She dropped her gaze, focusing on the brownie plate between them. "There's not much more to . . ."

A loud crash jolted both of them.

Sean jerked his hand away and jumped to his feet as an alarm blared from a near distance. He glanced down at her. "Lock the door behind me." He yanked his sidearm from his holster. Slamming the front door open, he sprinted across the street to the police station without looking back.

Maggie stood stunned for a moment before she scurried in his wake and flipped the lock closed. Her heart raced and her thoughts slammed through her mind in a mass of chaos as she watched Sean.

He charged into the police station as

smoke billowed out the front corner. In moments, township fire trucks and county sheriff vehicles swarmed the area, blocking off Main Street.

Maggie swallowed deep breaths, trying to deter the fear that was nipping at her. *Lord, please keep him safe.* For countless minutes she observed the flurry of activity as firefighters hurried into the station and cops taped off the city block. She hoped to see Sean emerge soon. She knew they were nothing more than business associates, maybe borderline friends, but she would feel responsible, if his being near her brought disaster.

The back door! She streaked across the café. She barreled through the connecting doorway and skidded to a stop by the back entrance. Testing the lock, calm washed over her. She must have locked it earlier in the afternoon when the interns left. Turning her back, she slid against the smooth, metal surface and dropped to the floor.

Wrapping her arms around her knees, she huddled in a tight ball and tried to regain her control. She willed the tears ready to spill to retreat. Sucking in a deep breath she counted in her head. 1 . . . 2 . . . 3 . . . 4 . . . 5 . . .

BAM! BAM! BAM!

Her head shot up and she stared straight ahead; her entire body shook like a tuning rod.

BAM! BAM! BAM!

"Open up, Maggie." She registered Sean's muffled voice.

"Sean?" She thrust off of the floor and sprinted to the front of the café.

Sean stood just on the other side of the glass, his face smudged with soot. "Maggie, would you let me in?"

She yanked open the door and propelled herself toward his chest, plastering her arms around his middle. "Are you OK?"

He patted her back. "Well, I won't be if you don't let me breathe."

Warmth spread up her cheeks as she released him. "Sorry." She stepped back through the entryway.

He lifted his hand to his neck and began twisting as he trudged through the front door and dropped onto the chair he'd left earlier. "No need to be sorry."

"Can you talk about it?" She slid onto the chair and locked her hands in a tight grip.

"What I know . . . not that it's much. It looks as if someone threw a brick, broke the front window of the police station, and followed that with a homemade smoke bomb. The smoke set off the alarm, signaling the

76

fire station. But somehow, the sprinklers weren't set off. We'll have to look into that later when the insurance company gives their assessment. Other than the window, and some public service time, nothing appears to be damaged."

"Well, that's a good thing."

His lips drew into a tight line. "I guess."

"You guess? That doesn't sound very solid, Chief. I would think you would be pleased that it was basically a non-event. No one was hurt. Nothing was destroyed. Sounds pretty good to me."

Shrugging his shoulders, the left corner of his mouth twisted. "Why would someone break the window of a police station and not take anything? Not destroy anything? It doesn't make any sense. Who would break in for no reason?"

Ice shot through her veins. She swallowed deeply trying to dissolve the instant bulge in her throat. "Who, indeed."

5

The unusually muggy air of the October morning enveloped Sean as his feet hit the pavement in a steady rhythm. He enjoyed his early morning runs. They gave him an opportunity to check out his town and spend some time in prayer. He wasn't good at sitting in a pew, a chair, or even a recliner, and centering his mind on talking with The Lord. His mind seemed to focus best when his body was in motion.

As he turned from Sycamore Lane to Columbus Street, his prayers fell in pattern with his morning route.

He started with his brother Mac, in South Carolina, who was facing uncharted territory. The owner of the company where Mac acted as the general counsel was nearing the end of a long cancer battle. The man was a mentor to Mac, a man of integrity and faith, and his brother's admiration for his boss was evident with each mention of his name.

The CEO's looming death gave Sean pause.

How would his brother react to losing another integral person in his life? With the death of their dad, and then their mom, Mac retreated into himself, turning his back on his family, friends, and even God. He was much further along on his faith journey now, thanks in large part to the man who now faced imminent death, and Sean prayed that Mac's relationship with the Lord was strong enough to withstand the blow of another loss. Perhaps this loss would cause him to turn outward, seeking comfort in others and Jesus, rather than trying to solve all of his problems alone.

Sean prayed for that truth.

The squeal of tires turning a corner fractured the peaceful cocoon the early morning provided. He ignored the distraction and continued to the intersection of Columbus and Main. Turning left onto Main Street, he quickened his pace, heading up the slight slope as he neared the town square, and shifted his focus to his younger brother, Joey.

Joey lived and played professional baseball in Minnesota. He'd ridden a slump from the All-Star break to the close of the regular season. His self-worth was yoked to his ability to perform on the field. The last few times he'd spoken to his brother, the youngest Taylor seemed to have lost some of his unending supply of self-confidence. The team was done for the season, but Sean prayed that God would give Joey a glimmer of hope in his exit interviews with the coaches. He often allowed his ability to play baseball to send him on a dangerous roller coaster, and one bad season could have his little brother turning his back on his one true love.

As he passed the police station, a piece of plywood, awkwardly nailed over the broken glass, shifted his prayer to a few thanksgivings for the day and the previous evening. The puzzle pieces didn't fit for him. Why would someone deliberately break in to a police station and not take anything? He was a little anxious to discover the answer. He always did like a good mystery. There were so few in Gibson's Run, he was worried it would take a few days to shake the rust off his gold shield. He hoped his long unused skills wouldn't hamper the investigation. Whoever chose to attack the police station deserved justice, and he wanted to be the man to serve it with a lock and key.

He closed his prayer with an "Amen" as

his gaze shifted to Only the Basics and his thoughts settled on the shop's owner. After the previous evening's chaos, he hoped she wasn't freaked. As irritating as she could be, he would hate to have to search for another baker to come to town. Although he could likely find a tenant less demanding, he doubted he could find one who could bake as well as Maggie.

He glanced down at his watch and wondered how early she clocked in to begin prepping for the day. Crossing the street, he closed the half of a block from the station to the bake shop in under a minute.

The front of the café was dark, but he saw a flicker of light from the kitchen area in the back. Turning down the side alley, he made a quick right behind the building. The crunch of gravel beneath his feet filled the stillness of the parking lot as he slowed to a walk, allowing his breath to settle.

The backdoor handle reflected a dull shine from the single security lamp posted on the opposite end of the lot. He cranked the knob to the left and shoved open the door, silently berating Maggie for not locking the dead bolt. Hadn't he just warned her that someone had tried to break into the shop? Wasn't a near bombing across the street enough to be vigilant?

He closed the door with a click and followed the fresh aroma of baking bread. He took a single step in the direction of the kitchen, intent on giving her the stern reminder about adhering to upped security measures. But his heart was stunned into silence by the angelic tones wafting over the scent of the bread and the notes filled his spirit with an otherworldly melody. He moved toward the sound; the music grew more intense and vibrant with each step.

Through the doorway of the kitchen, Maggie's shoulders rolled as she kneaded the dough on the marble slab. The rhythmic movement was one he had witnessed much of his childhood when his mother stood in nearly the same spot. But Mom never sang like Maggie. No one ever sang like Maggie.

He leaned his shoulder against the door frame, lacing his arms, and listened.

Her voice was full and rich; she hit notes that sounded as if they'd been transported from the original Christmas Eve angels' choir when Christ was born.

He recognized the song from a musical he endured during a trip to New York years earlier. His girlfriend at the time thought he needed to be culturally aware. Three rows back, he'd achieved cultural awareness via osmosis. But if the lead that night had a voice like Maggie's, snoring would have been the last thing on his mind.

She lost herself in the final bars, tilting her head back as if she were singing for God alone. When she finished, she dropped her head for a moment and then began leisurely kneading the mass of dough, a hum still softly slipping through her lips.

He stood frozen, reveling in the music swimming through him before he clapped his hands in a steady tempo.

She spun, a stray curl falling from her bun across her forehead.

His hands stopped mid-clap.

Stark terror shone in her gaze.

He stepped toward her and stopped mid-stride as a quick glimmer off the large chef's knife in her right hand caught his eye. "Whoa. Maggie, it's OK."

She held the knife steady, pointed directly at his heart, not flinching at his words.

He shoved back the black hood of his sweatshirt, taking another step toward her. "Maggie, it's me. It's Sean." His voice sounded soft and smooth to his ears in complete opposition to the pounding of his heart. "We're friends, now. Remember?"

Her hand held steady, her face washed in the gray tone of fear; her eyes nearly black as her pupils expanded against her clear, blue irises.

His gaze locked with hers, trying to find his Maggie inside the house of horrors where she had disappeared. He shuffled closer to her, his hands raised in submission. She could easily thrust her knife in his belly. He was willing to take the risk. He trusted her. He needed to get her to trust him. "Maggie . . ."

Her head tilted to the side. The blade of the knife tipped toward the ground. "Sean?"

A silent moan escaped his lips. He cautiously laid his right hand on her shoulder and removed the knife from her slack grip with his left hand. Setting the knife toward the back of a wire shelf, he kept his focus trained on Maggie's downturned face. With a slight nudge, she slid limply onto the step stool beside the baker's rack. He squatted in front of her and took her hands, gently rubbing the backs with his thumbs.

She dropped her focus to her pinstripe, black cotton chef pants.

"Do you want to talk about it?" His voice was low.

She lifted her gaze to his. The pain etched in the crystal blue depths of her eyes twisted his heart. What had happened to her?

She shook her head and rolled her shoulders. The corner of her mouth curled. "I'm fine. You just startled me."

"Someone who's startled throws flour in the air or screams. She doesn't pull a knife on someone with the intent to slice his belly."

Yanking her hands from his protective grasp, she forced him back on his heels as she shot up. She swiveled toward the pile of dough and began banging and punching as if she were in a self-defense class. "What are you doing here, anyway? You shouldn't be sneaking up on people when bombs are going off in the neighborhood. That's just rude."

Sean stood, his gaze trained on her back. How had she gone from singing angel, to scared rabbit, to outraged she-cat, in barely a heartbeat? "My question, first . . . what's going on with you, Maggie?" He crossed his arms.

Silence hung in the room punctuated by her rhythmic pummeling of the dough. Her back was taut with pressure as she kneaded.

He leaned against the shelves. He could wait. He was a patient man. His patience had helped him break more than one squirrelly witness. A hot-tempered baker should be a snap.

The simple question hung in the air. His

gaze drilled holes in her back. His voice, sharp with the edge of police steel, sliced through her mind as his question danced through her seeking an answer.

She fought to control the tears threatening to spill down her cheeks. What could she say? Oh, sorry about the knife. I thought you were the maniac who used to track my every move. He was released from prison. It's got me a little jumpy. You understand, right? No harm. No foul. Have a nice day. Yep, that would do it. Sure, right after he kicked her out of the shop and apartment for being a whacko who attracted stalkers.

To be fair, there was only one stalker and she was fairly certain he didn't know where or who she was anymore. She sucked in a deep breath. Between the attempted break-in Sean mentioned a few nights ago at the bakery and the explosion at the police station last night, she felt herself slipping into old patterns, jumping, screaming and apparently pulling knives with every creak and noise in the shop.

This morning, when she was fully given over to singing for The Lord, her defenses were down and she had panicked with the first clap.

A knife? Really? How was she going to wiggle out of that brilliant move? She sighed. Eventually, she needed to face him. The dough was nearly smooth to her touch. She wouldn't be able to hide behind it much longer or she would have to trash the whole batch for over-kneading.

He wasn't moving. Why couldn't he be like other men who stomped off when she ignored them? Why did he have to be special?

She patted the dough and stretched to lift the damp dishcloth draped across the sink. Wiping the residue flour from her hands, she centered her mind, trying to convince herself that thick framed glasses weren't still superimposed over Sean's face. Be brave. Just take a peek. You can do it. She twisted the damp cloth between her hands as she turned, slowly raising her gaze. Peace washed over her like a tidal wave.

No glasses.

Only Sean. He didn't look happy. Not mad or angry. He looked resolute. Leaning casually against the tall baker's rack, his arms were crossed loosely over the logo embroidered on his sweatshirt.

Even now, when she was trying to think up a viable excuse for her crazy-lady-wielding-a-knife routine and her world seemed to be slowly cracking like the top-crust of her zucchini bread, she couldn't help the slight clench of her stomach at his handsome face.

Why did his heart have to shine through his melty, chocolate-brown eyes? She'd never been able to resist chocolate. *Shield up, sister. You can't afford any extra calories today.* She stretched her mouth wide, laced her arms over her stomach, and lifted her shoulders in a quick shrug. "Thank you for your concern. But there really isn't anything to discuss. I got spooked. What with the bomb last night and all. I wouldn't actually have cut you."

He uncrossed his arms and took a step toward her. "You could have fooled me." A slight grin tugged at his mouth.

"I've been on my own for a long time. A girl needs to at least appear as if she can defend herself." She turned from his intense stare, praying he couldn't read the fibs fumbling out of her mouth. She flipped the hot water lever and placed her hands directly under the steady stream, scrubbing her hands with intensity.

Sensing him directly behind her, his presence a tangible reality, she didn't turn. Her carefully constructed veneer would shatter if she faced him again. One look into those eyes and her wobbly constitution could topple like Humpty-Dumpty. And, she didn't have a single king's man on speed dial.

Butter. Sugar. Bake. She needed to bake something, to create something rich and decadent. The intake and the sharing of heavenly loaded caloric gifts was always a cure for patching up the cracks in her life. She knew only God could give her the ultimate tending, but, for a momentary fix, she couldn't pass up a delicious alternative starting with butter and sugar.

Sean's hands rested lightly on her shoulders, giving her a gentle squeeze. His touch was reassuring, not romantic, but she welcomed the tender pressure. With the weight of his hands, the tension of the last few moments eased from her body.

"I will leave you to your work." With a light pat on her shoulders, he stepped away. "Although, it appears you can take care of yourself. I'll lock the back door on my way out. Something you should remember to do."

The door wasn't locked? She shut her eyes and swallowed the bile rolling up her throat.

His running shoes squeaked as he made his way toward the back exit. The squeaking stopped at the doorway.

She held her breath. Keep going. Keep going. Please don't ask me why. Her self-preservation was nearly spent. One understanding look from those soulful brown eyes and she would spill faster than a corporate whistle-blower. And then, she would have to vanish. Again.

"Be careful today," he said. "I don't want any unnecessary knife fights on my hands. I like my town nice and quiet." There was a chuckle in his voice as he retreated.

With the soft click of the lock, she released a breath. A burning sensation registered in her muddled brain and she yanked her reddened hands from the now scalding water. She leaned against the stainless steel sink and tears streamed down her cheeks as she laid back her head and prayed. "Will it ever just go away, God? Will I ever be free?"

Sean jiggled the handle to make sure it was locked before taking a short cut to his small 1920's home on Maple Street. His run through town would have to wait until tomorrow. His detour had taken more time than he'd anticipated.

After all these months, nothing should surprise him when it came to Maggie McKitrick, but knife-wielding-freak-out was one he hadn't anticipated. Her excuse that she was "spooked" seemed somewhat reasonable, but the cop in him never was satisfied with the obvious answer. Six months ago, a wall of red-tape and a lily-white rap sheet greeted him when he ran a background check on her. He had waivered on signing the lease, but Jane gave him the my-puppy-just-died look and he handed the keys over to Maggie. Now, he wasn't so sure that had been the best choice.

He slid his key into his front door. A twig snapped in the near distance. He yanked the key from his door and leaped over the railing of the front porch. He jogged down the side of the house, careful to keep his steps soft and virtually silent. Approaching the rear of his house, he pressed his back against the wide, wooden siding, determined to surprise whoever was skulking around his property. Slowly, he slid around the corner of the house.

His neighbor's cat, Fred, was sprawled across the backdoor mat, as he tried to scratch an unseen itch.

His heart slowed. "Hey Fred."

The white and tan tabby, whose belly revealed pink flesh between cracks of fur, tilted his head to the side before he resumed his intense scratch.

"Guess you're my prowler."

The incident with Maggie must have affected him more than he thought. One little knife and he was jumping over railings at the sound of a snapped twig like he was a TV cop rather than a small town chief. Stepping over Fred, he jerked open the screen door and slid his key in the back lock. He needed to think like the rational, well-trained detective that he was. His intruder may have been Fred, but something was needling his instincts. Something wasn't right in Gibson's Run. He could feel it. And his gut told him that something started with his pretty little tenant.

The door slammed as he jogged up the narrow back staircase. He needed to take a shower and get to the station. It was time for him to do some real investigative work again.

He stood from his crouched position, brushing the dead leaves from his dark jeans. He hopped the four-foot wooden fence enclosing the dimwitted cop's backyard, then tightened the blue scarf at his neck, and tugged his ball team's hat low on his brow more out of habit than fear of being recognized.

This morning was too close. He couldn't stay in this rundown town. He needed to take a break. Go back to Maryland. Regroup. The pieces hadn't fallen into place as he'd strategized. He would have to wait a little longer. Patience wasn't a natural virtue, but he had learned to wait as he pursued God's gift to him. He anticipated a few bumps in the road, but he forgot how small towns worked. They all had a busybody. He should have anticipated her. And yet, he was caught unaware when he glimpsed her telephoto lens between the drapes of her ill-kept home. Not that the nosy old lady was a big obstacle. But, her gossipy ways reminded him. No one could hide in a small town.

He tugged a crumpled pack of cigarettes from his jacket pocket and clamped a stem between his lips and flashed his lighter to ignite the revolting bi-product of his time away from society. He sucked in a lungful of smoke and then released the cloud of nicotine gray through his lips and nostrils as he paused to admire his gift.

His lovely Mary Margaret lifted chairs from tables. Fury burned in his belly at the thought of her sweet, soft hands being laced with unsightly calluses. When they were married, as God ordained, she would never work again. The police and that meddling godfather of hers had driven her here to a life of servitude and menial labor. If they would have left them alone, Mary Margaret

93

would be presiding over the Georgia mansion his grandmother bequeathed him, singing him private concerts in the conservatory on the second floor.

His eyes fluttered shut as the image of his most treasured fantasy floated into his mind. She was leaning against the gleaming, black grand piano, the moonlight sparkling through the bank of windows, draped in a silky, white dress. He clutched at his flannel shirt as he swayed to the music only he could hear. His angel. Singing only for him, the way God intended.

He had been listening to her sing this morning, standing at the base of the back stairwell. A preview of what would one day be. Then the cop rudely interrupted the concert, forcing him to slink away into the darkness, like the criminal so many had unjustly accused him of being. He would not allow another such interruption. He had been raised to know how to deal with uninvited guests.

He shifted his attention away from the shop, and his lips lifted to a sneer as he admired the clumsy patchwork over the broken police station window.

The previous evening, he should have had more control, but the burning vision of that cop's hand touching his gift exploded in a billowing rage through his body. Before he could fully comprehend his actions, a loose brick from the sidewalk released through his fingers with the accuracy of a Sunday afternoon quarterback. He had to think quickly, relying on one of the lessons he'd learned from his fellow inmates. Distraction was always the best strategy.

He stubbed the remainder of the cigarette in the palm of his hand and threw the base into the mildew-encrusted fountain behind him. Glancing down at the gold sedan, he scanned the cabin for a remnant. Overlooking details was what separated him from Mary Margaret these past years. He wouldn't be so careless again.

He had dealt with men who had interfered in the last decade.

Sean Taylor would not get in the way of destiny.

His and Mary Margaret's destiny was epic. They were ordained by God to be together. And they would be. Either in this life, or the next.

6

Glancing up at the clock above the oven, Maggie closed the box on the last of the twenty dozen bagels for the Smith brothers' breakfast meeting. She had ten minutes to spare before she had to open and someone would be by for the order. This was the second time this month the Smiths had ordered such an enormous blowout of bagels. Oh, hail the carb-lovers!

Reflecting on the morning, Maggie cringed. The day started so wonderfully, spending time baking and praising Jesus, until Sean surprised her. For all of her bravado and surly attitude, she'd pulled a knife on a cop. There would be consequences. Truce or not, she would be facing some well-deserved interrogation. Minutes, now hours, later she could admit to herself that the fear was real.

Over the last few months, the terror she'd kept in a well-insulated room in her mind, while her tormentor was tucked away in prison, had been gnawing its way free. She'd been able to keep the lock secure with the knowledge that her new life was untraceable. But, if she wasn't vigilant, her fear would escape and consume her, paralyzing her with the thoughts of what could and had happened. Shaking her head, she let out a slow, cleansing breath. She couldn't worry about what might be. She had a business to run.

The bakery hadn't been her dream when she was a girl, that dream died with Mary Margaret, but this shop was hers and she could feel God's warming smile on her. He had given her this tremendous gift and she wouldn't waste a moment of the opportunity.

With a grunt, she heaved the tray of boxes off of the prep-counter, waddling from the kitchen to the main café, and shoved the loaded carrier onto the shelf.

The snickerdoodle-flavored coffee dripped into the dispenser. She snapped the lid shut and then popped the pump lever so that it would be ready to flow freely when Mrs. Shively came in for her morning fix.

She filled the cubbies for sugar, zero-calorie sweetener, swizzle sticks, and straws with the speed and ease of one who could accomplish the simple task in her sleep. She straightened the handles on the milks and creamers. The symmetry would be lost as soon as Marty McSeverin and his mother arrived for her on-the-way-to-daycare coffee. After experiencing Marty for five minutes every morning, Maggie understood why his mother often stopped for her on-the-way-to-daycare coffee after she dropped him at Tiny-Tots Daycare.

Tables clean. Counters clear. Napkins stocked. Display case set and filled. Coffee brewed. Flip on her tunes, unlock the door, and another day would begin. The flutter of butterfly wings tickled the walls of her stomach. She was ready for another day. *Oh, Lord, Thank You for this life! I wouldn't be living it without You.*

She walked behind the counter, opened the small compartment housing the sound system, and contemplated what kind of melodic mood she was in today. Music was her first love. She loved baking and it helped to fill the creative void leaving music had created, but nothing would ever replace the feeling she had when the Holy Spirit flowed through her body in song.

She shuffled through various mixes before landing on an alternative Christian rock set. The music would help to put her focus on

God. Maggie wasn't much of an evangelist, but she tried to share her faith in her own subtle way. She slid the compartment door shut, stood, and straightened her chef's coat.

Showtime.

She unlocked the door and flipped the "closed" sign to "open" in one smooth, synchronized motion. And bam! There it was: the twisted tingle in her stomach she always had before she stepped on a stage. Now, it was a constant reminder that every day of her life was a show. Who knew when she was training to dance and to sing for the Great White Way that she would be playing a role for a lifetime rather than a nightly performance? She tugged the small string downward and the Roman shade lifted with a zip to reveal the picture of Main Street, Gibson's Run, Ohio.

She leaned her left shoulder on the glass of the door and scanned the street. Two pick-up trucks were parked north of the town's fountain, both owned by regular customers. Her gaze shifted south, and she caught a glint off of a gold sedan she didn't recognize. Her stomach rolled as her brief conversation with Mr. Hopper replayed in her mind.

His information was limited to Sissy Jenkins's suspicion about an unknown vehicle, and like so many others in town he had ignored the balance of what the resident-expert-on-everyone-else's-business had to share.

Maggie wished she could have, this one time, given Sissy a little of the attention she obviously craved. If he had, Mr. Hopper may have been able to provide Maggie with enough details to erase the wave of worry threatening to drown her. She drew a deep breath through her nose. The air in her lungs was forced out slowly through her lips as she prayed for peace from her worries. Could anyone add a single hour to one's life by worrying?

The reminder from Jesus' own words often brought her comfort. Today was no different. Worry was a waste of energy. At the moment, she had no way of confirming if the unknown gold car was the suspicious sedan Sissy was prattling about to Mr. Hopper. The new car of a town resident was the most logical conclusion; nothing nefarious.

Maggie looked away from the vehicle. When Sissy came in for her post-Jazzercise latte today or tomorrow, she could subtly question the ever-knowing Mrs. Jenkins about her suspicions. Her gaze drifted up the street and settled on the plywood covering the front window of the police station.

Or she could ask the chief.

She was on a bit of a teeter-totter with the police chief. Although their relationship seemed to be balancing out, this morning's knife-wielding exhibition probably used up all of her free question tokens. Payment for her curiosity would undoubtedly require answering some of his questions about her life. Best to stick with Sissy.

Sissy's intel would be smattered with more fluff than facts, but any details would help move Maggie closer to the peace she craved. She shoved away from the door. Before she made it behind the counter, the bell announcing a customer chimed, and she turned with a broad smile "Good morning, Mr. Grey. How are you today?"

"Maggie girl, I thought we discussed this? Mr. Grey was my father. Please call me Henry or Hank." The gentle farmer stood six foot two inches and had the look of a weathered cowboy with salt and pepper hair and a thick mustache covering his top lip. He held his tattered ball cap and the arms of his light-weight flannel shirt were cuffed to the elbows. His worn denim spoke of years, not mere months. There was authenticity in his clothing, the kind that couldn't be purchased from a catalog.

"Well, Hank, what can I get for you this

morning?" Maggie moved behind the counter.

"You know Bitsy's in South Carolina, helping Emory, our youngest, settle back into her apartment for her last year of law school. Although I suspect the two are just shopping their way up one end of King Street and down the other. But, she's left me all alone to fend for myself for three days without her cooking. I woke up this morning and decided that I just had to try one of your scones. I love those carrot muffins you make, and your coffee is as good as my wife's, please don't tell her I said so, but for some reason I just got a hankering for one of those scones. Every time I stop in for some coffee or a visit with the guys, those scones scream my name from across the shop, but Bitsy's voice is always louder. Now that Bitsy's in Charleston, I think we might be out of shouting distance, what do you think?" His smile shone through his eyes.

Maggie was definitely not immune to his charm. And since Bitsy dropped by the store a week ago with a list of items Henry was allowed to have and not allowed to have, she was fairly certain she could give into his request without offending anyone and, of course, sticking to the crucial list. Bitsy

Grey's naughty list was not a place she wanted to be. "I think we can make that happen. Would you like a to-go cup for some coffee?"

"That would be fine. Thank you." He took the empty cup and ambled to the rack of coffee selections. "There's such a wide variety."

Maggie watched him through the glass of the display case as she used large tongs to lift a carrot and ginger whole wheat scone, with extra sugar, from the neat stack, dropping the little treat in a small paper sack. He lifted each of the miniature easels describing the coffee and appeared to be reading them in earnest. He turned. "Where's the regular coffee?"

She couldn't suppress her grin as she folded the top of the bag. "The one Bitsy picks up for you is the first one on the left."

He moved to the first dispenser and shook his head. "Who knew I was drinking a 'full-bodied aromatic bean' that has the 'bold intense flavors synonymous with the beautiful country of origin'?" He pressed the lever on the top of the dispenser and sealed the lid on the cup. He took a generous sip and moseyed back to the counter. "Maggie-girl, this is one mean cup of joe. If I wasn't already head-over-heels for my wife, she might have a little competition on her hands," he said with a quick nod of his head.

She giggled. "Well, who knew all I needed to get the most handsome man in town's attention was to put a little water and beans together?"

"We're simple folk here. Nothing like those city dwellers."

"Did you just say 'city dwellers', Hank?" Sean asked, the jingle of the entry bell echoing behind him.

Maggie's heart shot to her throat at the sight of the chief of police.

A twist of a grin pulled at his lips.

That's promising.

"Well, what would you call them?" Henry said. "You arrested enough of them."

"I would call those guys criminals." He extended his hand to Henry. "How's it going without Bitsy?"

"It's a struggle." He turned and winked at Maggie. "But this lovely lady is helping to keep me fed."

"The lady definitely knows her way around a baking pan. Have you tried her brownies?" Sean's eyes held warmth and welcome, not a question in sight.

Maggie expelled the anxious breath.

"Well, I don't believe I have, son." He turned back to Maggie. "Will you be making those for Sean and Jane's big brouhaha next week? I guess I could try one there. Bitsy never corrects my eating in public."

"You're going to the Policemen's Ball, Mr. Grey?"

"Hank . . ."

"Hank.

"Yep. Bits loves any reason to dress in something sparkly. And I think it's always wise to support the local police. You never know when you might need one or two on your side."

"Well, I'll definitely encourage Jane to include brownies on the dessert menu. And, maybe a couple of those special oatmeal-raisin-spice cookies your wife doesn't know you like so much."

Henry set his coffee on the counter and reached into his back-pocket, pulling out a well-worn wallet. He handed her a few bills, and tilted his head with a nod. "Maggie-girl, I think we can keep those cookies a secret between you and me. Bitsy wants to know everything, but she doesn't need to know everything."

"Your secret is safe with me, Hank." She cashed out his receipt and gave him the coins.

"I knew I liked you for more than your cookies. Hope you have a great day." He smiled, slipping his wallet into his pocket. He fitted his tattered ball cap on his head and lifted his coffee and the bag. Turning to Sean, he said, "This one's a good tenant. Don't you let her get away."

"Will do. See ya later, Hank." Sean turned to face Maggie as the bell trailed the farmer's exit. "Quick question . . ." he started.

Feeling the heat of embarrassment rise, she lifted a single eyebrow.

"Do you have any sharp objects behind that counter?" His tone was warm with a slight dash of teasing.

She stepped up to the counter. "Is the big, bad chief of police scared of a little bitty baker?"

"My momma always told me to fear women I'd angered. And Maggie, I've angered you more times than I care to count."

"You've nothing to fear here, Chief. Nothing, except some extra fat and calories. And, maybe a groveling tenant who needs to apologize for being so jumpy this morning."

"No apology necessary. But, would you like to explain?" he asked.

Dropping her gaze from his, she was afraid that if she saw compassion in his eyes she would tell him more than she dared. Even her years evading any personal attachments hadn't prepared her for the moment she would encounter his sympathy. She must stay strong to remain safe and to keep him safe. "I thought I explained this morning. You sneaked up on me and I was startled. Just about anyone would have been shaken if you had let yourself in to their business, unannounced, before five o'clock in the morning."

"If you say so . . ."

"I say so. Now, what can I get for you this morning?" She smiled.

"A large cup of coffee and a sun-dried tomato bagel . . . with some of that vegetable cream cheese."

"Will do," she said, sliding a paper cup and lid across the counter.

He'd capitulated too easily on the morning's incident. Something didn't feel right. He was a cop. He should be demanding to know why she had nearly severed his spleen in her kitchen. Why had he let her off the hook so easily?

She snatched a bagel from the back counter basket. She slathered each slice with cream cheese, sandwiched the halves, and then wrapped the order in waxed paper. She dropped the bagel and three napkins into a bag. Setting the package on the pick-up counter, she focused on the object of too

107

many of her wayward thoughts.

He wore a lightweight, navy blue jacket with GRPD in bold white font stretched across the back. His pants were uniform blue and his weapon was on one hip. She had seen him countless times in full uniform, but before last night she couldn't recall seeing the gun. Shivers chased up her spine.

He poured skim milk into the coffee and lifted it to his lips. When he turned, his dark brown gaze was on her.

Butterflies swarmed in her stomach.

He reached into his jacket, retrieving his wallet. "How much do I owe you?"

She lifted her hand as if she were a crossing guard stopping traffic. "On the house." Her lips twitched as she spoke. "It's the least I can do."

He shoved the bills back into the weathered leather. "So, you're meeting with Jane about the banquet today?"

"Yes. She's coming by this afternoon. I believe with her partner, Millie. Hopefully, the shop won't be too busy. Today could be a . . ."

The jingling of the bell over the door stopped Maggie midsentence.

Marshall Smith, the youngest of the Smith brothers, strutted through the door with a gleam of mischief lighting his eyes. He breathed in confidence and exhaled charm. He nudged Sean away from the counter with a meaty hand and reached for Maggie's with his other. "Good morning, Miss Maggie. How's the day treating you so far?" He lifted her knuckles to his lips.

"Just fine, Mr. Smith." She giggled.

Marshall's jeans were distressed but neat. The polo he wore strained across his shoulders and chest causing the logo for Smith Brothers Construction to ripple above the pocket.

Sean elbowed Marshall. "You can wipe that smirk off your face, Marsh. The lady's trying to run a solid business here. She doesn't need to be harassed in her own store."

"Just so happens I am here to do business with the lady." Marshall crossed his arms. "What about you? Is this police harassment?" He lifted an eyebrow and tilted his head toward her.

"No. Sean was in here to get breakfast, just like you. I have your order all ready." With a smile, she slid the bagel containers to the opposite counter in front of him. "Let me grab your cream cheeses from the back fridge." With speed driven by the fear of potential bloodshed, she hustled to the back snagged the containers and slid to a stop, breathless, behind the counter.

The men were in a silent showdown. Both had their arms crossed; their gazes were on opposing walls.

Catching her breath, she shook her head and set the cream cheeses in the open spot between the bagel boxes.

Marshall twisted to her. Uncrossing his arms, he flashed a smile. "Hey, sugar. This looks great."

She bit the side of her cheek, suppressing her own matching grin. "Your brother already paid the bill, so you're good to go."

"Thanks." With a wink, he straightened and lifted the carrier. He turned to exit, but stopped just inside the door. He flashed a grin that could melt the paint off the Mona Lisa. "I'll see you this afternoon for my P.M. fix, sugar." The door jingled with his exit leaving only music to fill the silent space.

Her gaze drifted to Sean.

The bag crumpled in his grip. His gaze locked with hers; his lips were drawn in a tight line. "Guess I'll see you later." But he didn't move — not even a shift toward exiting. Was he waiting for her to reply?

She tried to think of something clever to say, but all she could do was nod her head, unable to speak. The breath she thought had returned was quickly sucked from her body.

After another long minute, he rammed his hat on his head and left the café.

"Whew." She slumped against the back counter. Her teeter was certainly tottering and it didn't have anything to do with crazy interns or burned cookie sheets.

Two steps outside the entry, Sean felt his shoulders drop. Was he actually jealous of Marshall Smith, his brother Joey's buddy? He shook his head. He was done. Seriously finished. Tension left his tightly gripped fingers, still clutching the bag holding his breakfast. He chuckled.

Jealous. But who could blame him? After months of ramming his attraction for Maggie to the back of his mind, keeping her firmly in the tenant-business-only-relationship file, he no longer could hold back his desire to pursue her. His attraction burst through him like the baseball he'd hit through Mrs. McGuernsey's front window in the 3rd grade. And like with that broken window, he wasn't quite sure what to do next. He was hung up on the pretty brunette with a smart mouth and killer eyes. He didn't know the path from jealous landlord to suitable suitor. Ugh! Even his thoughts were turning girlie.

Lifting his coffee to his lips, he jaywalked across the traffic-less street to the station, and caught the gold sedan in his peripheral. His cop instincts flared, and thoughts of Maggie returned to their well-marked file as the pages of Sissy's stalker notebook flipped through his mind. The car had Maryland plates and foggy windows from the early morning dew. With the sleeve of his jacket, he wiped the moisture from the driver's window and peered inside.

Not a single cup, map, or newspaper littered the inside. The car was as clean as the day it rolled off the assembly line. As far as he could tell, the vehicle had been sitting in that parking spot for at least twelve hours, if not longer.

How had he missed it that morning on his run? But, he hadn't run in front of the bakery. He'd made a detour. He straightened and looked over his left shoulder. From the driver's seat, one would have a perfect view of the café without ever being seen by Maggie. The hair on the back of Sean's neck prickled.

Alvin better have that background on the license plate.

7

The late afternoon sun beamed through the front windows, warming the café in an autumn glow. Maggie knew she should lower the shades, but she loved the way the colors transformed the shop in the afternoon. And it didn't hurt that the heat of the sun kept the senior ladies to one free refill instead of two, allowing Maggie time to linger over coffee and dessert plans for the Policemen's Ball with Jane.

They had sketches and notes strewn about the table and Maggie nodded her head at the appropriate intervals as Jane discussed her plans. "So the idea is to make the entire ballroom seem like a homecoming dance. I know it's a little cheesy, but Sean and I thought, fall, what goes with fall? In Ohio, the only correct response is football. Not that I get it." Jane's eyes twinkled as her long brown ponytail swayed. "But most of the policemen played football, or at least watch football. And even though the current Columbus Chief of Police is a woman, there seems to be an assumption that the men and women in blue like nothing more than a little pigskin when the temperature begins to drop below freezing."

"I haven't really watched football since college, but I can see the appeal. And I think the homecoming theme is a fun idea. We can make really special desserts that go along with the theme, well beyond leaf-shaped cookies. I'm thinking about making these little chocolate cups in the shapes of footballs, filling them with this amazing chocolate mousse that's so light and fluffy it can't possibly have any calories that stick with you. Oh, and then I just pulled together this new idea for a cherry-filled puffed pastry that is like taking a whole pie and popping it into your mouth in a burst of flavor. Maybe we can make it with pumpkin instead, more autumn-like. What do you think?"

Jane's eyes closed as a broad smile stretched across her lips. "Maggie, you are killing me. I think I just gained six and a half pounds listening to you describe these desserts. I won't be able to fit into the ridiculous costume Millie has picked out for me."

"What is she making you wear?" Maggie asked as she poured coffee into Jane's cup.

"My best friend has decided that we need to go dressed as hockey cheerleaders. Which is totally ridiculous since hockey doesn't have cheerleaders."

"Cheerleaders? Were you one in high school?"

Jane snorted. "No. And I definitely shouldn't play one now. But she's my best friend. She has been since she traded me her peanut butter and jelly sandwich for my ham salad in the first grade. So how could I say no?" Her smile twinkled in her eyes. "Come on, the girl saved me from ham salad. She has me for life."

Maggie's head fell softly to the side, and she rested her chin in the palm of her right hand. She missed friends. More than friends, she missed friendships. The kind that spanned decades, not weeks. She missed the knowing looks and the intricate conversations that consisted of single word sentences. She missed trust. She had that once, when she was Mary Margaret. She sighed and shifted to fence-post straight in her seat as she listened to Jane. Friends would be nice, but they were a luxury.

Her business was a necessity. She needed to make this party, at least her part of it, spectacular. She may want friends, but she needed her business to be a success.

Jane patted Maggie's hand. "I'm sorry. I do tend to run off when I'm telling a story or talking in general. Let's talk cake."

Sean could hear the giggles from the curb. The volume grew with each step toward the café. He yanked the front door open, causing the bell to jingle.

Three heads swiveled in response. One face held a warm smile shining through brown eyes he had known since childhood. The second face held the tentative grin of something more, but he couldn't be sure as her gaze dropped to the table. And the third face was nothing but trouble, from the tilt of her long, blonde-haired head, to the twinkle in her million-dollar eyes.

"Hello ladies. It seems you are elbow deep in event plans."

Maggie stood. "Can I get you something, Chief?"

"Umm . . . sure. But you don't need to get anything for me. I can just . . . well . . . umm . . ."

Millie flipped her blonde hair over her shoulder, twisting in her seat. "Spit it out, Taylor. Do you want the girl to get you a coffee or are you just loitering because there isn't any crime in this town?"

Tipping his hat in her direction, Sean said, "Always good to see you, Mrs. Horton."

"None of that 'Mrs. Horton', nonsense. I will always be Amelia Tandis. Got it, Taylor?"

"That's Chief Taylor to you, Tandis. Steal a baby Jesus lately?"

"Sean, we were in the eighth grade, and I believe you were the look-out for that little mission."

"I plead the Fifth." He couldn't help the grin. He loved these ladies as if they were his own sisters. "How are you, Janesie?"

"I'm really well, Sean. Thanks for asking." Jane smiled.

"She gets a 'how are you'? All pleasant and nice, while I get hammered from the moment you enter the joint. You were never fair, Taylor. No wonder you became a cop. You can bully people professionally," Millie huffed.

"Millie." Jane laughed. "Bullying you is like the Canadian Mounties bullying the U. S. Army."

"True. But still one would think there would be a little loyalty after two decades of friendship." Millie slumped in her chair with a pout.

"And what was with you beating me up

the moment I walked through the door?" Sean asked.

"That was just a little love hit. You know I love you."

"Gee, thanks, Mill. Love you, too." Sean turned toward the counter and met Maggie's stunned gaze. "Don't look so horrified. We've been going through this routine since I was ten years old and madly in love with Millie, following her around like a stray puppy."

"Well, that is quite a picture." Maggie chuckled. "A stray puppy? Really?"

"Really. Not very manly, I'm afraid."

"But charming," she said. "Now, what may I get for you?"

"Just a cup of coffee."

She took a ceramic mug from the shelf, laid a dessert plate on the counter, and then lifted a single eyebrow.

"How can I resist?"

Her eyes twinkled before she plucked a single brownie from the display tray.

She handed the brownie and coffee cup to him, and their fingers lightly brushed against one another. A rocket went off in Sean's belly, warming him from deep within. He couldn't tear his gaze from her. His feet were rooted to the ground, the simple touch shaking him to his core. He was startled when Millie leaned on his shoulder. He hadn't even noticed she'd stood up.

"Taylor," she whispered in his ear. "You might want to pick your tongue up off of the floor. You're kind of obvious." She sauntered toward the racks of coffee carafes.

"What do you mean?" he whispered. He set his plate and coffee cup between them and reached for the skim milk, prepping his cup.

"You might want to wipe the drool off your lip, Champ."

Instinctively, he swiped at his mouth with the back of his free hand.

Millie snorted and grabbed the milk from his hand. "You are such an idiot. There must have been something causing emotional and romantic stuntedness out there in farm country for you and Jane to be such late bloomers."

Leaning a hip against the counter, he crossed his arms, hoping the two inches of height he had on her might add a sense of intimidation. The more reasonable conclusion to her pontification would come when she ran out of ways to torture him.

"Are you just going to stand there?" She blew across the rim of her cup before taking a sip.

"I didn't hear a question in your diatribe

119

on my pathetic single life."

"Do you have a thing for Little Miss Baker-Girl?"

Sean stood a little straighter; his heart sped with the question. "I don't know what you mean."

"Mmmhmm. Dude, you're like a billboard at the corner of Broad and High. Everyone in Columbus can read you." She flipped her hair as she walked back to the table.

"I have no idea what you mean." He mumbled under his breath as he filled his mug with snickerdoodle coffee. But he did. He'd never been able to hide his thoughts from Millie or Jane, but his manly sense of self-preservation and thin string of remaining pride refused to acknowledge it. For now. He grabbed his plate and followed Millie to the table.

Jane and Maggie were beaming with excitement.

"Oh, you should totally have life-size cutouts of the different police chiefs attending," Maggie said.

Sean slid onto the seat between Jane and Millie, across from Maggie. "Why would you want to have pictures when we'll be there?"

Jane shook her head. "Not of you today, but you when you were in high school. You know the whole, 'Fall Homecoming Dance' theme?"

"Ahh." He lifted the brownie to his lips. He was probably better off keeping his mouth filled for the duration of the conversation.

The talk of centerpieces, bands, food, and attendees caused Sean to fall delightfully deeper into a sugar coma. Despite his innate boredom of the topic, the merry-go-round conversation allowed him the luxury of focusing his attention on an unaware Maggie.

As she spoke, her face was alight with joy over the variety of pastries and desserts she would prepare. She offered suggestions on savory items for Jane to pass along to the caterer.

Sean enjoyed watching her enthusiasm, a welcome conversion from the early hours of this morning. He lifted his coffee cup and drained the contents as his mind shifted to the One he could always rely on for direction. *God, do you think you could give a brother a hand? I don't need a big sign, just a little nudge to know I'm doing the right thing. We should just be friends, right?*

The front door to the café opened.

Maggie's shoulders slumped as she pushed away from the table. "Duty calls."

She hurried behind the counter, drawing her latest customer, an older woman, into a simple conversation. Her ability to make every customer special awed him. He tore his gaze from Maggie and tuned in on the conversation at the table. But instead of talk of centerpieces and cake, he found two women staring at him with the intensity of his former Captain the day he found out Sean had a felon from the FBI's Most Wanted list in a holding cell. "What?"

"You like Maggie." Jane smiled as she lowered her chin to rest in her hand.

"I don't know what you are talking about." His cheeks burned. He could mask his emotions from major criminals but against these two he was hopeless. "She's my tenant. She doesn't even like me."

"He tried that maneuver on me, too." Millie snorted.

"Seanie, you are so obvious."

"What is it with you two?" he mumbled.

"Sean," Jane covered his hand with her own. "You are like my brother. I've known you my whole life. I have known the moment you started liking a girl since we were ten and you had that ill-fated crush on Mills."

"You two are like the same person."

Jane patted his hand. "All I am saying is

122

that if you don't admit that you like Maggie in the boy-meets-girl way pretty soon, your face is going to turn into an eggplant. And possibly explode."

"What are you talking about?"

"Lack of oxygen. Purple," Millie said, snapping her fingers. "Keep up, Taylor. The point she's trying to make is you are in total like with Maggie. And, you might want to do something about it. Something like, I don't know, ask the cute coffee-girl out for something other than coffee?"

He ran his hand through his hair and began kneading his neck. "It's complicated."

Millie's eyes scrunched together. "What's complicated? When Mrs. Crossett leaves, go up to the counter, and say, 'Hey, Maggie, how 'bout we grab some dinner on me sometime?' " She lowered her voice and mimicked his hand motions.

"I do not sound like a surfer-dude."

"You do in my head."

Jane's mouth went into a tight line as she sent some mysterious girl message telepathically to Millie. He'd always wanted to know what they were silently saying to each other with those looks.

Jane's face softened with a smile as she focused on him. "What Millie means to ask is why do you think it's complicated?"

"Well, for starters, I'm her landlord. And until a few days ago, every time I talked to her it was like ripping a bandage off and exposing a puncture wound. I don't know what I'm feeling, but I don't think I should do anything rash. We're just beginning to be friends." He thought it best to leave out the near slice of his belly at the end of her knife.

"I can see where there might be some complication with her renting the building from you, but can't you just put Mac or Joey over this building so there isn't a conflict of interest?" Jane raised her brows in question.

Tell Joey and Mac? A shudder ran through his body. "I could, if there was anything to tell. Which there isn't. I don't know what I feel. Well, at least not beyond relief that I can come into the café without an engraved invitation." He lifted his hand to his shoulder again and kneaded the muscle that seemed to be perpetually tight.

Jane tilted her head to the side. "Sean, you like Maggie."

"Hypothetically, let's say that I do. How do you two presume to know what I'm feeling?"

Millie laced her arms. "We always know."

He slumped deeper into his chair, stretching his legs under the table. "Gee, thanks.

I'm glad all of that time as a detective paid off."

"Don't get all twisted up about it." Millie grinned. "With everything else in your life, you're a medieval castle with a fifty foot moat keeping guard, but when it comes to your heart you've always been wide open spaces. That's why we would never have worked. Even in the fifth grade. I would have chewed you up and spit you out like yesterday's daily special."

"Again, thank you. My ego is feeling so full I will barely be able to live with myself."

Jane squeezed his fingers. "Sean, you know we both love you. And, although Millie has never been one for tact, she is right. Your heart rests solidly on your sleeve. It has since you were little and there's nothing wrong with that. More men should be so transparent with their feelings."

He was mildly comforted by the generosity he saw in the depths of her gaze. But no self-respecting male wanted to be thought of as 'transparent' with his feelings.

"I wish I had acted on my feelings for Lindy sooner," Jane said. "Everything worked out for us, but it could have easily turned a different corner. I know this isn't even remotely the same situation, but if you really like Maggie as much as your face says

125

you do, then do something about it. Don't let responsibility or expectation or what your brothers will say stop you from experiencing something life-changing."

"Thank you, friend. I do feel something for her . . . man this feels weird. Dudes totally don't talk about stuff like this."

Millie dropped her hand on top of their still-connected fingers. "I didn't think you were a surfer."

Jane's brow drew to a tight line. "Millie, we are having a moment. Don't go all Millie over it."

"Whatever." Rolling her eyes, Millie lifted her chin towards the front window. "New subject . . . what happened to your cute little police station? I didn't think there was crime in this town."

The flame of anger Sean had been keeping on a slow boil roared to a bonfire. "There was an explosion last night."

"What?" Jane's hand plastered across her wide mouth.

"Is everyone OK? Were you in the station? Who would do something like that in Gibson's Run?" Millie questions tripped over each other in their jostle to free themselves from her lips.

His heart melted into a puddle. He loved these women. In the midst of treating him

126

like a character dissection in their favorite love story, their minds collectively shifted with whiplash speed to concern over his well-being.

"No one was hurt. I was actually here at Only the Basics when the pipe-bomb shattered the window."

Millie lifted a single eyebrow as she leaned back in her chair. "What were you doing over here, Mr. We're-just-friends?"

Jane pursed her lips. "Clearly that is not important right now, Mills." Jane frowned. "Was Alvin or one of the part-timers on duty? No one in town was hurt, or my mom would've called. The trail of Bitsy Grey's gossip contacts spreads wide. I'm sure the news would have made it to Charleston by now if someone was injured."

"Thankfully, no one was hurt. The station was empty. Beyond the fire department and Maggie, hardly anyone in town was bothered. Of course, Sissy Jenkins called me at home this morning to ask about it."

"Wow, if Sis waited until this morning, it must not have been a big deal," Millie said.

"That's what doesn't make any sense. No one knows anything and there doesn't seem to be a reasonable explanation for why someone would want to blow a hole through the side of the station," Sean replied.

"Did you ask Jamison? As the high school principal, he might know if one of the kids was looking to pull an epic prank," Millie offered.

"Spoke with him this morning, but I don't think it's a bored student looking for a step up from cow-tipping. The whole thing doesn't fit with normal vandalism and school pranks. Gibson's Run teens aren't this neat and organized. This is the work of someone who knows their way around explosives and how to keep the outcome quick and clean." His brain flashed to the empty sedan and its showroom new interior. His chair legs scraped against the floor under the pressure of his added weight. "Ladies, I hate to run out on this conversation, but there's something I need to check out." He rammed his hat on his head and nodded to Maggie as he jogged through the front door.

Discussion over his love life would have to be shelved. He had a suspicious car's owner to track down. Cleanliness may be next to godliness, but he had a gut feeling that his neat freak had little to do with God-like behavior.

8

"I'll see you tomorrow, Sean," Alvin hollered.

Before Sean lifted his hand in a wave good-night, the front door closed behind his deputy.

The background check on the abandoned sedan had come in fifteen minutes earlier. According to Alvin, the system was down during the week, and that was why he wasn't able to get any of the information until this afternoon. Alvin had probably forgotten about the assignment until Sean reminded the deputy earlier today.

Now that he had the information on the rental car and its renter, his curiosity could be satisfied. The car was picked up at Dulles Airport by a Stephen A. Smith. A common name, but not one he could connect to a local. He wished the town council had approved his project plan to install a link to the FBI and the State of Ohio databases.

But they had turned him down because there wasn't anything but petty crime in Gibson's Run.

He couldn't argue with their logic at the time. He swiveled his chair to the computer and did a search for the car rental branch at Dulles and dialed the number. He waited on hold for several minutes before a woman informed him that their manager wouldn't be in until the next day, but she would be sure to leave a message for him to call. With one dead end, he dialed a sure thing, his old partner in Columbus, Chuck Riley.

"Riley," the voice was gruff.

Sean grinned at his partner's tone. "Taylor."

"Hey, man, how's the party planning going? Guess you suburb yokels have all the free time in the world to pick out plates and pastries. The rumors are true, small town cops are just girls who shave."

"Listen here, old man, I'm the one doing you a favor to keep your butt from getting all toasty in the fire when Shelia finds out you were really supposed to pull this whole thing together. Your wife would never have forgiven you if you stole the opportunity from her to get all dressed up. And the FOP will be singing your praises, all because I kept you from burning and saved the day."

Sean leaned back in his chair and kicked his feet on top of the desk.

"Don't you mean Jane Barrett? And it isn't exactly a success yet, or don't you remember a few of your other exploits? Need I remind you of a certain drug bust that went south when you found out you had an FBI informant locked up with a Ten-Most-Wanted? Wouldn't want to see you crash and burn like that, my friend."

"Hrmph," Sean cleared his throat and sat up. "I didn't call to talk about the party. I need a favor." He could hear Chuck's chair scrape the floor.

"What do you need?"

"I've got a rental car parked in town, and I'm fairly certain the person who rented it used a fake ID." He passed on the information in Sissy's log and his own observations. Sean scrubbed his face. "I know it might seem minor, but with the explosion at the station something doesn't feel right about it. I'm probably making it a much bigger deal than what it is, but I like my little community quiet. I don't want anything messing it up."

"I'll run the background on the driver's license and the tags. You might want to call the rental place at Dulles and see what info they have on the renter."

"Thanks, 'Dad.' I already have a call in to the manager."

"Hey, it's been a long time since you've done any real police work. You may have lost your touch, what with all the party planning and quiet streets you've been dealing with," Chuck snorted.

"I don't mind being thought of as a yokel. But, it doesn't mean I work like one. This is a sleepy town and I want it to stay that way. Goodnight, Chuck." Sean hung up the phone and returned to his online search.

The pounding on the front door drew his attention away from the computer. The plywood made a less than ideal window to the main entrance. Rising, he blanked his screen and then ambled to the door.

Shadowed in the front entry's burned-out security light, another thing on Alvin's to-do list, he couldn't make out who was on the other side of the frosted glass. He yanked the door open to Maggie McKitrick.

Her cheeks were tinged pink and her chin had a tiny smudge of chocolate screaming at him to wipe clean. He motioned for her to enter. "What brings you by the station at this hour?"

"I was locking up and saw your light. I thought maybe you didn't get any dinner. I brought you a sandwich and some chips. I didn't have any soda, but figured you might have something here. But I wasn't sure and so I didn't bring a beverage. I guess I should have." She bit her bottom lip. Her nervousness was endearing. Her cheeks seemed to bloom a deeper shade of pink while she spoke. He could get used to a nervous Maggie, except maybe when she pulled a knife on him.

"Is there just one sandwich, or did you make enough for two?"

"Well, I didn't like to think of you eating alone, so there might be a couple sandwiches in the bag. But if you are hungry I have food at home and can leave you to your work."

Resting his hip against Alvin's desk, he looked into the open bag. "Although I am sure I could eat both of these sandwiches, I would much prefer to share them with you. Do you mind making do with my desk for a picnic table?"

"As long as you don't mind. I wouldn't want to get in your way. Or keep you here any later."

She moved toward his office and he caught the aroma of chocolate that she wore like the finest perfume. She wasn't just beautiful, she was delectable. He shook his head. *We're working towards friends here Taylor, just friends.* He motioned for her to sit in the chair opposite his desk as he slid into his own chair. He opened the bag and pulled out the two sandwiches and potato chips.

"This one is chicken salad. It has nuts, so if you are allergic . . ." she said pointing to the sandwich closest to her.

"Not allergic."

She reached for the second sandwich package. "This one is ham and Swiss with some apple chutney. They're both on potato bread. It's a new recipe. I'm thinking about carrying bread. Not quite sure if it's a good idea." Her voice had a slight quiver.

"Apple chutney? Potato bread? Chicken salad with nuts? What happened to a little yellow mustard on white bread with a couple pieces of ham and cheese in between? You know this is Gibson's Run, Ohio, right?" He smirked.

"Yes, I know this is Gibson's Run. I do live here. But just because this is a small town in the 'Heart of it All,' doesn't mean you can't try something a little unique." She mirrored his crossed arms and let out a sigh. "And who thinks nuts in chicken salad are exotic?"

"I didn't say exotic." He chuckled.

"Well, regardless. You need to broaden

your horizons beyond mustard and white bread. There's a whole foodie world out there just waiting to be nibbled on." She thrust a half of the chicken salad sandwich within centimeters of his face.

He took a bite, brushing her fingers with his lips. The combination of flavors burst through. He could taste basil and a hint of garlic, softened by the juicy grapes and sweet pecans. The combination was held together by a rich dressing that was creamy, but not heavy. Maggie had created a taste of heaven in between the softest pieces of bread he had eaten since his mother was alive.

His eyes closed as he devoured the monster-sized bite from the half sandwich she held. Small murmurs of pleasure escaped his lips.

Her fingers tingled from where his lips had touched her. She was paralyzed by the wave of desire-laden guilt rolling to her toes. She lowered her hand to the desk, the half-eaten sandwich barely in her grasp.

He seemed to be enjoying the salad. His eyes remained shut and his mouth stretched into a soft smile as he chewed.

She was thankful for the relief from his intense scrutiny. She had been a bundle of nerves when she crossed the street. Jane and

Millie convinced her that Sean wasn't eating properly, that he was consumed with discovering who broke into the station, and would forget to feed himself. When she lowered the front shade for the night and saw the light in his office still burning, she decided she owed him more than a simple apology for nearly slitting his belly. Within twenty minutes, she had bread sliced, dressing mixed with chopped chicken, and warmed chutney all packaged nicely. Crossing the street, her stomach began to question her spontaneous decision.

And now, staring at the slight dusting of five-o'clock shadow on his square jaw, reeling from the barest touch of his lips to her skin, she wasn't sure spontaneity was wise. Where had the impulse come from? She wasn't exactly a fly-by-the-seat-of-your-pants kind of woman. She was strategic and planned. She was thoughtful and organized. She knew escape routes and tactical maneuvers. Uncle Jack had taught her well. When was the last time she had done something — anything — on a whim?

Sam. Ten years ago. Sam Riegle, the red-shirt junior running back for the University of Maryland, with his sweet Southern drawl and knack for showing up at her dorm at two in the morning to go for a coffee or on a moonlit stroll through campus. He was joy-filled and ruggedly handsome with his over-long brown hair and his deep-set, gray-green eyes. He'd made her laugh until her sides hurt. He'd enjoyed the simple pleasure of holding hands while walking to class and watching an old horror movie in a dark room. He was what every girl wished for in a first love and more than anyone could have created in her imagination. Her stomach twisted as the echo of what might have been floated through her mind. She closed her eyes and rubbed her temple.

"Earth to Maggie." Sean's voice broke through, zooming her back to the present.

"I'm sorry. What were you saying?" She shoved down the overwhelming desire to drown in the welcoming warmth of his chocolate-brown eyes.

"I was saying that you may have turned me into a foodie." He grabbed the half-eaten sandwich from her hand and took another generous bite. "This chicken salad is the best thing I have eaten in more weeks than I can count."

Her heart warmed as he devoured the food. Maybe spontaneous wasn't such a bad idea. She slid the remaining half of the sandwich in front of him, shifting the untouched ham and Swiss to her side of the

137

desk. "I'm glad you like it." She lifted the sandwich to her mouth. Before she could take a bite, his hand touched hers.

"What, no sharing?"

The slight challenge in his face caused the tension to drain from her body, slamming the door to her memories. Possibilities filled her heart. "Well, I guess since you asked so nicely."

He chomped a quarter of the half in one bite. His eyes fluttered shut again while the groans of pleasure escaped his lips. "Wow . . ."

Slouching in her chair, she munched on plain, salted potato chips and enjoyed the show.

His complete surrender to the pleasure of eating melted more of the ice protecting her heart. Anyone who became swept away in her food couldn't possibly be too much of a distraction.

She crunched on a chip.

Maybe this one impulsive dinner wasn't a bad idea.

9

"So there is Mr. McArthur banging on his front door at two o'clock in the morning in nothing but blue and white polka-dot boxer shorts and black socks." Sean's eyes twinkled as he turned to lock the door of the station.

Laughter bubbled in Maggie as the image of the balding, slightly overweight, high school band teacher took center stage in her mind. "What did he do?"

Zipping his jacket, he took the canvas bag from Maggie's hands and slung it over his shoulder as they began walking along the sidewalk. "We approached him from behind and he called out over his shoulder, 'Sean, this isn't any of your concern. Wanda's fallen off the wagon again.' And he starts banging on the door, screaming for Wanda to open up."

"So you just left him there?"

"Nope, we cuffed him and brought him

down to the station for drunk and disorderly. Seems Wanda wasn't the only one whose wagon had tipped over. It was all cleared up in the morning, no formal charges or anything. But now when we get a call after midnight, I call it a WandaMac and generally send Alvin over to check it out."

"That doesn't seem very fair to make Alvin do all of the night calls."

He looked down into her upturned face and grinned. "Well, it doesn't seem very fair that Alvin sleeps through most of his shifts, either, but life isn't always fair, is it?"

She nodded her head and tugged her coat tighter. The chill seeped in through the opening, nipping at her neck. She'd looked all over her apartment for her favorite blue scarf — one of the only gifts from her parents that she'd kept — but it was missing. She probably left it at church on Sunday. It wasn't like her to be so forgetful, but with the events of the past few weeks her mind was stretched thin.

"Cold?"

She lifted her gaze to Sean and shook her head slowly. "Just a little. I wish I wasn't so absentminded. I couldn't find my scarf. It wasn't with my coat where it normally is. Who knew the temperature would drop so quickly."

"Welcome to Ohio. Our weather is nothing if not inconsistent." His head tilted slightly. "Are you missing anything else? You know, from the break-in?"

A chill raced up Maggie's spine. Swallowing against the lump in her throat that formed as quickly as instant oatmeal, she shook her head. "I don't think it's missing. I probably just left it at church." She flashed him a grin and was thankful for the darkness that hid her growing fear. "Nothing's missing, but I'll keep a look out." Burrowing her hands into her pockets, she shifted her attention to the small pool of water at the base of the elaborate fountain gracing the center of town.

Water rarely flowed from its spigots, and the exterior needed a good scrub against the mildew that had wall-papered itself over the ornate structure, but people loved the old thing, even placing the structure on the flag designed for the town's sesquicentennial celebration last month. She withdrew a penny, kissed Abe Lincoln's face, and tossed the coin into the dank water with a plunk.

"Did you make a wish, Miss Maggie?"

At this particular moment, she desperately wished she could chuck the pieces of her past and her mounting anxieties into the shallow water along with her one-cent piece. To not allow a missing scarf send chills of fear through her body or to not greet a simple friend's visit with a knife wielded in terror. If only it was as easy as tossing a coin in a fountain to rid herself of the ugliness of her past. "Even if I made a wish, I couldn't tell you. Wouldn't come true, would it?"

"No, I guess not."

She enjoyed the casual silence that lingered between them, creating a private cocoon against her worries, allowing her to just be in the moment.

Then Sean cleared his throat. "So, this morning when I stopped by your kitchen . . ." He leaned his hip against the wrought iron fence surrounding the fountain.

Her stomach rolled into her heart and she waited for the rest of the question. What would she say? *I thought you were a psychopath stalker who was released from prison. I'm sorry. We cool now?* Nope. They certainly wouldn't be cool if she dropped her past with a splat in his lap.

Her past held consequences well beyond the answers to deceptively simple questions. Knowing her past, he would no longer be safe. He would end up like Sam, or worse.

And Sean would just be the start. She had to keep her new friends and her new town safe. She needed another solution, another story. Think.

"I was just wondering . . ."

"You were wondering why I tried to slit your belly open like a fish?"

His mouth lifted and his shoulders relaxed as he crossed his arms. "Naw, I get you were freaked, and when you're ready you can tell me why."

Relief washed through like a tidal wave. Her cheeks burned. Once again, she was thankful for the shadow of night. "Oh, OK."

"I was wondering where that voice has been hiding."

"What do you mean?"

"Maggie," he said as he lifted his hand, brushing a loose curl behind her ear and sending a trail of tingling heat down her cheek. "I don't think I have ever heard a voice more beautiful than yours. I know I'm not a great judge of talent, but even I could tell the last place you should be headlining is a broken-down kitchen behind a bakery in a town no one outside of Columbus, Ohio has heard of."

She tried to recall anything prior to the stranglehold of terror when she looked up and saw thick rimmed glasses and jet black hair superimposed over his face; his hands clapping with the same slow, eerie, nauseating rhythm that haunted her for nearly a decade. "I was singing?" She stared at the pool of water below and squeezed her arms around her middle.

"You don't remember singing?"

"Sometimes I sing when I am alone." She kept her attention on the murky water. "It's not a big deal. I bet you sing in the shower."

He moved to her side, leaning his elbows on the fence. "What I do in the shower is not defined as singing. Screeching, maybe, but definitely not singing. What I heard you doing . . . honey, that was ethereal."

Ignoring the gentle flip of her heart at the easy endearment, she lifted a single eyebrow. "Ethereal? What am I, the singing dead?"

"No. I meant angelic." He chuckled.

"Chief, you should know by now, I'm no angel."

"I know. Even more reason for my surprise. How could that voice come out of you?"

"Hey!" She punched his shoulder.

"What I meant to say was that I was surprised that someone so beautiful on the outside could also generate such beauty from within."

"Nice save."

"I was a closing pitcher. Saves are my specialty."

The last thread of tension broke and she was once again at ease. "Pitcher, huh?"

"Yep, my sinker got me through college and a couple years in the minors."

"Did you ever play in the majors?"

"Nope. I wasn't that good. I was just an OK college player, but pitchers get some special looks, so I was drafted out of school and spent a couple years in the minors. My shoulder was fairly shot by the time I closed out season number two playing for this Double A team in the Carolina League. I knew if I ever wanted to comb my own hair when I was forty, I should hang up my cleats and try something else."

"I'm sorry. Did you always dream of playing baseball?"

"I guess. My dad was a big baseball nut. He used to play catch with Mac and me all the time. I guess baseball was something we kept doing to keep his memory alive." He dropped his gaze. "To this day, if I hear the clean snap of a fastball in a catcher's mitt, I can still smell my dad's cologne."

"What a wonderful gift." Her heart puddled at the image of a little tow head with a mitt bigger than him sitting at his daddy's feet learning all about their game.

"Yeah, I guess it is."

"So you played in college. Did your brothers keep playing?"

"Joe still plays. He was the one with all the talent. Broke into the majors about five years ago. He's a centerfielder." Sean named the team and Maggie, despite her teaspoon worth of baseball knowledge, was suitably impressed.

"Mac was really good, too. He was a catcher, so he could see the game better than Joey and me. He made it longer in the minors. He was what they call a journeyman ballplayer. I think he played one or two games in the 'Show,' but he found his true passion on the business side. The owner of the last team he played for became a mentor to him. Mac now runs the baseball operations for that team as well as acts as general counsel for the guy's holding company."

She knew that the youngest Taylor was a professional athlete. Anyone who'd ever spent more than ten minutes in Gibson's Run knew about the legendary Joe Taylor, but she'd never heard much about the elusive Mac Taylor. "Lawyer, huh? I guess baseball worked out for him."

"Hey, don't get too impressed. I can still rev up some heat and throw a fastball past

146

him. Emphasis on a single fastball. He's just a pudgy old suit now."

"Noted. Maybe I should watch out for that fastball myself." She gazed at him. "Regardless of what your brother is doing, I think you have achieved something quite remarkable here. You can feel the vote of confidence this place has in you. You have to be the youngest chief this town has ever had, and yet, I never hear anyone mention your age. They just talk about how good you are at what you do. For the whole town to be blind to your age is quite a testimony to your achievement."

"I don't know about youngest, but it is a nice, safe little town and I like to keep it that way."

"Well you do a fine job, Chief."

"And I am smart enough to know when someone is purposefully shifting the conversation away from herself. Weren't we talking about your singing ability before we got side-tracked on the talented Taylor brothers?"

She turned toward her apartment. "It's getting late. I should get home. Early morning," she spoke with an exaggerated yawn. She began walking, stuffing her hands into the pockets of her jacket.

"Hey Maggie, wait up." His hand

squeezed her shoulder, stopping her forward direction.

She turned.

He lifted his other hand to her shoulder, softly caressing her upper arms.

The wall she kept rebuilding in her heart began to crumble once again.

"Maggie, why won't you talk about yourself? Why don't you trust me?"

She wanted to tell him everything. She wanted to close the space between them and wrap her arms around his waist, rest her head on his chest and sink into his protective embrace. She wanted to pretend for a few minutes that her whole world wasn't held together by of the barest thread. But life — her life — wasn't about getting what she wanted. She couldn't afford to give people her trust. Her life was about survival, and despite her weakness, she had to keep the secrets. She pivoted away from him and unlocked the door to her shop. "I trust you just fine, Chief. I just don't feel like recapping my life story. History is history." The tinkle of the welcome bell echoed through the empty space. "Thanks for walking me home." She turned to face him with a practiced, over-bright smile. "I can take the bag."

He came into the shop and leaned against

the long table. Why wasn't he moving? He needed to go. At that moment, she craved being alone like it was the last brownie in the pan. She needed space to rebuild the protective barriers that her dinner companion had eradicated. Her shoulders dropped. She closed the space between them and yanked on the handle of the bag, but he didn't release his grip.

With the flip of his wrist, he tugged her toward him. She landed awkwardly against his chest, the air thrust from her lungs. He tilted her chin up, forcing her gaze to meet his, the warm, welcoming depths offering comfort and something beyond her understanding. His thumb traced the soft line of her jaw. "Maggie, I like you. You are a beautiful, exasperating, fascinating woman with more layers than a wedding cake. And, I am interested in all of them, the ones I can see and the ones hidden beneath the surface. Regardless of how long it takes, you will trust me. God sent you into my life, all loud and demanding, and I'm not about to let you shut me out because you are scared of something you won't share with me."

A shiver shimmied through her as his hand slid to the nape of her neck, gently drawing her face closer.

"Maggie-girl, this is fair warning. I am

not backing off. I am officially playing the game and I always play to win."

Her lids fluttered shut as she waited for his lips to drop to hers. As the bag's sudden weight dropped into her hands, she stumbled forward in the space he'd just filled. She struggled to open her eyes and saw the long table in front of her. She slowly spun on her heel, dragging the bag in her wake. She looked up and her foggy brain cleared.

Sean shoved his hands in the pockets of his GRPD jacket. A twinkle of a smile twisted at the corner of his lips. "Goodnight, Maggie." He went out her door, crossed the street, and then disappeared around the corner of the police station.

"Oh, dear. I'm in trouble with a giant, capital 'T.' "

10

The boom of the tribute cover band completing their sound check trailed behind Maggie as she elbowed the swinging door that connected the ballroom and the back prep room. She dropped the three empty pans into one of the multiple crates she had used to transport all of the individual desserts to the party.

Jane had settled on a mix of high-end desserts and simple classic treats, but no multi-tiered cake. Praise Jesus! Driving boxes of individual desserts and pastries the forty-five minutes of freeway between Gibson's Run and downtown Columbus was significantly easier than navigating the bumps and bruises of the trip with a cake.

She lifted the two-foot chocolate center-piece from the cooler. With measured steps, she walked back through the swinging door to the ballroom. If she could assemble this piece without mishap, the rest of the set-up would be a breeze. She could be on her way home to her second-hand sofa, a cup of tea, and a luxurious night of reading before the first police officer arrived.

The music tickled her ears and flooded her mind with memories of lazy days in Sam's car a lifetime ago. She released a deep breath and willed her tears to retreat. She didn't have the time or the energy for an unplanned trip to the past. Her priorities were in the here and now.

Balancing the wide box, Maggie maneuvered the obstacle course of tables. The dessert station was elegantly draped in navy and cream tablecloths. Each of the serving dishes and display trays was artfully arranged, some already laden with desserts. She laid the large box on a prep table the staff had thoughtfully set up for her use. Slicing the tape binding the box, she lifted the lid to reveal the nine separate pieces of molded chocolate that would form a large police badge inside a hollow outline of the state of Ohio. She had molded a large piece to look like a swooping ribbon with the FOP initials and the date etched in the surface. To complement the whimsy of the homecoming themed event, she had a football with a king's crown circling the end. The showpiece was intricate, but nothing compared to what she had completed in her final exam for cooking school. That particular piece had received a passing grade and a glowing recommendation, which landed her a job at a high-end Columbus hotel and eventually led to her own shop.

God had given her an escape route and a whole new life.

And she wasn't about to waste it. She arranged the pieces and slid the main components into the structure's framework. She set the final touches in place and then stepped back and surveyed the chocolate for any defects or possible opportunities for failure over the next five hours.

"Oh, my, it is beautiful!"

A broad smile stretch across her face as Jane Barrett walked toward her. "I think it will hold."

Jane gave her shoulders a quick squeeze as she took in the chocolate centerpiece. "I knew you were good, I mean, I've tasted your work. But this is beyond spectacular. This is art."

The compliment glided through her ears and into her heart. "Thanks."

Jane dropped her arm from Maggie's shoulders and took a slight step away to survey the rest of the table.

Maggie's mom had told her before one of

153

the annual family Christmas parties that a table should be interesting, with lots of different levels, so that all of the food would get a fair shake. "But don't get too fussy, Sweet Girl, all the bits are going to the same place." How many times had her mother called her that lovely old nickname? If she closed her eyes, she could almost smell her mom's classic perfume.

"Well, Maggie," Jane said, hugging her clipboard to her chest. "This is magnificent, and yet, so subtle. You have certainly outdone yourself. I adore the footballs filled with mousse. They turned out fabulous. I love, love, love the cherry pies, and are those oatmeal raisin cookies? My dad may melt into a pool of slush at your feet. And the sheriff badge cookies . . . are they shortbread or sugar?"

"The badges are shortbread. The FOP symbols are sugar — chocolate sugar cookies. And, yes, I may have promised your dad some oatmeal raisin cookies."

"Genius. You've managed to give everyone something that is bound to be their favorite. From fruit to chocolate, you've hit all of the major dessert categories. Both upscale and homespun. I am very impressed." Jane scanned a mysterious list of details on her clipboard. From her tightly coiled bun to her sleek, black sheath that accented and concealed in all the right places, Jane was the perfect picture of a behind-the-scenes event planner.

"Jane, you look amazing and calm. How do you do it and in those heels? And what happened to the hockey cheerleader outfits?"

"Millie finally bent to my will and we opted for professional rather than costuming. Praise my dear sweet Jesus!" Jane glanced down at her four-inch nude heels. "The shoes? The platform under the footbed helps." She snapped her fingers. "And as far as the event, well, I love it. It's such a joy to throw parties and it's even more fun when you are spending other people's money."

"You make it seem effortless. No one would know you took over this event only a few weeks ago." Glancing around the beautifully decorated room, Maggie could almost envision it filled to capacity with happy guests. "This place looks amazing. You'd never guess that this place was a cavernous ballroom with putrid carpeting from 1987 only two hours ago."

"Thank you, but it's only partially me. Much of the elaborateness is thanks to Millie and her ability to coerce even the stingiest of supporters to give generously. She had all of the cut-outs donated by a local supplier for a simple mention in the program. And she was able to not only secure tonight's band for half of their normal fee, but to get them to back out of a gig in Cincinnati."

"Wow, that's impressive. What, is she in the mafia or something?"

Jane giggled. "Nope. Millie is in the Millie-Wins-At-All-Costs club of one. She always gets her way. You would think I would be bitter about it after nearly three decades, but alas, I love her, so I am pretty happy when she wins. And I usually benefit from those victories."

As if saying her name caused her to magically appear, Millie sauntered up to the table in a deep burgundy halter dress with a fitted bodice and an A-line skirt. Her long, blonde hair flowed behind her. "Hello, girls, what's doing?"

Jane rolled her eyes and slid her hand to her hip. "Really Millie, does that dress scream professional elegance to you?"

Millie matched her best friend's stance. "Janesie, I have an image to maintain. And just because I am moonlighting with your little event planning business doesn't mean potential PR clients won't be swirling around this joint. I need to always represent Amelia Tandis Consulting. You never know when the next head-case will show up and need a beautiful spin in the Millie Machine of Magical PR."

"You really need to come up with another *M* word if you keep up with that drivel," Jane said, grinning at her friend.

"Hey, that drivel procured you all of these lovely expensive decorations for free and a band willing to make nice with the FOP on the off-chance that they might get out of a speeding ticket in the near future."

Jane's mouth dropped open. "Millie, please tell me you didn't promise the band they wouldn't get a speeding ticket if they were stopped?"

Millie shrugged her shoulders. "I may have implied that serving the state's finest one night out of the year couldn't hurt if they ever needed help with sticky legal situations."

"Millie! You can't promise things like that. It's lying. Haven't we talked about lying?"

"Oh, Jane, the virtuous wonder, I didn't lie. I implied. There's a difference."

"We'll talk about this later." Turning to Maggie, Millie smiled. "Everything looks beautiful. I can't wait to sink my teeth into a few of each."

With a quick scan of the table, Maggie swiveled to face Jane and Millie. "I'll just pass the final list of instructions to the caterer and be on my way. She's being kind enough to drop my serving dishes back at the shop, so there shouldn't be anything for you to worry about on my end. Have a good night. I can't wait to hear about it."

"Maggie, you aren't leaving, are you?" Jane asked.

"I hope you don't mind. I spoke with the catering staff when I arrived, and they felt very capable of filling the trays as needed and tearing down the tables." She shrugged her shoulders. "Should be pretty straight-forward." Without her interns, Maggie barely caught two hours of sleep per night over the past week. Her current fantasy centered on a solid eight hours of closed eyelids after unwinding with her tea and new book.

Jane's head tilted to the side. "I don't mind you not filling the trays. I was hoping you would stay for the event, as a guest."

"I really can't." She glanced down at her flour and butter crusted chef's coat, a small reflection of the work that had consumed her for the last week. "Even if I had clothes to change into, I'll barely make it through the forty-five minute drive home."

"Oh . . . I just thought that you might want to stay. You know, spend some time with Sean when you aren't in a chef's coat and he isn't in a police uniform?"

A flash of she and Sean dancing to the lilted melody of a love song twirled through her mind and sent a streak of shivers down her spine — but that daydream wasn't strong enough to overpower uninterrupted sleep. She was so exhausted, only Jesus coming back and tapping her on the shoulder for a dance would convince her to give up quality time staring at the back of her eyelids. "I am sorry. All I want to do is go home, take a long shower, melt into bed, and stay there for the next eight to twelve hours."

"Seriously, Maggie, you can't up and leave before your Columbus debut." Millie crossed her arms. "Everyone who's anyone in this town will be here. Or if they aren't, they'll wish they had been after the wonderful press coverage tonight."

Press?

Warning bells shrieked in Maggie's brain. Press meant photos. Rule number one in the nice-peaceful-life handbook was never get photographed. She swallowed. Her throat felt as if sandpaper lined its walls. "I guess I'll have to remain a mystery tonight.

No need to scare future patrons off by watching the baker fall asleep standing up. Not a very good image for a responsible business owner."

Jane stepped forward and laid her hands on Maggie's shoulders. "Understood. You get home and get some rest."

"Thanks." Maggie glanced over her shoulder at the table. "I think you should be in good shape." She refocused her attention on Millie and Jane. "Thank you both for giving me this opportunity. The faith you have in me is unwarranted, but appreciated."

Jane stepped back. "No thanks necessary. You did us a huge favor. With the last minute changes, you really pulled a rabbit out of your hat. I tried one of those little footballs back in the kitchen and that chocolate mousse is something to write sonnets about."

Maggie felt the heat rise to her cheeks and wrapped her arms around her middle to keep from yanking Jane into a bear hug, splattering her lovely dress with the flour and chocolate adhered to her chef's coat.

"Well, Mags, since we can't persuade you to stay, not that we tried very hard," she said with a lift of an eyebrow to Jane. "You better skedaddle out of this joint before tall, blond, and handsome catches wind that our plot to convince you to stay has been foiled by a hot shower and a long snooze. I'll lose all street cred if that comes out."

"Enough said. I'll be on my way. I can't wait to hear about the details at church on Sunday."

"You're closed tomorrow, right?" Jane asked.

"Thankfully, yes. It's under the guise of inventory, but I've secretly been completing the inventory all week in little spurts. I can't wait to have a day all to myself that isn't a Sunday. Two days off in a row seems so decadent."

Jane pulled Maggie into a quick hug, seemingly unconcerned with her chef's coat. "Well, enjoy the much needed rest. And be careful not to fall asleep on the drive home. Those roads can get a little curvy closer to Gibson's Run."

"Thanks. See you on Sunday." Maggie nodded a quick goodbye. She exited through the side door, leaned against the wall, and released a low sigh. Exhausted and over-whelmed with the kindness of Millie and Jane, tears were building. She slumped against the white painted cinder block hallway wall leading to the prep kitchen. Swiping at the wetness, she sought the only

One Who truly knew her. *Lord, please give me strength and let me know what to do. These wonderful ladies are so generous with their friendship — please forgive me for continuing not to share equally with them. Help me to know what to do. I need You now. I need You so desperately . . . to show me what to do. I just want to be me again. Is that even possible?*

She scrubbed her cheeks and shoved off of the wall. Each bone in her body felt like it weighed over a thousand pounds. She just needed to rest. Rest would solve everything. Maggie slammed her hands against the bar on the door to exit.

A rush of cold air whipped, wrapping her thin café pants around her legs, and reminding Maggie that winter was about to bare ugly teeth. The frigid wind offered a strange sort of comfort. Nothing like October zooming into November to freeze out a pity-party for one.

11

An upbeat melody filled the cracks of conversation as Sean wound his way through the series of cleverly situated cocktail tables. He couldn't suppress the slight smile as he faced the life-size cut-out of himself at eighteen in his letterman jacket. He shoved his hands in his pant pockets and rocked back on his heels, taking in his younger self's blond mullet and wide-mouthed grin.

The night that the photo was snapped, he thought life couldn't get any better. He was dating a cheerleader named Brittney who liked to dot her i's with hearts, and he was quarterback for a winning football team. He had reached the pinnacle of high school supremacy.

His fragile little bubble burst only two weeks later when Brittney proclaimed her love for the lead scorer for the basketball team, leaving Sean and his heart smashed.

For the next month, he wandered the halls of GRHS like a forlorn puppy.

"Flash from the past?"

Sean looked over his shoulder.

Jane's smiling face and constant friendship had been his comfort in the midst of that harrowing month and most of the other trials in his life. "Hi, Jane. I was just remembering Brittney and her heart-dotted i's."

Jane narrowed her eyes. "Just hearing that girl's name makes me seventeen years old and mad as a lion hungry from a forty-day fast."

Sean looped his arm over Jane's shoulders and yanked her to his side. "I love you, Janie." He kissed her soundly on her forehead, causing her to chuckle.

"Now, it's not every day you walk up on your wife being mauled by a police chief who is declaring his love for her. What is a poor husband to do?"

Jane's husband of a little over a year, hockey legend Lindy Barrett, stood behind them. Despite his relaxed stance, his glare was piercing as he stared down at Sean, giving a glimpse at the jealousy simmering under the surface.

Sean dropped his arm from Jane's shoulders. He didn't want to stretch the bonds of friendship too far. He feared he might have

164

his face stretched against Lindy's wicked left hook.

"Oh, Lindy, don't be silly," Jane said, sliding her arm around her husband's waist. "Sean and I were just reminiscing a little about high school and this awful girl who broke his heart."

"Was it Millie?" Lindy asked.

"Nope." Sean chuckled. "Millie broke my heart at ten. This was another cheerleader."

"Enough about high school. It's a depressing topic. I want to know what you think." Jane spread her left arm out toward the ballroom filled with mingling guests.

The wide buffet wrapped the back left corner of the room, and several cops stacked their plates with a variety of hot and cold appetizers. The parquet dance floor was partially filled with guests swaying to the music, and the simple yet elegant dessert display, sitting opposite the appetizers, was starting to draw a crowd.

"Janesie, you and Killer definitely outdid yourselves. This place looks amazing. You will probably have to plan the next twenty of these things."

Jane's cheeks flared pink as her husband tugged her closer to his side. "That's what I told her," Lindy said, pride lacing his voice. "She was born to make people happy. She's certainly made me happier than I ever thought possible."

Lindy brushed a soft kiss to Jane's forehead.

A wave of awkward washed over Sean as he watched the blatant adoration his dear friend's husband had for her. He was ecstatic for Jane. He didn't know anyone who deserved this kind of love more, but he couldn't quite squelch the envy creeping up his spine as he took in the blissful couple. *Snap out of it! You're a dude. Dudes don't get gushy over happily-ever-after, chick-flicks, or sappy commercials.* Sean stuffed his hands in his pockets and searched the ballroom for a viable exit from the oppressive sweetness.

Scanning the desert table, the image of the pretty, petite brunette once again came to the forefront of his mind. Would she attend the party? He mentally reviewed their conversations over the past week and couldn't remember an actual invitation slipping into their discussions. He did remember their near kiss and the way she felt in his arms, as if God had created her to fit his embrace, and the stunned expression as he told her his interest was in more than friendship. *Dude, seriously? Man-up. The next thing will be reading romance novels in a*

166

bathtub with scented candles.

Jane cleared her throat, drawing his attention. "Gentlemen, I need to see about a few things. Sean, would you be the wonderful friend I know you are and introduce Lindy around?"

Sean nodded. "No problem."

"Thank you." Jane lifted her lips to her husband's cheek, and then wiped away the slight residue her lipstick left. "I will see you later, Mr. Barrett."

"You can count on it, Mrs. Barrett."

Jane walked to one of the servers carrying a tray of appetizers and then guided him back toward the prep room and out of sight.

"So, would you like to get something to drink?" Sean asked.

Lindy shrugged his shoulders and the two moved to the ten-person-deep line at the bar.

"How was tonight's game? I was in a bit of a rush leaving town, and I only caught the second period. The team was winning, right?" Sean asked as the two scooted forward.

"We managed to tank in the third." Lindy shook his head. "This new goalie the team brought up is like Swiss cheese, filled with holes and sharp flavor. The coaches have their hands full with him. Not that he's a dream for us on the player ops side, but at least we only need to make sure he's communicating with the front office and has a place to sleep."

"Huh, I didn't really know what you were doing with this new job. I thought you were really digging retirement, although it's kind of weird to say you're retired at thirty-six. You seemed like you had a few good years left in you."

Lindy shrugged his shoulders. "My knees just couldn't take it anymore. This job in hockey ops, dealing with the players' acclimation, is a good way to still be in the game without having to travel all the time with the team or be away from home too much. I knew that if I wanted to be with Jane, I needed to be in Columbus. Simple as that. She is more important to me than any career. More important even than the Cup. I would walk on hot coals and through a wall of glass just to be with her." He shook his head, let out a low whistle, and rocked back on his heels. "Nice . . . maybe I have been married too long. I sound like one of Jane's sappy movies."

Sean matched Lindy's stance, shoving his hands in his pockets. "No worries, man. I'm glad you're a little sappy about her. She's like my sister and I would hate to think I would have to challenge you to a fight because you weren't completely sold-out on your relationship with her."

"You think you could fight me?" Lindy chuckled.

"I am a trained police officer, so yes, I think I could fight you. But no, I don't think I would win. I've seen enough videos and witnessed your exploits in person to know that you are more than scrappy."

Lindy nodded his head in approval. "Good to know Jane has had someone like you looking out for her."

"We farm kids stick together."

The two took the final steps to the front of the line.

Lindy rested both of his hands on the bar and shifted his focus to Sean. "What'll you have?"

"A diet soda."

Lindy nodded and glanced at the bartender. "Make that two."

"Make that three."

Both men shifted their focus from the bartender to the scruffy blond standing at the corner of the bar.

Jason "Hooty" Horton was the star defenseman for Columbus and an imposing figure at nearly six feet three inches. His face bore the beginnings of a shiner on his left cheek and his mangled mullet was still damp from his post-game shower.

Lindy grinned and slid the first of the three drinks down to his friend. "When did you get here? And, when did you stop drinking beer after a game?"

"I've been here fifteen minutes listening to my wife berate some poor waitress while I waited for you to get to the front of this molasses paced line. I gave up drinking two weeks ago, at the urging of my wife. Have you ever had a gorgeous pit bull nag you about something? You eventually give in because she doesn't have the capacity to release her hold on the bone. Nearly two years with Millie and I have become the biggest of push-overs."

Lindy snagged a lime from the bar fruit tray and plopped it into his soda. "Dude, you were a goner the first time you met Little Miss Millie. She could probably convince you to wear pink and start watching soccer."

Jason's face contorted into a twisted reflection of internal agony. "The pink I could handle, but soccer. I think that might be my line."

Sean chuckled as he sipped on his soda. He didn't know Millie's husband as well as he knew Lindy, but Jason's description of

170

Millie's tenacity was spot-on. He almost felt sorry for the guy. Of course, Jason was married to a former supermodel who also happened to have a super brain and the uncanny ability to speak truth into any situation. From his perspective, Jason Horton was one blessed man.

Jason downed half of his soda in one swallow. He sucked in a single piece of ice and loudly crunched as he spoke. "I'm starved. Please tell me we have more than little pizzas and chicken wings to hold us over until we head to Morton's?"

Lindy nodded to the dessert table. "Sean's girlfriend made all of the desserts, and from the samples Janie brought home you'll be more than satisfied, Hoot."

Sean shook his head at the mention of Maggie. "She's not my girlfriend."

A grin twitched on Jason's lips. "Really. That's not what I heard."

Sean's neck burned with heat and his tie seemed to tighten around his neck. "Maggie is definitely not my girlfriend. On a good day, we may call each other friend. And on a bad day . . . well, I don't want to think of what she would call me."

Lindy barked a laugh. "Come on, Lover Boy. Let's eat some dessert."

The trio wound their way through the

ballroom. Various officers stopped to greet Sean and were introduced to the two hockey legends. Both superstars took the handshakes and back-thumps with good humor.

Sean was impressed that they seemed to genuinely embrace the attention without seeking the spotlight. His brother Joey could learn a few things from these two.

The men arrived at the pillaged dessert table. The chocolate sculpture of the state of Ohio with its various intricacies was breathtaking. Maggie was truly an artist.

Sean glanced over his shoulder, looking around so he could congratulate her. And, maybe ask her for a dance to see if he had imagined how well they would fit together cheek-to-cheek.

Jason smacked Sean's shoulder as he leaned forward and snagged a delicate chocolate football from the table. "Girlfriend or not, this Maggie can sure roll out the spread." He popped the whole dessert into his mouth, simultaneously releasing a moan. "Forget about loving my wife, I would marry this girl on the spot and gain two hundred pounds in a year. This is amazing." His gushing words were quickly followed a loud thwack to the back of his head.

Millie stood just to the rear of Jason with both hands resting on her hips, her face reflecting the intimidation often associated with her husband. "Listen here, mister. You are tied to me until death do us part and unless you want that 'in good times and bad' to be more bad than good you better say that you had a temporary seizure."

Jason slid his arms around her waist and yanked her to his side. Kissing her temple he whispered in her ear and her face relaxed, accepting his hug with one of her own.

She leaned into his arms and smiled. "Don't ever say forget about my wife again, OK? You really hurt my feelings."

He kissed her lightly on the lips, releasing her from his embrace. "Yes, dear."

"Wow," Sean started. "I never thought I would see the day when someone could actually hurt Millie Tandis's feelings. There were days when I thought you didn't have any."

"Please, you can't even get up the nerve to ask the girl you are all gushy about on a non-date date. So don't get up in my grill with feelings talk. You've always been a little overly emotional and kind of a girl, Taylor."

"No need to get all Millie, just because your husband is enraptured with my girl's culinary skills."

"I'm really starting to dislike that Maggie-girl. It's a good thing Janesie sees something in her. That always helps me keep an open mind."

Sean snorted. "Yep, Millie, you are always open-minded."

"Hey . . ."

Jane stepped in the middle of the two old friends. "Stop. You two could never just play nice in the sandbox, could you? You've been friends too long to have a knock down drag out in the middle of a party."

"Yes, ma'am." Millie nodded. "Sorry, Sean. I'm a little on edge. This party is a pretty big deal, and we've pulled it together in less time than any of the rest of the events Jane and I have planned together. I guess the lack of sleep is finally catching up with me."

Jason slid his left arm around her waist and patted her tummy with his right hand. "And, she might just be grumpy about something I did to her as well."

"OH, MY GOODNESS!" Jane screamed and wrenched Millie out of Jason's arms and into hers. "Is it true? This is so awesome. Oh, my goodness. When? What? Where? How?"

Millie stepped back with a true blush on her cheeks. "Uh, I don't think we need to go into the how, but the when is in about six months. We only found out two weeks

174

ago, and we were waiting until we had the doctor's visit today to say anything."

Doctor's visit? Sean was confused. "What's going on?"

Lindy chuckled. "I believe Millie and Jason are going to be a mommy and a daddy." He stretched out his hand to Jason with a smile. "Congratulations, man. That's great."

Jason nodded as he shook Lindy's hand.

Awareness rolled over Sean, the heat of embarrassment warming his neck. "Millie, congratulations." He gently pulled her into a hug and whispered in her ear. "I am really happy for you. Sorry I was such a jerk."

Millie stepped back and swiped at an errant tear on her cheek. "Thanks, and you can't really help being a jerk. You are a Taylor brother. You guys pretty much excel at being jerks."

Sean rolled his eyes. "Glad to see being a mother-in-waiting hasn't softened your tongue."

Millie shrugged her shoulders. "Can't change. And even if I could, why would I want to? I am fabulous." She flipped her hair, spinning toward the dessert table. "Now let's eat some sweets. I can't wait until we go to dinner. This kid is hungry. And so is his momma."

The group of friends spread out, each lifting a plate from the stack, adding a variety of treats to the smooth surfaces. They found an empty table near the back and settled down to try the variety of delicacies. Whispers of mmm's and oh my's were the only sounds at the group's table for a solid five minutes.

Lindy finally broke the group's quiet murmurings. "Sean, I agree with my outspoken friend, your girl can cook her apron off. These chocolate footballs are ridiculous and the oatmeal cookies . . . I think I am out of words." He looked at Jane. "Did your dad try these?"

Jane nodded. "Maggie hid a small box with his name on it in the backroom. I have a sneaking suspicion it's filled with oatmeal cookies. Mom will not be happy."

"Why won't I be happy?"

Elizabeth "Bitsy" Grey, Jane's mother, had stopped just to the left of her daughter. The petite, platinum blonde was Jane's complete opposite both physically and emotionally, but the love the two of them shared was tangible as Jane rose and leaned into her mother's embrace.

Sean shoved away from the table and stood to greet her as well. Bitsy had been one of his mother's closest confidantes. She'd quickly stepped in to fill the gap his mom left behind in Sean and his brothers' lives.

She stretched up on tiptoe, yanking him down to her in an embrace that had the strength of his best handcuffs. "How've you been, Sean-dear? I've been in South Carolina with Emory so long I feel as if it's been simply forever since I last saw you or you came over for dinner."

He patted her sequined-covered back. "Missed you too, Bits. But, I've been busy."

She stepped back, but kept her hands on his arms. "So I hear. What with that awful incident at the police station and the mysterious stranger in town. But it's nice to hear that you've finally started to play nice with our sweet little baker."

Sean's cheeks burned. Why was everyone obsessed with him and Maggie? "We've been planning the party and I stop by for a coffee in the mornings."

"And I hear that you are there nearly every night in the café when it closes. Sharing a little after-hours dessert?"

"Mother!" Jane exclaimed.

Bitsy looked over her shoulder. "What? Jane-dear, I am just repeating what I heard from Sissy Jenkins at class this morning. It's not really gossiping."

Sean longed to rip his tie off and suck in

some much-needed oxygen. He slipped his hand behind his collar and kneaded the base of his neck.

Henry Grey slid up behind his wife. "Well, dear, by the sound of Jane's voice and the stain on Sean's cheeks, I am guessing you missed another opportunity to keep your mouth shut?" He extended his hand to Sean. "Hey son, this is a great party you and my peanut pulled together."

"Thanks Hank, but Jane, Millie, and Maggie did most of the heavy lifting. I just agreed and wrote the checks."

Hank smiled, shoved his hands in his pockets and rocked back on his heels. "Well, then, you did everything a man is supposed to do." Turning to his wife, he laced his fingers through hers. "My dear, I believe you owe me a dance and this sounds like a slow one. Not that I can really tell. This stuff is a little too rock 'n' roll for my taste. But for the opportunity to dance with my best girl, I can sway to just about anything."

Bitsy fluttered her eyelashes and leaned into Henry's side. "How can I refuse?"

The couple of forty-plus years began to walk toward the dance floor, but two steps in Bitsy looked over her shoulder and shouted. "Congratulations Millie and Jason. That's just wonderful news about the baby.

And, Jane-dear, I saw that box with Henry's name. You can just take that home with you. He doesn't need any additional temptations."

Millie slumped into her chair. "How could she possibly have known I'm pregnant? She's been in South Carolina. We only found out two weeks ago and didn't have it confirmed until today."

Jane leaned her elbow on the table and rested her chin in her cupped hand. "I told you her tentacles reach far and wide. She has an in with God. By the age of twelve I had an inkling, but I grow more convinced each day of every year. I don't question how she knows. I just always know she knows."

"My mom's the same way. It's a mother thing. You'll have it too, I imagine. Nothing to freak out about when we've got this stellar spread of sweets to devour," Jason said as he tossed a cherry tart into his mouth.

Millie perked up. "Do you really think I will have the Bitsy Grey All Knowing Gossipy Superpower when I have the chicken nugget?"

Jane giggled. "Probably. My sister acquired it when she had Chelsea. And it freaks me out." She bit into an apple-filled turnover and sighed. "But I agree with Jason. Who cares right now? I want to wallow

179

in all of the sugary goodness on my plate and not worry about the five pounds I gained the moment I looked at the table." She turned toward her husband. "I hope you were serious about liking those cookies, because I think we just inherited a box."

Lindy draped his arm on the back of Jane's chair. "They're all right. This Maggie chick can bake. She's pretty." He raised a quick hand. "According to my wife. And she lives in your dinky little town. So what's wrong with her, Sean?"

Sean's throat contracted. So close to moving on to a new topic. "Nothing's wrong with her. We just haven't had a date yet. I thought she would be here tonight."

"She would have been, Boy Wonder, if you had actually invited her," Millie said.

"What do you mean? I did invite her." He distinctly remembered thinking about inviting her. He must have invited her. Right?

Jane laid her napkin on the table. "Well, she didn't understand if you did invite her."

Millie leaned forward. "Did you actually say, 'Maggie, do you want to go to the dance with me?' Or did you pull a Taylor and invite her by telepathy?"

Sean lifted an eyebrow. "Again, with the surfer dude?"

Millie opened her mouth to challenge as

Lindy interrupted. "Ladies, not that we don't love having your attention showered on us, but we don't want to keep you from your duties." He squeezed Jane's shoulder. "It looks as if there is a significant back-up at the bar, sweetie, and Millie, isn't that Shayne Delroy from Columbus Monthly?"

Both friends instantaneously swiveled in opposite directions.

"I told Raymond to open another bar twenty minutes ago." Jane looked over her shoulder. "Sorry to rush off." She kissed her husband on the cheek before bulleting to the side door.

Millie rose with the languid pace of a lioness rising from a nap and kissed the top of Jason's head. "Boys, I'll see you later. I am off to make this the most talked about event of the year." She glanced over her shoulder at Lindy. "And don't think for one minute that you are smarter than me, Barrett. I know a diversionary tactic when I see one."

All three men watched as Millie sauntered across the ballroom to the waiting reporter and photographer.

Lindy lifted his drink to his mouth. "Jason I applaud your patience and your intelligence. I don't know many men who could go toe-to-toe with her every day."

A smirk stretched across Jason's face.

"She's a handful, but I can't imagine my life without her. Not to get all movie-of-the-week on you, but she's made me believe in God's goodness in a way I never knew possible. He truly created that one woman for me."

Lindy sighed as a slight grin tugged at the corner of his mouth. "I know the feeling."

Apparently sentimental gush was contagious amongst men.

"And," Lindy shifted his gaze to Sean. "If what I've heard from my wife and can see with my own eyes is true, I imagine you know the feeling, as well."

Sean grazed the edge of his glass with his finger. "I don't know what I feel. Maggie is a complicated, frustrating, engaging, beautiful, and confusing woman. Half of the time I want to yell at her and the other half I want to squeeze the stuffing out of her."

Jason lifted a single eyebrow. " 'Squeeze the stuffing'? Are you an eighty-year-old grandma or a single dude? Do you like her?"

"Yes."

"Do you want to date her?"

"Yes."

"Then what's the problem?"

"I don't really know anything about her."

Lindy leaned back in his chair. "Isn't that why you date someone?"

Sean rammed his hand through his hair and began kneading his neck and his shoulders. "That's just the thing. Every time I get close enough to ask her out or even when we are spending time together, I'll ask her what I think is an easy question, and she evades the answer like a rookie running back avoiding a tackle."

Jason shrugged his shoulders. "Doesn't sound like you really like this girl."

Sean gritted his teeth together. "How would you know?"

" 'Cause if you liked her, you wouldn't care how many blocks she threw up. You would keep trying to get through to her. You'd keep trying because you believed she was worth it. Do you think getting Amelia Tandis to fall in love with me was easy?"

"No." Sean chuckled.

"Exactly. I had to use every stick in my hockey bag and find a few new ones to crack her thick exterior. Millie's issue was trusting that anyone could love her for something more than her looks. Once she accepted and trusted that I loved her in spite of how she looked, rather than because of how she looked, it was a whole new ballgame. I wouldn't settle for anything less than having it all. Dude, I know this is a little too chat-time-over-lattes-with-the-ladies, but being a real man doesn't mean hiding your feelings. It means not being afraid to let them shine."

Lindy nodded. "Although I do think marriage has made us both overly in touch with our emotions, Hooty's right. I almost let a wayward sense of nobility and my own fear keep me from being with Jane. Loving someone has more to do with understanding what that person needs from you than it does trying to figure out what you need from the other person. If you are focused on how confusing this girl is to you then your focus is still on you. She doesn't need you to decode her. She needs you to be there for her. What you have to do is figure out what it is that only you can provide her. You determine that and the rest of it will fall into place. It won't be easy, but trust me," he said as he looked over his shoulder at his wife. "It's totally worth it."

Sean leaned back in his chair and contemplated the two men who had married his two oldest friends. No one would ever consider either of the professional hockey players weak or unmanly, but here they were professing love for their wives and encouraging him to seek out the same kind of love with Maggie. Listening to Lindy and Jason made him want to discover if there was a chance. He stood up and nodded.

Lindy grinned. "Good luck, man."

"Dude's a goner." Jason leaned back in his chair and tossed another piece of chocolate in his mouth.

Sean wove his way through the crowd with his heart pounding, drowning the shouted compliments of party-goers. He didn't slow down to talk with anyone. He needed to get home. He needed to see Maggie. As he slammed open the door to the main lobby of the hotel, a heavy hand dropped to his shoulder halting his momentum.

Chuck Riley. He stepped into a manly hug, one-armed with three quick pounds on the back. "Hey Riley, sorry I didn't talk with you and Shelia. Something's come up and I need to get back to Gibson's Run."

"Understood. Party's great. I won't keep you, but I thought you might want to know what I came up with on that little project you called me about."

"The car?"

"Yep. Seems that your questionable car was actually rented by a recently released parolee of the State of Maryland, Mitchell O'Donnell. Name ring a bell?"

"Should it?"

"Not really. Just wondered. Name didn't mean anything to me, so I did a little digging." He stepped through the doorway and

185

leaned against a supporting beam. "He's from a pretty well to-do family in upstate New York. He was high up in a semi-popular Jesus cult called The Mission, before he upped his criminal advances. There was some hub-bub about him and a pretty little singer he tracked all over the country before he tried to kill her for not appreciating his overzealous fawning. His sentence was reduced to stalking and aggravated assault, thanks, it seems, to his parents' long-reaching influence. He's been a guest of Maryland's for a little over three years until a few weeks ago when he was released on good behavior."

The hair on Sean's neck bristled. "But, if he's a parolee, he shouldn't be allowed to cross state lines. I'm not sure if he can cross county lines in some states."

"Which is likely why he rented the car under a pseudonym."

"But why would he come all the way to Gibson's Run, and then leave the car that got him there?" Sean kneaded his neck and shoulder.

"That's a question for you to figure out, Chief. I will help anyway I can, but I have enough criminals of my own to keep track of, I can't take on another state's lunatics, too."

186

"Thanks. It would have taken me months to get this information. I really appreciate you going out on a limb for me." Sean's lips tightened.

"Partners don't stop being partners just because one of them quits." Chuck grinned. "Anyway, maybe now I can get you to come up and have dinner with us. Shelia's been in my craw for weeks, but I didn't want to bug you."

"You mean you forgot to ask."

"That too."

"I'll try and come up in the next week. Tell Shelia I am sorry for not getting back to her sooner."

"Thanks, man."

"Who was the girl?"

"Not a clue. Her name was sealed in the record."

12

Maggie scrolled through her expansive music collection. Her fingers lingered over certain songs, flashes of memories crowding her mind. Every song told a story. She swallowed against the lump expanding in her throat, choosing a playlist that was melancholy and matched her mood.

She settled on the sofa and cracked the spine on her latest find. Books held the same allure as music and cooking. Each acted as a buffer to the outside and often toxic world. She read the opening chapter. She read it again. And again. And a fourth time. Slamming the book on the garage sale trunk doubling as her coffee table, she stood. She picked up the steaming mug of tea and shuffled to the large windows that spanned the back of the apartment. The graveled space behind her shop had a quiet view with a shining security light. The view of the gravel and broken-pavement parking lot just out the backdoor of her shop made her feel safe; a bird's-eye view of the easiest entry point to her apartment.

The parking lot was empty except for her delivery van. The lone security light flickered, signaling that it would soon need to be replaced.

She pursed her lips. Another thing to add to the list for Sean.

Jane and Millie seemed surprised tonight that she didn't stay for the party.

Even if Sean had invited her, she would have declined.

Despite her more than flicker of attraction toward him, she knew the best thing for both of them was to remain friends.

Friendship implied a subtle distance that would keep both of them safe.

She tilted her head to the side and the vertebra in her neck cracked. Every bone in her body ached, as if she were in her late nineties, not her twenties. Lifting her free hand to her shoulder, she rubbed the muscle trailing her collar bone. Her eyes floated shut, allowing the simple massage to soothe more than her weary bones, and she melted against the brick windowsill.

Her mind wandered back to the conversation she had with her Uncle Jack when she'd arrived home. He confirmed that her tormentor had made all of his scheduled appointments with his parole officer, except one last week. When Jack asked his PO about the missed appointment, he assured him that his parolee would likely have an excellent excuse. Her godfather wasn't as convinced and planned to drive up to Maryland to pay a surprise visit to the ex-con.

She tried to convince Uncle Jack that visiting him would bring more risk than reward, but her fierce protector couldn't be swayed.

She rubbed her temple at the mental replay of the phone call. She regretted placing her beloved Jack in jeopardy, but she knew her arguments were futile. Convincing a man to do the safe thing was rarely successful. She never should have risked an unscheduled call.

But Sissy's mystery car had her scared.

She tried to casually question Sean the evening after she saw Al's Always Available towing service hauling the sedan down Main Street.

He told her that the car appeared to be abandoned, and he wanted to return it to the rental company.

Who would rent a car and leave it in Gibson's Run?

The thought of whom the "abandoner"

could be sent Maggie's mind rocketing in a thousand directions, but she'd simply nodded to Sean and filled his coffee cup in silence. If she'd asked one of the questions that had shot through her mind, she knew his curiosity would be piqued. She wasn't prepared to quench his thirst for answers. Instead, she called Jack. But their conversation left her more worried and fearful than she'd been in over three years.

He missed a scheduled check-in with his PO.

There'd been an attempted break-in at the shop.

And the explosion at the station . . . could they all just be coincidences?

Don't borrow trouble.

She closed her eyes and exhaled a slow breath. Drawing in a lungful of air, her eyes fluttered open. The warmth of the air from her lips fogged against the window. The flash of wind against the glass pane seeped through the poorly sealed frame, forcing her to turn from the view.

Her gaze landed on coat hooks that held her well-worn wool coat and a fleece jacket she'd had since college, but nothing else. Her stomach twisted.

Have you noticed anything missing recently?

Her blue scarf, one of the last presents

she'd received from her parents, hadn't been at church last week. From the night of her parents' deaths, she had wrapped herself in the scarf like a security blanket whenever she needed the comfort of their arms. The past five days were jammed with preparations and the missing scarf hadn't crossed her mind until this moment. Setting her tea cup on the foot locker, she pivoted toward the jackets. She yanked them off their hooks hoping to see the tattered, midnight blue cashmere strip float to the ground.

No scarf.

Her heart sped.

She closed the few steps to her small bedroom. In the center she slowly spun, studying the space. Her bed was neatly covered with a second-hand quilt, and nothing else. The nightstand and dresser were empty. Jerking her minimal clothing from her closet, she flung the hanging pieces on the bed one by one. A knot grew in her throat.

No scarf.

Sean had asked her over a week ago if she was missing anything, and she had methodically searched the café, looking for any sign that her life had been invaded. Everything appeared to be in order downstairs. She'd never thought to look in her apartment.

She slithered to the floor. Her legs suddenly became boiled spaghetti. A warm tear streaked down her face. Dragging in a breath, she forced it out through her lips.

The break-in? The car? The missed appointment? The scarf? Was he here? No. No. It couldn't be him.

Her lungs burned with the pressure of the air she gulped. She shook her head. Coincidence did not dictate pattern.

He hadn't been in Gibson's Run. The madman wouldn't risk his freedom to spy on her and not make contact. He didn't work in stealth, subtle gestures. If he had been here — she swallowed against the knot in her throat — he would've wanted her to know it.

She must have left her scarf somewhere reasonable.

One more breath. Slowly in. Steady out.

A haunting melody about being courageous for Christ cracked the cocoon of fear that had quickly consumed her and wafted into her consciousness. She inhaled the words and allowed them to swallow the worry that seemed to perpetually plague her.

How she longed to be a strong and bold example for Jesus, but could she really live a life for Christ when everything she did was based on a lie? How could she fully embrace God's love for her, if she wasn't able to be honest about who she was, even with herself? She flattened her palms against the floor and stood. She scrubbed a circle over her face and rolled her shoulders. She was safe. Staying safe was her number one priority. She was succeeding, for now.

She padded into the living room and slid onto her second-hand loveseat, grateful when the music shifted to a hopeful worship song reminding that God's love wasn't dependent upon anything she did or didn't do.

"Father," she began to pray aloud. "I don't know where to start. I haven't been doing a bang up job of making sure I align my will with Yours and I want to change that. I want to be more in-tune with You. I am so afraid. I know You've told us not to fear, but Lord, I've been holding on by a thread. Please," her voice trailed to a hiccupped whisper. "Please, Lord, send me some help. Send me a champion, someone to protect me. I don't know how much longer I can do this all alone." She dropped her head against the arm rest and swiped a single tear from her cheek. "Yep, this isn't pathetic at all."

Shaking her head she lifted her gaze heavenward; a twist of a grin at her lips.

"Single girl sits at home, alone, on a Friday night. Drinks tea. Listens to sad music, and talks out loud to God. I'm surprised every cable network on the planet isn't beating down my door to make a reality series."

Three loud bangs on her door had her jumping from the couch as if the cushions were hot coals. Her heart sped, but she forced herself to walk to the door and look through the peephole.

Sean leaned against the door frame, his tie yanked loose and his dress shirt open at the neck. He looked rumpled. He looked agitated. He looked breathtaking.

She twisted open the deadbolt and un-latched the chain lock. Glancing toward the ceiling, she imagined God in heaven and lifted an eyebrow.

Silence was the only response.

Releasing a long slow exhale, she opened the door. "Hi."

One hand was propped against the door frame as he leaned forward. "I missed you tonight."

Maggie dropped her gaze, biting her lower lip.

"Why didn't you stay at the party?" he asked.

"I wasn't invited."

"About that," he said as he dropped his

arm and stood straight. "I am sorry. I meant to invite you, I think I even thought I asked you, but my mind gets a little mushed when you are around."

Her heart flipped over with the simple confession. She motioned for him to enter. He passed her without touching, but she caught the light, woodsy scent that always followed him. She lifted the chain and slid it back in place over the closed door. *Lord, please direct my steps and give me strength. You were listening, right? Is he my champion? Are we just supposed to be friends? Can You give me a clear answer? This can't be just some whacky, cosmic coincidence.*

She glanced down at her torn and paint-splattered University of Maryland sweatshirt and matching men's sweatpants with a faded number seventeen on the thigh. Her hair was twisted in a bun, still damp from a shower. Her shoulders slumped. Dressed in decade-old hand-me-down clothes, a mop of wet hair, and not a smear of make-up on her face. The Lord was making sure she'd be more than safe tonight. Definitely friend-zone all the way.

Sean wasn't waiting for her to give him permission or direction. He was examining her apartment like a detective looking for clues.

She glanced at the clock on the micro-wave. The policeman's ball should still be hopping. What was he doing here? "Can I take your coat?" she asked.

"Thanks."

She hung the jacket on the coat rack, shoving the worry over her scarf to the back of her mind. "Can I get you some tea?"

"Tea would be nice."

She moved to the kitchen and lifted her tea kettle. She filled the kettle and shifted the flame to medium high, then she set the water on to boil. "Should be ready in few minutes." She shuffled around the island, her arms wrapped together, the sweatshirt bunching over her chest. Stopping three feet in front of him, she dropped her gaze toward her bare feet and waited for him to start.

Did she mess something up at the party? Was she not going to get paid? Was she losing her shop because she accidentally poisoned someone with the baklava she added at the last minute to the dessert buffet? Was the person dead? Was Sean here to arrest her? Her arms tightened around her middle as her heart sped up.

Say something!

He yanked at his tie, slid it off, and tossed it over his jacket. Turning back, he let out a soft sigh. "Do you mind if we sit?"

Sitting was good. He couldn't arrest her if they were sitting.

He sat and fidgeted, driving the bubble of nerves rolling in her stomach to a steaming boil. She sat opposite, drawing her knees up under her chin and folding her arms around her shins. Watching him out of the corner of her eye, she began to gnaw on her bottom lip.

He shoved his hand through his short, blond hair and began kneading his neck. He was upset about something. He lowered his hand and shifted his focus to her. His eyes were dark and unreadable. "Maggie . . ."

A high pitched whistle came from the kitchen and they both twisted toward the noise.

"Tea." She stood.

"Oh, right, tea."

She moved to the kitchen, lifted a mug from a hook, and plopped in a mint tea bag.

He followed her, taking three strides into the kitchen space.

Trying to ignore him, she lifted the tea kettle and clicked the stove knob off. Steaming water sloshed into the cup as she bobbed the bag up and down to steep the tea. She handed the mug to him. Leaning against the counter, she laced her arms, and watched him blow above the rim of his mug. "Sorry, I only have mint tea up here. I try and keep caffeine out of the apartment. It's nice to have a place that's relatively stimulus free."

"Mint is fine."

"It'll need to steep about five minutes. If you want, we can sit back down and you can tell me why you are at my home on a Friday evening when you should be at a party you are hosting."

The corner of his mouth twisted into a partial grin. "Sounds good."

They both resumed their previous positions.

Instinctively, she hugged her arms around her chest as she watched him settle into his seat. Forget water-torture, the silence of this man could break even the strongest of soldiers.

Sean set his mug on the trunk.

The woeful sound of a sad song rose.

"Maggie, I should be at the party. I should be shaking hands and laughing with my friends. I should be eating dinner at Morton's with Jane, Millie, and their husbands. I should be a lot of different places, but the only place I wanted to be tonight was right here, on this couch, with you."

The blood seemed to rush from her head and pool in her heart making each beat thud in her chest. "Huh . . ."

Tilting his head, his brows drew together. " 'Huh?' I tell you I want to spend time with you and you respond with, 'huh.' "

"Sorry," she said. "I'm not really sure what I should say. I thought we were spending time together. It seems like we are spending time together every day. Aren't we friends, now?"

Sean began pacing in front of the trunk, twisting the space between his neck and his collar bone until she thought he might actually rip his shirt.

Maybe I said the wrong thing. She stood, reached up and laid her hand on his shoulders to stop his pacing. "Sean, I'm glad you came over tonight. I like that we are friends. It's nice not fighting with you." She chuckled. "Well, at least not as much."

He pivoted mid-pace and stared directly into her eyes.

Her stomach dropped to her feet. "Ummm . . . hi?"

"Hi, yourself." His lips twisted into a soft smile. His hands lifted and tugged the half dozen bobby pins from her hair. He dropped them to the trunk with a tiny clatter and unwound the heavy, curly mass from its bun. "You have the most beautiful hair, but you always have it tied on top of your head."

The release of the weight sent tingles shooting over her head and down her spine, detonating a warning siren in her head. She swallowed against her heart that seemed to be lodged in her throat. Biting her bottom lip, she willed the pink heat spreading across her cheeks to retreat. "Oh, well . . . it's kind of a mess. I took a shower as soon as I got home. I'm actually kind of a disaster."

"I think you look wonderful." He ran his hands lightly over her hair. "Comfortable, relaxed . . . wonderful." His hands rested on her shoulders and gently kneaded the stiff muscles.

Shivers careened through her system triggering a cacophony of alarm signals in her mind.

Who was this? When did Sean Taylor start doling out compliments like a romantic hero in . . . well, any chick flick ever made? Just yesterday they'd debated the finer points of using two percent over skim milk in a latte and he bored her with statistics over the coming college basketball season. He'd treated her like a buddy, a friend, an acquaintance — not like someone whose hair he was going to untangle or whose shoulders were in need of a massage.

She jerked free from his hands. "What are you doing?"

"I am trying to relax you."

"To do what, Chief? Why are you here? I don't think we've established that properly." Crossing her arms, she wished the sweatshirt wasn't four sizes too big.

"I told you. I wanted to see you tonight." He smiled and shifted a step closer.

Sliding backwards, she hit the half exposed brick wall leading to the bedroom doorway. She was stuck. She extended her hand. "Stay where you are."

He closed the gap.

"Hey, I said stay."

"I'm not a dog, Maggie. And you're going to listen to me." He rested his hand on the wall, forcing her to lean back as he lowered his face to hers. "You aren't going to run, or make tea, or find one of the million other distractions you have used in the last few months to avoid me." His voice was low and deep, as if he'd just woken from sleep. "I like you, Maggie McKitrick. I like how you treat your customers as if they are the only people on the planet when you are with them. I like how you get all fired up about the silliest thing and then realize it's silly and blush with embarrassment. I like how your nose crinkles when I say something

202

you disagree with, kind of like you are doing now. I like you. And I would like to get
to know you better. I get that you have stuff
in your life you don't want to discuss. That's
OK, for now. I just want the chance to get
to know you and to see if what I'm feeling
for you is as big as I think it might be." He
rested his forehead against hers. "Maggie, I
don't want to be just your friend or your
landlord. I want to be something more.
So . . . what do you think?"

Her breath came in shallow spurts.

His nearness seemed to suck all of the
oxygen from the room.

Forget about words forming or an opinion.
She would be happy with a simple air-in-
lungs scenario.

A soft grin tugged at the corner of his
mouth. "In the six months I've known you
Maggie, you've never been speechless. Give
me something."

She sucked in a shaky breath. "Whoa . . ."

"I'll take it." He chuckled and lowered his
lips to hers. His touch was light and with it
a shock wave of heat shot through her,
sparking like kindling to a wild fire. He
moved slowly, deepening the kiss with
determination, but with the unspoken
understanding that she could stop anytime
she wanted. His mouth moved against hers,

teasing with breathless anticipation, banishing the last of her resistance.

Maggie curled her arms around his neck and she fully opened to the kiss.

He lifted her to her tiptoes, crushing her to his chest.

And she let go. For the first time in nearly a decade, she was wholly in the moment. Pure heat poured through her veins and she rode each wave as it crashed through her system. Time seemed to speed up and slow down simultaneously. And as she felt Sean slow the kiss and loosen his hold on her, she stepped forward, seeking him as an anchor.

He lifted his lips to her forehead and kissed her with a sweet gentleness that turned the fire burning inside her to a warm pool of calm anticipation. He leaned back, his arms still laced around her, and tilted his head. "So, now that we've gotten that out of the way . . . I think we need to talk." With a chuckle, he laced his fingers through hers and guided her back to the sofa.

Resuming their positions, she was thankful for the space for the Holy Spirit between them on the couch. Her mind seemed to be filled with cotton and she couldn't trust her heart to not pull a Jeremiah 17 and deceive her into thinking that a little cuddle on the couch was a good thing . . . even if it seemed a stellar idea at the moment. *C'mon brain. Kick back into gear.* Conscience? Morality? Anyone listening?

He stretched his arm across the back of the sofa, nearly, but not quite, touching her shoulder. "So," he started. "Before I say anything else, I want you to know I have wanted to kiss you since the first moment you walked into the empty space with Jane."

Her head tilted to the side. "Why?" The question floated through her lips in a breathy voice she did not recognize.

He chuckled. "I don't know, exactly. I can't explain why I am drawn to you. I just am."

He leaned his head against the back of the sofa as his eyes closed. His steady breathing punctuated the subtle sounds of the sorrowful tune acting as the evening soundtrack.

She could feel her hair turning gray as she waited for his eyes to open. "Sean, I am very confused. I thought we were starting to be friends?" She was just becoming comfortable with being his friend. And now what?

He shifted his head. His eyelids opened to half-mast. "We are. But I want more. I want to take you out to a nice dinner with tablecloths and waiters. But that doesn't really matter unless I know what you want." His

205

voice sounded husky and soft to her ears. "What do you want, Maggie?" His words melted through her, breeding new questions and revealing old worries.

She rested her cheek against the back cushion of the sofa. "I don't know what I should want," she whispered.

He inched his hand forward lightly toying with a wayward curl.

Sliding out of his reach, she swiveled her head to face the far wall.

The cushions on the couch shifted as he slid toward her and cupped her chin, forcing her to make eye contact. "Hey, where did you go?"

"I'm here."

"Maggie, don't." His lips drew tight.

"Don't what?"

"Don't shut me out. For some reason me asking you out on a real date to a real restaurant freaks you out. Why?"

"You finished?" She asked, pointing to his mug. Not waiting for an answer, she took the cold cups of tea and retreated into the kitchen. She yanked the tea bags from the mugs, tossed them in the trash can, flipped on the faucet, and scrubbed past the point of clean. The anger and the terror burned like sulfur in her stomach, warring against the hope that only moments ago had been budding to the surface.

One mug clanked against the stainless steel sink with Sean's light touch on her shoulder. "Maggie," his voice was low. "Listen to me. I don't know what makes you fear dating or relationships, or even men, but I want to understand. I want to help you. Let me help you."

The warm streak of a single tear fell down her cheek. She turned and wrapped her arms around his waist, pressing her cheek against his chest. He drew her in and rested his chin on her head. A shudder ran through her entire body, as the tears she didn't know she needed to cry flooded his shirt front. His arms were a safe haven she didn't know existed. She was thankful for the comfort.

He's my champion.

God gave her the answer.

Let me help you.

She'd been waiting nearly a decade for the security of those four words. He would have no way of knowing what providing her help would require.

Eventually, she would need to explain everything to Sean, but not tonight. Tonight she wanted to revel in the simple joy of answered prayer.

The images were grainy on the six-by-four

207

inch monitor, but he watched clearly as his beautiful Mary Margaret ran her fingers down the stupid police chief's chest. Rage boiled him. He inhaled deeply through his nostrils. A cleansing breath meant to calm and retain control. The boil slowed to a simmer. He moved the joystick control to the left and followed the couple's movement through her dank apartment to the used sofa.

Couple.

The word felt like acid burning holes in his brain.

The small-minded cop didn't deserve to walk on the same soil as his beloved, let alone be in a room alone with her. He would teach him that lesson very soon. The cop was just another in the long list of loose ends Mary Margaret forced him to tie. But he would gladly bind a knot around this frayed ribbon.

He zoomed the camera lens on her face. Although the monitor was diminutive in size, reflecting only varying shades of gray, he imagined the color of her sapphire blue eyes sparkling up at him almost as if she could see him. He reached his hand forward and stroked her cheek, his fingers running along the cold smooth surface of the screen.

Rolling his chair to the far side of his desk,

he flipped on his printer and a whirring sound filled the tiny back storage room that served as his office at the demeaning job he'd been forced to acquire to adhere to his early release. A means to an end.

Swinging his attention back to the monitor, he depressed a single button to the left of his camera controller and blinked as the screen shuttered nearly twenty times in rapid succession. The printer expelled all twenty photos in under sixty seconds — the benefit of having countless used computers and digital devices at the ready in his role as a computer repairman, skills he acquired at the behest of the penitentiary system. Not a glamorous job, but one that had served him well as he prepared for his reunion with Mary Margaret, allowing him access to the technology, low and high, to reach his goals.

He lifted the first picture from the newly printed stack, the ink still moist to his touch. Unlike the monitor, his pictures were in full glossy color and revealed the subtle beauty of his bride to be. His eyes became transfixed on every feature.

High cheekbones. Full lips. Clear porcelain complexion. Long wavy hair, once angelically blonde, the only mar of his beautiful gift. She was a stunning masterpiece The Lord had created just for him.

He lifted the blue scarf around his neck and inhaled her delicate fragrance still lingering in the weave.

Without looking, he reached for the stack of photos and flipped through them like the pages of a live action comic strip. He watched her smile widen and her eyes flutter close. Lifting a glass of water to his lips, he smiled as he took a long deep drink.

The final photo in the stack stuck to the picture before it and he pried them apart with the force of his thumb and forefinger. With a snap, the pictures fell away from each other and he saw his beloved with her lips touching that man.

The water glass shattered in his grip. Blood dropped on his pants leg from a gash in his palm, severed by the glass. He looked at the pieces scattered across his lap, floor, and desk, shimmering like crude diamonds. Lifting the largest fragment from the floor, he turned it over in his fingers as he stared at the photo. He depressed the piece of glass against the cop's face, dragging the jagged edge across the picture in swift, sure strokes. Each movement became quicker, as he slashed the cop's face and superimposed his own features in the blank spot.

Calm washed over him.

She was alone again. Waiting for him.

He lifted the now nearly perfect photo of Mary Margaret and drew a heart around her face with his bloody finger. *Soon, my sweet. Soon.*

13

Sean arrived at her apartment the next morning with a picnic lunch and a pair of hiking boots in her size.

"How did you know my size?" she asked, suspicious, as visions of Mitchell's acute attention danced in her head.

"I asked Jane and Millie to take a guess. Millie was right." He grinned.

They spent the day rambling through the six-mile loop connecting Old Man's Cave and Cedar Falls in Hocking Hills. Stopping midway near the falls, they enjoyed a lunch of peanut butter sandwiches and apples.

The mist dampened her hair and clothes, sending chills through her body. She couldn't suppress the shudders that rolled through her or the whine that slipped through her lips.

Sean pulled a small burner and a tiny pot from the backpack and filled the pot with water. He set the liquid to boil and began rummaging through the bag. In two quick moves, he shoved her massive, curly mess of hair under a toboggan, and dropped tea bags into two pop-up mugs that had also been stashed in the bag. Her champion.

Maggie nibbled on her bottom lip, trying to ignore the flutter of her heart as he poured the steaming water into the two cups and handed her a mug with a wink. The cadre of butterflies stationed in her stomach stretched their wings.

She sipped, ignoring the scalding burn as the tea chased a path to her stomach. She could barely feel the cold chilling her toes, the rain on her face, the hard rock under her bottom, or the scorching heat of the metal cup in her hands. Her mind raced as she tried to form protective walls against the full-court press of woo he was giving her. If she wasn't careful, her heart would soon be a puddle for him to splash through and she would be forced to run again.

He blew across the top of his mug, his face mostly hidden by his tattered baseball cap. "How's your tea? Too hot?"

She took another tentative sip. "It's perfect."

"Naw, but I think that you just might be."

The butterflies zoomed to a swirling twister in her tummy. Looking at the water surrounding them, she ignored the pull of his gaze on her and sipped her tea, the sound of the rushing waterfall pounding out the silent lull in their conversation. Her giant mound of ever growing hair popped the toboggan to the top of her scalp. Sighing, she set her cup on the rock beside her and tried to readjust her cap. "So much for perfect," she muttered.

Sean chuckled. He leaned forward and yanked the cap over her ears and just above her eyes. With his forefinger, he raised her face to meet his gaze. "Maggie," his voice was low and barely audible over the crashing falls. "I am all in. Crazy, beautiful hair included. I know it's a lot to take in. And it must feel as if I flipped some switch, but sweetheart, this thing between us, it's been burning a slow, steady flame since the moment I laid eyes on you."

With a gulp, she tried to ram her expanding heart back down her throat. Dipping her chin, she broke the connection with his eyes. "Sean, I think we should just stay friends." She twisted the cup between her hands and stared at the falls. "You don't know me. And I don't want to run the risk of losing your friendship. Of having to leave."

He grabbed her hand, forcing her to look

214

at him. "Leave? Maggie, who said anything about leaving?"

"No one, but what if you and I . . . what if we try and date . . ."

"I like the sound of that," he said with a grin.

Her eyes did a synchronized somersault. "What if we try and it doesn't work out? You are my landlord. We live in the same extraordinarily small town, one on which you have dibs."

"Dibs? Gibson's Run isn't the last cookie in the jar."

"No, but your life is here, always has been, and mine just started. If we try and fail, I would end up having to leave and start over." Again.

Raising a single finger to her face, he traced the subtle curve of her high cheekbone. "Then let's not fail."

"Sean, I'm serious."

"So am I." Leaning forward, he pressed a soft kiss to her lips.

"What kind of game are you playing?" she whispered.

"Game?" His forehead pinched, creating a deep crease between his eyes. "I don't play games with people."

"Some people do."

"Maggie, I'm not some people and I'm

not giving up so easily." He tossed the remainder of his tea over his shoulder and threw the used teabag in the wrapper from his sandwich. He thrust the trash and his pop-up mug into his backpack. "Maggie," he said, tugging on her shoulder and forcing eye contact. "I'm warning you right now, I'm pushing this thing between us as if I'm the last out running to first."

"I have no idea what that means."

Sitting back on his heels, he shot her a toothy grin. "Well, my dear, your new suitor, if you'll have me, is a former ball player. You'll just have to figure that one out." He reached out his hand to her and she laid her empty cup in his open palm.

Suitor. Such an old-fashioned word, but gentlemanly, befitting the man. She had a suitor if she wanted one. A shiver ran through her body that had little to do with the cold. She waited for the inevitable fear to consume her, but all that followed was a sense of calm, of knowing that she was on the right path. She stood, wiped her hands down the front of her jeans, and adjusted her hat.

He linked his hand with hers, guiding her down the subtle slope and back to the main trail.

"So you were a baseball player . . ."

216

He yanked her close to his side and draped his arm over her shoulders. "Just ball player. Drop the base." He smacked a kiss against her wool-covered forehead. "But no worries, we've got a few months to teach you the ins and outs of the game. We'll make you an aficionado before spring."

She wiggled free and scooted a few steps in front of Sean. "Spring?" she called over her shoulder. "You are awfully presumptuous, Chief Taylor."

He grabbed her hand. She stumbled over her feet, landing with a thud against his chest. "You can stop being difficult now," he said, lifting her chin. "I'm not giving in, Maggie. You'll just have to get used to the idea of us." He tossed his backpack over one shoulder and hugged her against his other side with a tug. His stride was double the length of her own, and she struggled against running.

She planted her feet and leaned forward, gripping her thighs.

Sean grunted as he tumbled head first toward the edge of the trail. Wet leaves formed a smooth path like a slide. His hand thrashed forward and clutched at her ankle for support. The force yanked her toward him.

She skidded to a stop, grabbing hold of a

sapling jutting out of the ground. Mud sloshed against her face; her heartbeat filled her ears.

"Hang onto the tree, Maggie," Sean yelled. The pull of his weight lessened against her leg. He tossed his backpack on to the trail as he clung to a tree root with his opposite hand. Dragging himself against the slope, he threw a leg toward the path and lurched for a rock partially submerged under a pile of brush. Within minutes, both of his feet were flat on the trail and his hands were reaching toward her.

"Take my hand," he said, his voice a rumble of a whisper.

She looked from the tree, strong and solid, certain it would hold her weight, to his waiting hands and hesitated.

"You're gonna have to trust me, Maggie. I won't let you fall." He stretched his hand slightly closer to her. "I promise. Trust me."

She closed her eyes and extended her left hand, grasping for his waiting palm. Gulping air, she felt his grip tighten around her wrist and her eyes snapped open. Her feet dangled high above the seemingly bottomless ravine. The bark scratched at her hand. A line of sweat dropped down her cheek disappearing into the pit below.

"Let go, Maggie. I've got you." His voice

was barely audible above the waterfall in the near distance.

She twisted, focused her gaze to his, and lunged.

He hauled her to him. The velocity caused them to stumble and fall in a heap just to the left of his backpack. His arms wrapped around her. Her face pressed tightly against his chest; his heart thumped against her cheek. His hands quickly trailed her arms and back. "Are you OK?"

She nodded her head. Words would be minutes or possibly hours, away.

"I'm so sorry." He puffed a heavy breath. "I don't know what I would do if something happened to you." He gently kissed her forehead.

Staring into his eyes, she wanted to be consumed by the genuine concern and care she saw in their depths. The lump dissipated in her throat. She, too, was all in. She trusted him. He was her champion.

On Sunday, they attended church together. The forty-pew, white-clapboard church on the corner of Walnut and Spruce was the second-oldest building in town. The little corner landmark was the place where Sean's family had worshipped decades earlier, in multiple pews. Now he was the lone remnant of the past, surrounded by the family of his heart rather than his blood, he'd told her. Sean beamed as he introduced Maggie to dozens of people she served daily in the coffee shop.

With each handshake and welcoming hug, she sensed a shift. She was no longer the anonymous new woman in town. She wasn't the baker who made tasty treats and the best coffee. She was officially being branded a local and the potential girlfriend of the middle Taylor brother. The innocent act of walking through the church doors together as a couple vaulted them to "IT" status and the topic of the hottest gossip in town. But Maggie didn't mind.

Since the day she sprinted from Maryland, she'd needed to hide and escape. She'd run stealth and off the grid. She moved often and with little notice. Strategically, she made surface-only acquaintances and kept her appearance nondescript. The lead actress in a play that only she knew was in production. And yet, since the day Jane sought her out at church, her self-appointed sequester had been eroding.

Jane poked at Maggie's evasive answers about her survivalist existence and in so doing, offered the possibility of a stable, serene life. One that could be filled with a modest business in a community that was safe and insulated. Maggie's burgeoning friendship with Jane led her to Gibson's Run, the quaint little bakery, and a whole new life out of the shadow of fear. Day after day, her true self revealed bits and parts until all that was left of her one-woman show was dyed hair and a newly minted name.

Now, for the first time in nearly a decade, Maggie's life was moving forward, out of a state of anonymity and into a place of grace. In the centuries-old building, she found a piece of her heart that had been stolen along with her identity.

Over the next few weeks, their lives fell into a particular pattern. Sean continued to come by every morning for his coffee and bagel, but when she handed him his to-go cup he kissed her on the forehead. Each evening, he swung by the shop as she closed up and they chatted about their day as the floor dried from its evening mop.

She was almost ready to admit they were dating even though they hadn't yet made it to the tablecloth and waiter restaurant dinner date.

On advice from Bitsy Grey, she reached out to Jenna Arnold to see if the young teacher would be willing to work part-time, after school and on weekends. The newlywed was thrilled. The added help allowed Maggie to breathe as her business quickly expanded, and more time to focus on her relationship with Sean.

With each passing day, Maggie was more excited to start and end her day with him. She was falling in love. She wanted to be completely honest, but not if her honesty put him in harm's way. Since the night of the of the Policeman's Ball, she hadn't heard from her Uncle Jack.

The suspicious activities around town seemed to stop cold. No more manila envelopes. No more strange cars. No unexpected phone calls. The fact that Jack hadn't tried one of his countless contact strategies meant that the monster must be where he was required to be by the State of Maryland.

But Maggie's scarf was still missing. The explosion remained a mystery, and the gold sedan was a consistent topic of gossip when Sissy came in. The questions lingered, and her worry over the potential answer to those questions grew apace with her anxiety over when and how she was going to tell Sean her truth. And what that truth would mean for them and if Maggie McKitrick would be able to survive the honesty.

14

Jenna poked her head through the doorway adjoining the kitchen and the café. "Are the pies for the Smith brothers ready? Marshall just called and said he would be swinging by in a few minutes."

"They're boxed up in the walk-in cooler. I'll be right there to help you." Maggie made a final swirl of the meringue covering on the seventh of ten chocolate cream pies that had been ordered by Sissy Jenkins for her family's Thanksgiving dinner. Maybe all the pie would keep Sissy quiet for a day.

If the sales came in similarly at Christmas, she would be able to afford a second industrial mixer or maybe a dough sheeter to help with all of the pie orders and fondant rolling for cakes.

She lifted two pies and slid them into the oven, flipping the egg timer to five minutes. Wiping her hands on her black apron, already plastered with flour, chocolate, and various other bits and pieces, she joined Jenna.

The past three days were a blur of butter, flour, and fillings.

Maggie, with the help of a few extra hands attached to Jane, her sister Molly, Jenna, and even Millie — who mostly sat on a stool and doled out orders — had baked over three hundred pies ranging from pumpkin to custard to fruit medley. She'd shipped eight pumpkin pies, ready-to-bake with explicit instructions, to Jane's sister, Emory, who was trying to impress her nearly mother-in-law. Another fifteen were going to a few different firehouses around the township and into Columbus early Thursday morning as a thank-you for working on a family holiday.

Her last sizeable order came from her favorite clients, the Smith brothers, who were hosting a family-business dinner for all of their construction workers and their loved ones. The brothers ordered twenty-five pies, fifteen dozen assorted cookies, and ten dozen brownies. She'd made two separate trips to the baking supply store, just for their order.

Jenna slid four pumpkin pies off the shelf and set them in the carrier on top of a stack of six pecan pies. "Those boys can really pack away the sweets."

Maggie chuckled as she added three cherry and one black raspberry pie to the carrier. She sealed the lid and lifted the pie to the wheeled cart housing the additional desserts. "I think they're feeding close to one hundred people tomorrow. They're having the whole thing catered by one of Bitsy's friends. At least we don't have to cook tomorrow. All of the baking will be done and the sweets will be in their respective homes, while all we have to do is stuff our bellies with turkey and oyster dressing."

"I can't wait. My mother-in-law is cooking and Tyler has promised not to study for the whole day, so we can sleep in and arrive with a pie and two smiles."

The buzzer sounded from the egg timer and Maggie stepped out of the cooler. She slid gloves onto her hands, removed the pies from the oven, and rested them on a rack to cool. "Jenna, you've been invaluable these last two days. I am so thankful the school district gives the whole week off and you were able to run the store so I could bang out all of these extra orders. You've been a real lifesaver." She swirled more pies with meringue and slipped them into the oven.

Jenna placed a pie box on the cart. "No need to thank me. I really enjoy working here. It's a nice balance to elementary kids every day." Jenna maneuvered the cart out of the walk-in and into the café.

Maggie followed. "I am glad Bitsy recommended you. I really needed help."

Jenna lifted the top carrier, shifting it to the counter. "Thank you. So, what are you doing for Thanksgiving? Are you spending it with the chief?"

Shoving the matching carrier on the counter, Maggie could feel her cheeks burn a hot pink. She still wasn't fully accustomed to people knowing her business. "Yes. Actually, I . . . we're going to Bitsy and Henry Grey's. It seems that the Greys have unofficially adopted Sean and his brothers. I'm to bring desserts."

"I'm guessing pies are on the menu?"

A shudder ran through Maggie's body. "I'm not sure I could eat a pie. At least not for a few weeks. But I've been testing out a few things that I haven't wanted to start selling in the shop, because I wasn't sure if I could maintain consistency. So, I think I might just spring something a little fancy on them."

"Well, I'm sure it will be delicious whatever you bring. How many people are the Greys expecting? They have a pretty big family, right? I get confused. Tyler grew up

226

here, but I am fairly new to town."

Maggie draped an arm over Jenna's shoulder and gave her a side hug. "Welcome to the club." She turned and packaged up the assorted cookies and brownies that would complete the Smith brothers' order. "They have three daughters, but only Molly and Jane will be at dinner with their families. Their youngest daughter is staying in South Carolina for the holiday."

"That's right. She had that big shipment of pies. So is it just Molly, Jane, and their families?"

"Nope, Millie and her husband will be there and both of Sean's brothers arrive tonight for the weekend." Maggie's stomach clenched and twisted. The Taylor brothers were coming.

Jenna leaned her hip against the back counter and laced her arms over her apron. "Meeting the in-laws? That's rough."

"It's not like that, not really. Sean and I are not . . ." What were they?

Her new friend lifted a single eyebrow. "You and Sean aren't what? Crazy about each other? With each other every free moment?"

"I know it must seem like we are. . . . well . . . a couple."

"Oh Maggie, you are the chief's girlfriend,

just accept it. Everyone else in town has." Jenna chuckled and squeezed Maggie's hand. "Girl, you've nothing to worry about. Everyone in this town knows how crazy that man is about you and his brothers will love you too."

"If it were only that easy . . ."

"Just remember to breathe. That's how I endure the holidays." Jenna gave her a little wink as she sauntered to the front door and flipped the lock. Twisting to face Maggie, she smiled. "Well, Miss Maggie, you better shove those worries in a basket on a tall shelf, because it's show time. Are you ready for today?"

Maggie folded the top of the carrier and glanced at her watch. "Better be. It's seven-thirty and we have a full one ahead of us. It'll be kind of exciting to hear the cash register ding." She squatted behind the counter and selected a music mix for the day. She wasn't quite ready for Christmas, but her Broadway mix was filled with upbeat melodies and would act as a livewire through her system until she could prop her feet up after close.

The front bell chimed.

She stood and her heart warmed as Marshall Smith ambled through the front door. Even in the early throes of winter, Marshall's subtle late-summer tan glowed against the collar of his white polo shirt. He was handsome and a charmer, but she wasn't tempted. A wave of realization washed over her. She wasn't tempted, she was taken. Her heart belonged to Sean.

"Good morning, sugar." A subtle grin twinkled in his clear blue eyes.

"I think we have everything pulled together for you."

He glanced over the boxes. "I think this will do it."

Jenna dropped the final coffee dispenser in its holder. "Are you feeding all of Fairfield and Franklin Counties, Marsh, or just seventy percent?"

"Hey, Teach, you and that undeserving husband of yours are welcome to join us, but I imagine Momma Arnold has you in your assigned seat at the family table tomorrow afternoon at three o'clock, sharp."

"You know her too well. We were instructed to arrive no later than two twenty or we would throw off the appetizer portion of the meal. I love my mother-in-law, but she's a little intense."

"Sounds like Momma Arnold. Ty and I got into our fair share of trouble with that woman for our tardiness after baseball games. She really went nuts when we didn't take off our cleats before we entered her perfectly perfect house. When I was twelve, she forced my dad to tan my hide about the mud I got on her fancy white rug one time. I don't think I sat down for a week."

"Sounds like Nan. She keeps bugging Tyler and me to have kids, but I'm afraid she'll need to resort to plastic covers for the furniture."

"Yep, she had those when we were kids. Her furniture will look like it's two years old by the time you have grandkids."

"Who knows? She could go rogue on us and allow grandchildren to rule the world. Even wear their dirty shoes in the house. Stranger things have happened."

"Well, I'd love to see it. You and Ty will make great parents."

"Thanks. Do you need help carrying the load to your truck?"

"Naw, just need to pay the pretty lady here," he said, turning back to Maggie. "And try to convince her that she is with the wrong man and should run away with me."

"Marshall, you are trouble with a capital T." The front bell jingled as Maggie giggled.

"Marsh, are you bothering Maggie?" Sean asked from the doorway.

Maggie's cheeks burned, but her heart

glowed at the sight of his tall frame, his face shadowed by his GRPD baseball cap. "Good morning."

He gave her a quick nod, but focused his attention on Marshall. "Don't you have something to build or destroy, Marsh?"

"Heard Mac and Joey are coming in tonight."

"So?"

"Just wondering how long they're planning on being in town. Thought I might see if JT wanted to grab a drink or shoot some pool."

Sean closed the gap between them in two strides and seemed to tower over Marshall even though he was only a hair taller. "Stay away from Joey."

"He's a big boy. Doesn't need Momma Big Bro to play protector, not anymore."

"Just stay away."

Marshall put two fingers to his forehead and offered Sean a mock salute. "Got it, Chief." He turned back to Maggie and handed her his credit card. "Sorry about this, sugar. Some of us can't handle being cordial this early in the morning."

She dropped her gaze to the counter and swiped his card.

Both men stood facing each other, arms crossed, jaws clenched, and eyes focused.

The café seemed to shrink.

Jenna snapped a dishcloth at Marshall and hugged Sean from the side. "OK, boys, stop being boys and making Maggie feel as if she is a rope and you two are playing tug-a-war. Agree to disagree. Wish each other a nice Thanksgiving. And then you get going, Marshall Smith, before I tell Nan on you."

Marshall's Cheshire grin returned and he slipped his credit card in the front pocket of his polo. Lifting the large carrier with ease, he swiveled to face Maggie. "You have a delightful Thanksgiving, sugar. And know you are always welcome to join your favorite customers for a big spread rather than some take out with the Taylor boys."

"Happy Thanksgiving to you and your brothers. I'm grateful for the invitation, but I'm excited to spend my first Thanksgiving in Gibson's Run with the Taylors and the Greys."

"Well, I guess if you get to spend the day with Bitsy and Hank, it won't be too awful. Not as fun as with me, but you can't have everything."

"I look forward to seeing you back next week for your breakfast meeting. Hope you have a good weekend." She picked up a dishtowel and threw it over her shoulder.

"You too, sugar." He turned back to Jenna

and Sean. "Happy Thanksgiving, Chief. Come on Jen, why don't you help me out to my truck."

"How can I resist such a winning offer?" She walked ahead of him and held open the door.

The bell gave a quick jingle as the door clicked closed behind them, but Sean continued to stare after Marshall as he loaded the desserts into the back end of his truck.

"He's not coming back today."

Sean turned to Maggie, his body relaxing. "Happy Day Before Thanksgiving." He flipped the bill of his cap, revealing a twinkle in his eyes. Resting his hands on the counter separating them, he brushed his lips against hers with a soft wisp of hello.

"Good morning to you, too," she murmured as her eyes fluttered open.

"Mmmm, it is now." He stepped back from the counter and reached for a large to-go cup.

She laced her arms and leaned against the back counter, watching his slow stride across the café. A million bubbles of excited anticipation simmered in her belly, all due to a simple touch of his lips. She couldn't believe he was actually hers. *How can he be yours if he doesn't know who you are?* The voice of accusation shouted in her head.

She yanked the dish cloth from her shoulder and began wiping the clean coffee mugs, setting them in even rows on the shelf. "You're making yourself awfully comfortable here, Chief. Are you gonna even ask for a cup of coffee, or since the crime is so low in town you thought you might take up stealing to give Alvin something to do?"

His answer was the sloshing of coffee into his cup. The wave of fear retreated calming the seas for the moment. She heard the soft slide of his cup along the counter behind her. Peering over her shoulder, she couldn't stop the tug at the corner of her mouth.

He's dreamy. This man made her feel as if she were fourteen, drawing hearts on the cover of her spiral notebook with Sean & Maggie 4Ever in the center of each.

"How much do I owe you, ma'am? Or did I pay enough before I picked up my cup?"

She placed a lid on his coffee, running her fingers around the rim to snap the lid in place. "Well, I've been told this is the best coffee in town . . ."

"Even better than the fast food joint?"

"Even better than that place . . ."

"Huh," he said, lifting the cup for a deep drink. "It is quite tasty."

"And, since it's such good coffee, I think I might need more than a little kiss."

"So what were you thinking?"

She slithered around the counter and stood a few inches from him. "Something like this," she said, wrapping her arms around his waist, stretching tall on tiptoes. His lips were a breath away from hers and she could feel his heart pound heavy in his chest.

He drew her closer, his arms giving her no room for escape. His gaze searched her face as if he were looking for a sign, advance or retreat.

She answered his question by reaching higher and touching her lips to his. The kiss consumed her mind and body. She was falling through the clouds, filled with wonder and excitement, not wanting the moment to end. Her heart pounded. Nothing else existed. She couldn't breathe, but oxygen didn't matter. Only him. Only her. Just the two. Nothing else mattered.

A bell chimed in the distance. Every time a bell rings an angel gets wings. Maybe it was when beloveds kissed, an angel got wings. Perhaps she really was enveloped by the clouds of heaven.

"Oh, dear. Didn't mean to interrupt," Jenna's voice was like ice water.

Maggie thrust away from Sean. Her head was filled with clouds and her legs seemed to be made of barely formed gelatin, but she walked behind the counter. Where was her common sense? Draping herself over her man in the middle of a store! Why isn't he embarrassed? *I'm embarrassed.* Embarrassment, like pie, should always be shared.

"Well, I guess I should be getting to the station. I'm sure Alvin isn't in yet." He picked up his cup and fit his cap back to his head. "Have a good day, ladies."

Jenna rested her hip against the display cooler. "Have a good day, Chief."

He nodded and gave a wink to Maggie as he walked out the door.

Maggie grabbed the dishcloth and began drying the remaining mugs.

"Girl, that was so hot!" Jenna squealed.

Maggie sighed and polished harder.

"You can't ignore me all day, Maggie. You kissed your boyfriend. It is not a mortal sin, regardless of what Sister Agnes told me in the sixth grade."

Maggie set the mug on the shelf and slowly turned to face Jenna. "I know. I just can't believe how quickly I can lose track of where I am. I would've continued kissing him until tomorrow morning if you hadn't interrupted us."

"Doubtful. Sissy Jenkins is on her way over. She would've totally stopped you, and then hammered you for details until you waved the white flag. That woman is relentless. I wouldn't want to ever get in her crosshairs. Although, she is a good one to know. She knows everything about everybody." Jenna slid her arm around Maggie's shoulders. "But you have nothing to worry about. You don't have anything in your life that everyone doesn't already know."

At the sound of the egg timer, Maggie rushed through the swinging door to remove the final chocolate pies. She slid the delicate pies on a cooling rack and then leaned against the metal counter and swallowed, fisting her hands against her tearing eyes. She couldn't risk anyone in this town knowing what they didn't already know.

15

The sound of racing paws scraping against hardwood and incoherent yells assailed Maggie as she walked through the front door of Bitsy and Henry Grey's home on Thanksgiving afternoon. She held one of the large carriers from the shop while Sean propped open the door with his shoulder and balanced two similar crates filled with desserts. Once she was through the door, Sean followed, allowing the storm door to slam as a golden retriever puppy slid to a stop at her feet.

Setting the carrier on the polished wood floor, Maggie picked up the wiggling ball of fur and was rewarded with rapid wet kisses on her chin. The subtle smell of puppy breath assaulted her nostrils but she wouldn't give up the cuddle. "I didn't know Bitsy and Hank got a puppy."

Sean set his boxes on top of Maggie's and scratched the head of the puppy. "I didn't know I would have to fight for your affections with a dog."

"GORDIE!" Jane raced down the hall barefoot with a leash in her hand, a harassed smile on her lips. "Hey, you two. You caught our little maniac."

"He's yours?" Maggie asked as she snuggled the wiggling puppy closer.

"No. Gordie is Lindy's niece's puppy. We're just dog sitting for the weekend."

"Oh. I guess you want him back?"

"Naw. If you can keep that little terror settled and away from my nieces, who believe he's some kind of animated stuffed animal, I will be eternally grateful."

"I think you might have to pry this dog out of my girl's hands."

Sean patted the puppy's head again before leaning down to lift all three carriers.

"Let me help you. Maggie, the kitchen is just through the living room. Everyone is congregating in there. Mom is in heaven doting on one man after another. The house is filled with them since Sean's brothers arrived fifteen minutes ago." Jane paused and whispered to Sean, "My girl, huh?" Her voice carried, settling in a warm pool in Maggie's belly.

"Drop it, Jane."

"OK, but let me take one of those carriers. I would hate to think that all of Maggie's work could be destroyed with a simple stumble of those clumsy feet of yours."

"Who's calling who clumsy, Miss I Trip Over All Inanimate Objects?"

"That's Mrs. I Trip Over All Inanimate Objects, Chief," Lindy said as he lifted the extra carrier from Sean's arms. "It's good to see you, Maggie."

"You couldn't defend me any better than that, dear?" Jane glared over her shoulder.

"Sweetheart, I thought you said being a Christian meant no lying. I simply corrected Sean where he was in error."

"Hmphf . . ." Jane flipped her head forward just before she rammed her shoulder into the doorframe of the kitchen. "Don't say a word."

Both men chuckled as they passed Maggie.

The kitchen was double the size of her industrial space at the café, with antique white cabinets and granite counter tops. The room was charming, warm, and inviting. Envy was a sin, but at that moment, Maggie envied Bitsy Grey to the point of needing confession.

Two separate stovetops, one a range with an oversized oven below, were being manned by Bitsy and Jane's sister, Molly, a petite

240

blonde, who was a younger version of her mother.

Sean's brothers, Mac and Joey, were crowded in the spacious breakfast nook with Millie, Jason, and a man Maggie didn't recognize.

Sean slid his carrier onto the island beside the other two before he sidled around the marble slab and wrapped Bitsy in a hug.

She squealed and smacked a loud kiss on his face. Squeezing his cheeks between her hands, she smiled up at him. "Now the day is complete. I have all of my boys and most my girls. I only wish dear little Emory could be here and the whole family could be together."

"Oh, yes, dear little Emory will be missed today. She does so much of the heavy lifting," Jane said.

Bitsy pursed her lips. "Jane, it's Thanksgiving. There'll be no negative talk, especially about your sister. Understood?"

"Yes ma'am."

Bitsy nodded. She turned to Maggie with a smile. "Oh, Maggie, I am so glad you could join us today." She lifted the lid of the middle carrier and peeked inside. Closing the lid, she looked back to Maggie. "My dear, you've really outdone yourself."

Maggie's cheeks warmed. "Just played

around a bit. The carriers have built in coolers. All of the desserts should be fine for over twelve hours. They could probably be put outside, to get out of the way, until you're ready for dessert."

"That's a wonderful idea. Joey, Mac, Jake, take these lovely boxes of treats to the mud porch. Please place them on the table. Do not put them on the floor." She lifted a single eyebrow toward Joey.

The lanky baseball player grinned as if he were waiting for a photographer to snap his photo. "Bits, would Joe ever do anything like that?"

"Joseph, you'd do much worse. That's why I keep my eye on you. Your mother would want it that way."

"Yes, ma'am."

The three men each picked up a box and disappeared through a doorway on the opposite side of the kitchen.

Sean, Jane, and Lindy whooshed into the booth.

Sean patted the open cushion beside him. "This is prime seating."

"I think I'll stand. I shouldn't have the puppy at the table."

"Gordie'll be fine at the table, won't he, Bits?" Lindy asked, draping his arm across his wife's shoulders.

"Of course. Until a couple years ago, Henry would have Koufax sit beside him in the nook while he ate breakfast and read the paper. It's nice to have a dog in the house, at least for the day."

"Well, if you're sure it's OK?"

"I'm sure, dear. Sit and enjoy the kids."

"Hey, why doesn't Jane have to help?" Molly asked over her shoulder as she whisked gravy.

"She has guests, Molly. When you have guests I don't make you work in the kitchen."

"Yes, you do."

"I'm sure you're wrong, but it doesn't matter. Jane needs to entertain her friends. Make sure that gravy doesn't get lumpy."

Molly returned her focus to her pan and whisked faster.

"My dears, can I get you anything to drink?" Bitsy asked.

"Mom, I can get the drinks." Jane slid from the back of the bench and crawled out the front.

"Jane, dear, that is no way to behave in front of company."

"Aww, Bits, we aren't company. We're family," Millie said.

"Yes, but this is Maggie's first time to our home. I want it to be special, memorable."

243

"Jane scooting under the table will definitely leave an impression," Millie cackled.

Jane shot her a wicked glance over her shoulder as she passed the men coming back from the mud room.

"Hey, you stole our seats," Joey whined.

"You are twenty-six years old, stop being a baby, Sprout." Mac knocked him on the back of the head. Mac was the same height as his two younger brothers, but his frame was larger, thick and muscular where his brothers were lean. His dark hair, just graying at the temples, was cut short, not quite Sean's style, but definitely more corporate than Joey's carefree locks. He was three years older than Sean, but sun had weathered his face with deep laugh lines giving him a distinguished air. Women probably swooned for Mac Taylor.

Not her, of course. Maggie grinned.

Joey shoved Mac into the table of the breakfast nook rattling the decorative pumpkins in the center.

"Hey, watch it!" Sean clamped his arm around Maggie's shoulders, protecting her and the puppy.

"Yeah, ballplayer," Jason pointed his finger at Joey. "My wife's a vessel. Don't make me go old school hockey on you."

Millie smacked a kiss on Jason's cheek. "I

244

love you, tough guy. But don't worry about me. I've gone a few rounds with little Joey in my day. I babysat him a couple times, he never crossed me again. Isn't that right, Joe-Joe?"

Joey's face shot through deepening shades of red before landing in the range somewhere between eggplant and passing out. He turned on his heel toward Bitsy, who held a wooden spoon in her hand. "Bits, you know he started it."

She began tapping the spoon in the palm of her hand. "I don't care. You are twenty-six years old, Joseph Malone Taylor, and at some point in your life, you need to take responsibility for your actions and your re-actions. I don't have time to deal with you right now. Go find Henry and the girls. They went looking for some dry leaves to make decorations, but they're probably at the tire swing."

He rubbed his neck where his slightly unkempt hair brushed the collar of his shirt and nodded his head. "Yes, ma'am." He scuffled his feet as he disappeared through the open doorway.

Bitsy turned with a sigh and pointed the wooden spoon in her son-in-law's direction. "Jake, go check on your son. He is probably awake from his nap."

Jake nodded and nearly ran out of the kitchen.

Bitsy swiveled on her heel and marched over to Mac. "And you," she said with a poke of the wooden spoon in his chest. "You know that awful nickname riles poor little Joey. He is a young man and you need to start respecting him."

Mac's cheeks flared. "Yes, ma'am."

She turned toward the table. "All of you need to respect him. He is not the little one trying to keep up anymore. Or the gangly boy whose arms and legs seemed to sprout faster than the rest of his body. He is an adult, as are each of you, and I expect you to start behaving like adults. Is that clear?"

"Yes, ma'am," Sean, Millie, and Jason mumbled in unison.

"I mean, my heavens, what must poor Maggie think of all of you? She'll think I raised a house full of heathens and I will not have it."

They all nodded.

She twirled and made her way back to Molly, who was vigorously whisking the gravy.

Millie started to giggle. "Man, it's like we're thirteen again."

Sean chuckled and kissed Maggie on the forehead. "That look just comes out of nowhere and shames you back to acne and dirt bikes."

"Never fails to put me in my place." Mac plopped down beside Millie.

Lindy shimmied under the table. "I think I'll go help Jane."

" 'Fraidy cat," Millie muttered.

He stood, wiped his hands down his jeans and shrugged. "If Bitsy's happy, everybody's happy." He kissed his mother-in-law's cheek and whispered something in her ear before he went looking for his wife.

Maggie stroked the puppy that had fallen asleep.

Mac, Millie, and Sean began to share anecdotes about dinners at the farm, but she was having a hard time focusing. Her brain was trying to calm her heart and her stomach while keeping her feet from bolting out the door.

She never thought caring — loving — would cause this much fear in her spirit. Hearing all of the yelling, laughing, good-natured fighting, and emphatic discipline was almost more than her senses could handle. She knew she should be happy, joining in with laughter and stories of her own. She swallowed hard, fighting against the tears ready to spill over her cheeks and the worry of the hurt these new bonds might bring. She wasn't certain she could survive another loss, let alone dozens. She was falling in love with more than just Sean. In her life, love equaled death. And there were no happy endings in her stories.

Sean listened to Millie's long-winded story about a youth group pool party Jane and Molly had thrown when he, Millie, and Jane were twelve. He'd heard Millie's recounting of her organization of the girls throwing the boys into the pool more times than he had recited the Pledge of Allegiance. But the story was funny, at least, Millie's enhanced, somewhat embellished version. He chuckled as she began to describe the climax of the story with more enthusiasm. Was Maggie enjoying his childhood antics?

She was stroking little Gordie's fur with a slow steady rhythm, clutching him tight, not listening to a word Millie said.

"Hey, you OK?" he whispered in her ear. Fear was mirrored in her dulled, blue eyes. The same as when she'd held the knife on him. "Maggie?"

"I think I need a little fresh air." She scooted from the bench and fled out the back door with the puppy, nearly colliding with Jane and Lindy, almost upending the tray of drinks he carried. She muttered a quick apology, but kept moving.

Lindy whistled. "Hey, Sean's not perfect, but no need to steal the dog."

"Lindy . . ." Jane scolded.

He set the tray of drinks in the middle of the breakfast table. "What'd you do to the poor girl, Taylor?"

Jane patted Sean's shoulder. "Let her go for a little walk. The fresh air might do her some good. It must be overwhelming to be bombarded by all of this family . . . umm . . . charm."

"But nothing happened. One minute we were sitting here laughing at one of Millie's stupid stories . . ."

"Hey, watch it, Taylor. I could never tell a stupid story. It's not possible. Right, sweetie?" she turned to her husband.

"Yes, dear." Jason kissed her on the top of her head.

"See. You're the stupid-head, Taylor." Sean waited for Millie to stick her tongue out at him, but was pleasantly disappointed when she sipped her water instead.

Jane slid in beside Sean. "Listen. We aren't the easiest bunch of people to be around. We are like a really bad opera, loud, fast-paced, and hard to understand. She'll come around. From the little bit she's told me about her life, I imagine it's been a long time, if ever, since she's spent the holidays with a large family. It was just her parents when she was growing up. She has an uncle, but I think he is more of a family friend than actual family. Give her time. Let her have a little break. OK?"

Mac rested his hip against a tall stool near the island. "Jane's right. Maggie seems like a real nice girl, but a bit skittish. Joe and I were only around her for a little while last night and she seemed pretty guarded. Sweet, for sure, but tense. Nervous. Can't imagine how whack it must be to meet your significant other's family for the first time, and then have to spend a holiday with them. Could be she just needed a break. But, if I'm not mistaken, there's a lot of layers under the surface of that girl. It's more than just nerves over Thanksgiving and our general obnoxiousness that's causing her to run. You sure you want to peel them back?"

"Definitely." The thought of what he would find chased a chill up his spine.

16

The air was cooler than she anticipated. Maggie snuggled Gordie, taking in the late autumn yard dotted with leaves. She wished she could find her scarf and revel in the comfort the little strip would bring on a holiday. She had to let it go. She couldn't — wouldn't — accept the implication of her scarf being more than simply misplaced. The panic bubbling out of her was just the remnant of the years living in constant fear. Releasing a slow breath, she tightened her grip on the puppy. She shouldn't have run away.

Sean and his friends were having normal holiday conversations about normal life.

The kind of life she desperately wanted.

The puppy yawned and wriggled as he woke from his nap. He licked her chin, lapping her with sloppy kisses.

"OK, do you want to play?"

His kisses quickened in response. She set

him down in the damp grass.

He ran, his feet moving faster than his legs, causing his head-over-heels tumble in the grass.

"Not much of a dancer, are you?" She squatted and patted the grass in front of her as the puppy charged forward.

"He better not be. He was named for Mr. Hockey and the dude might come and correct the dog if he becomes more of a dancer than a fighter." Sean's hands were shoved in his pockets.

She patted the dog on the head and tossed a tiny stick for him to chase before she stood. "Who's Mr. Hockey?"

"Don't let Jane or Lindy hear you ask that question. You'll be tortured with a dissertation on one of the greatest hockey players in modern history."

"So," she looked over her shoulder at the puppy that was systematically destroying the stick. "That's who the dog is named after? Some hockey player? You don't think it's a little weird that Lindy's niece named her dog after a hockey player?"

"Nope. Lindy's Canadian, so I'm assuming his niece is Canadian. They take hockey pretty seriously up there."

"Oh . . ." Weird. Named the dog after a hockey player, huh . . .

"Maggie, I don't know if you are aware, but your new friend, Jane, is one of the biggest sports fanatics on the planet." His smile was soft and teasing.

She shrugged her shoulders. "I guess we haven't talked about it much. When I first met her, it was through church, so that's mostly what we talked about. I knew she was married to a guy who worked for some hockey team, but I didn't realize she was a fan. We mostly talked about cookies and Jesus."

He stepped closer and slid an errant curl behind her ear. His warm fingers trailed down her cheek and rested lightly on her shoulder, his touch warming her better than a steaming cup of hot chocolate. "Cookies and Jesus. Two of my favorites. I can see how sports wouldn't have come up."

"I don't really know much about sports. I used to watch football, but that was a long time ago." She bit her lip, dropping her gaze to the puppy.

"That's OK." His voice was low and it melted through her. He lifted his other hand to her cheek and slid his fingers to her neck, gently stroking as he tilted her chin up, forcing her look at him. His voice dropped to a whisper. "I don't want to talk about sports, Maggie."

"OK . . ." Her voice matched his tone.

"I want to know why you ran out of the house. What happened that scared you?"

Unseen ice sliced through her. Jerking away, she folded her arms across her middle and focused on the stumbling puppy. "I don't know what you mean."

He placed a hand on each shoulder, his touch feather-light. "Yes, you do." His voice was still low and laced with calm reassurance. "I want to understand. Help me understand."

She felt a wet tear race down her cheek. She swiped at her face. She shouldn't be crying. She should be ecstatic. She was living her dream, one that she'd wished, hoped, and prayed for most of her adult life. And yet, she remained chained by irrational fears.

She pivoted and wrapped her arms around his waist and hid her face from the inquisitive gaze. "I'm being silly. I think I'm just tired and missing my mom and dad." She closed her eyes and snuggled deeper into his warmth. He felt like an electric blanket on an endless blizzard night, and she was colder than the center of Antarctica — a cold that had little to do with the November weather. "I can get a little weepy at the holidays. It's so nice to be here with all of you. But it's just a little overwhelming."

His hands glided up and down her back. "You aren't being silly. I miss my mom and dad every day. And the holidays are a hundred times worse. I am blessed to have my brothers and the Greys. I still have family to help bridge the gap and not allow me to feel so empty. You've not had that, at least not for a long while. I can understand why this could be difficult." He kissed the top of her head. "I just want to make it a little easier."

Tears pooled behind her tightly shut eyes. He was right, more right than he knew. She was a mess and he wanted to be with her in spite of that. Her nearness to them — to Sean in particular — made them targets. She couldn't be certain when, but she knew now that the monster was free, each of their lives were in danger. They were vulnerable and blissfully clueless.

"Maggie, I don't know what is going on in that mind of yours. I get really nervous when you go quiet." His hand continued its soothing strokes. "I promise I'll protect you. Nothing you could ever say or do would make me love you less. Let me help you." He pressed another soft kiss to her temple.

Slice. All of her resistance, her fears, and her secrets, all of it fell away in the safety of his arms. Sean would protect her. She knew it. Her champion. And he would protect everyone else, her whole family. She would help him.

"I love you, Sean." Her voice was a whisper, barely audible through the rustling of the leaves and the growling puppy. But she knew he heard because his hand stilled on her back and he drew her tighter in his embrace.

He lowered his lips near her ear pressing a soft kiss just above her sweater. "I love you, too."

A sigh rolled through her body. The fear, anxiety, and distress, tangled like a vicious web her entire adult life, evaporated in the breathing of one breath. She rested her chin to his chest. "Really?"

Lowering his forehead to hers, his face reflecting his tender sincerity, he whispered, "Really." His lips brushed hers lightly with barely the weight of a breeze.

Sparklers lit in her belly, tiny bright bits of light bursting through her.

He rested his chin on her head. She was content to simply stand in his embrace.

Voices grew louder, a mix of deep, male tones and sweeter, high-pitched girl voices, breaking the tender bubble they'd created.

She took a step away from him, his arms

still hung loosely around her waist. Lifting her gaze, she met twinkling brown eyes reflecting the feelings bubbling inside of her. She had no doubt that he truly loved her. No doubt. And with the assurance, she needed to tell him everything. She couldn't wait any longer. She had to tell him. Tonight. "Hey," she whispered. "After dinner . . . are you doing anything with your brothers?"

"Nothing definite . . . why?"

"I just thought you could stay for a little while after you bring me home. We could talk about some stuff."

"If you want to."

"I do."

"Then it's a date." He laid a quick kiss on her forehead. "We have company."

Henry was walking with two little girls, about five and seven years old, who were spinning around as they each talked.

Joey was behind them talking to Jake, who was carrying something wrapped in a blanket.

The puppy scurried to meet the girls.

"GORDIE!" The younger of the two girls dropped to her knees and scooped up the dog. His hind legs dangled nearly to her toes as she struggled to carry the puppy.

"Hey Lizzie, why don't you let Papa carry

Gordie into the house?" Henry lifted the puppy with one hand and carried the dog like a football under his arm. His thick mustache hid most of his wide grin as he stared at his granddaughter. "Hey kids," he shouted to Sean and Maggie. "Joey and Jake say that Bitsy's raring to go with dinner. We best be getting inside."

"Yes, sir." Sean draped his arm over Maggie's shoulders and they strolled toward the house.

Joey slid up beside Maggie and mirrored his brother, throwing his arm across her shoulders. "What were you two doing?"

Sean smacked Joey in the head. "None of your business. You already got sent outside once for being an idiot. Idiot is not a streak to keep alive."

Joey rubbed the back of his head. "Good thing Joe doesn't need his head to hit the long ball."

Sean snorted. "Boy, you better pay closer attention to this off-season training and less attention to the off-season girls."

"Hey," Jake came up beside them. "Little ears." He pointed to his two daughters trailing their grandfather.

"Looks like you got the littlest ears tucked away in that blanket."

Jake lifted the top of the afghan and

revealed a tiny tuft of white blond hair and the fullest cheeks Maggie had ever seen on a baby. "Oh, he's adorable. What's his name?" she asked.

"Henry. After his grandpa."

"Good choice," Joey said. "One of the best men I've ever known. Couldn't have asked for a better fill-in dad." The corner of his mouth lifted to a grin. "Taught me how to make the throw to second with barely a hop."

"Not a bad father-in-law, either." Jake followed Henry and the girls through the backdoor.

Joey turned and blocked their entrance. "Just so you know. Those girls saw you two making out. I would be prepared for some serious interrogation at dinner. If not by Bitsy, then by Lizzie, who might be worse." He left Maggie and Sean on the back patio.

"Which one's Lizzie?" Maggie asked.

"The little one who tried to pick up Gordie."

"Well, she's too small to ask any real questions." Maggie nodded for confirmation.

Sean laced his fingers through hers. "You haven't met Lizzie."

"Bits, I couldn't eat another bite. Everything was so good." Henry leaned back in his chair and patted his stomach.

Bitsy lifted her linen napkin to her lips and dabbed. "Oh, thank you, Henry. But it wasn't just me. Molly did all of the work on the gravy."

Molly looked up from feeding the baby. "Thanks, Mom."

"Of course, dear. But I do hope you all saved room for Maggie's desserts."

"I'll go get everything set up." Maggie pushed away from the table.

"I'll help you." Jane followed her into the kitchen.

Sean resisted the urge to follow. He didn't want to leave Maggie for even a second. But he sensed that Jane wanted to talk with her alone. She was the closest thing to a best friend that Maggie had. Girls needed friends. He wanted Maggie to have everything. He would give the world if he could.

Mac rested his elbows on the table and leaned forward. "She seems better."

"Not sure why, exactly, but she's definitely less anxious."

"Probably the make-out session in the yard." Joey leaned his chair back on two legs spreading his arms wide. "Joe knows a little action always calms him down."

Millie threw her napkin at Joey. "Sprout, can you even see maturity on the horizon, or is it so far out of your view you'd need to trek Mount Everest to find it?"

He dropped the legs of his chair with a thud and shoved away from the table. "I'll go see if they need any help in the kitchen."

"Not without me." Millie stood. "Who knows what will come out of that unfiltered mouth of yours?"

Jason lifted his glass and took a quick sip, watching them fade. "That's my wife, the ultimate protector."

Lindy patted him on the shoulder. "She'll make a great mom."

"I just hope our kid is as good as little Henry." He nodded toward Molly holding the sleeping baby.

"I don't know whether it's because he's a boy or I've had three, but I would have ten more if they were all as good as Henry." Molly patted the baby's back. "After Chelsea, it took me over a year to even consider another baby. And then, there's our little Eliza . . ."

"Wha'd I do?" Her little blonde head popped up at the mention of her name.

A low chuckle rumbled through all of the adults.

"Nothing, Squirt," Jason said. "I was just telling your momma that I wanted a baby like your little brother."

"But what if yer baby is a durl instead of a boy? It won't be jus' like Hen-wee, if it's a durl."

"I guess you're right. Maybe if we have a girl she'll be just like you."

"I guess. But jus' so you knows, it tooked a lots of work to get me this ways."

"Really?"

"Yep," she laid her hand on top of his. "Kids don't jus' come out like me. You gots to work at it. Momma says I'm 'a piece o' work' almost every day."

"I see. Thanks for the advice, Lizzie."

"Anytime." She turned back to her grandfather and the game of tic-tac-toe resting between them.

Molly stood, cradling the baby in her arms. "The one thing that is certain. You'll never be bored as a parent." She turned to her husband. "I'm going to lay him down. I want all hands free to tackle those desserts."

Jake stood. "I'll help you."

Gordie raced in from the baby's bedroom where he had been sequestered during dinner.

Lindy leaned to the right and lifted the dog into his lap with a single hand. "Settle."

The puppy let out a deep sigh and stretched across Lindy's lap, his head draped over his forearm so he could watch the table.

"So, how did you end up with this puppy?" Sean patted the dog's head.

"He's my niece, Isabelle's, dog. Gordie was a gift from her boyfriend . . . the musician. The genius thought giving a grad student a puppy was a good idea."

"But how did he end up with you?"

"She's in Chicago watching the same boyfriend perform this weekend. Izzy is starting her PhD program in physical therapy at Ohio State this winter. Jane and I thought it would be a good idea to have her stay with us. I travel with the team for some games, leaving Jane home alone. My sister and my mother didn't like the idea of Izzy living on campus, so it seemed like a good fit. She's the only granddaughter and likely the favorite even if my mother won't say it. She's a sweetheart and we're both glad to have her, we just didn't know we were getting the peeing machine, too."

Mac's eyebrows drew together. "You have a niece old enough to be in a PhD program?"

"Well, she's super smart and a little young for the program, but my sister, Flora, is ten years older than me. So, Iz's more of a little sister than a niece."

"And the boyfriend?" Mac questioned.

263

"Skylar . . ." Lindy shook his head. "He's in a band. Lead singer with tattoos covering his left arm. They've dated for six years. I'm not really sure what she sees in him. She probably wants to save him, or something. He's beyond flakey. He got her the dog when she told him she was moving to Ohio. He thought she would be lonely. Idiot."

"So . . . how do you really feel?" Jason leaned back in his chair, a smirk lifting the corner of his mouth.

"I know. I'm a little protective. She's so young and innocent. She's wasting the best part of her life on a moron."

Carrying a tray of assorted desserts, Jane laughed. "Talking about Sky, dear-heart?"

"He just gets under my skin."

"Well, Isabelle loves him, so he's family until she changes her mind."

"I guess."

"I know." She slid the tray on the back sideboard and leaned forward to kiss his cheek. "Telling a girl who she should love never works out."

Millie followed Jane into the room with a matching tray. "Yep, cause look how it worked out for you."

Lindy snatched Jane into his arms, jostling the puppy, who jumped from his lap. He kissed Jane with a loud smack and smiled.

"I think she did pretty well. I know I sure did."

"Aw, man." Joey was quick on Millie's heels, carrying a tray laden with coffee, cream, sugar, and mugs. He dropped the tray on the table. Cups clanked together, several landing on their sides. Milk sloshed onto the clean surface. "I just ate. That stuff should be reserved for dark corners of clubs or your personal space, not in broad daylight after I had enough turkey to make an entire football team comatose."

Bitsy swatted his hand. "Shush up. It's wonderful to see my girl so happy." She turned to Henry. "Don't you remember how we used to worry that poor Janie would never find anyone?"

Patting her hand, he lifted his gaze from Lizzie and the tic-tac-toe. "Yes, dear. Very worried."

"Thanks, Mom." Jane pushed herself off of Lindy's lap and distributed the cups to the adults, dabbing up the spilled milk with a napkin.

"Do I smell coffee?" Molly asked as she and Jake returned to the dining room.

"Maggie even brought specialty coffee to go with the sweets. And just look at the variety." Jane swept her hand across the trays of petite, individual desserts.

Henry stood and moved the tiny plates around with a single finger. A grin stretched across his face.

"I thought you were full, dear?" Bitsy laced her arms.

"Oh, well, I wouldn't want to make Maggie-girl feel bad after putting in all of this effort." He snatched up an oatmeal cookie, consuming half of it in a single bite.

Sean chuckled as the dessert line formed.

Molly led her two daughters. Lizzie pointed to each individual treat while Chelsea only wanted a single chocolate mousse tart. Molly lifted a raspberry short-bread bar and topped it with homemade whipped cream for her own plate before filling a cup of coffee and leading the girls back to their seats.

Gordie trotted behind them sniffing the air for falling crumbs.

Jason held Millie's hand as they each filled a plate with an array of tiny treats.

His brothers weren't as shy, filling extra dinner plates rather than the petite dessert plates.

Jane and Lindy shared a single piece of pumpkin pie.

Smiling, Sean pushed away from the table, dropping his napkin on the chair, and left the room with enthusiastic murmurs of delight trailing behind him. The chef should be showered with the sounds of delight not futzing around the kitchen.

Maggie was wiping the gleaming marble of the island. The popping of a second pot of coffee brewing echoed off of the kitchen walls.

"Hey lady, you've some new adoring fans out there who are singing, or at least 'mmmming' your praises. Clean-up can wait." He lifted the dishcloth from her hand and kissed her forehead.

"I just like to have everything in place before I settle down to dessert." She turned to the coffee pot and filled an empty carafe; steam pillowed around the top as the liquid slid into its new container.

"Do I smell snickerdoodle coffee?"

"Well, it's someone's favorite and everyone should have their favorites on Thanksgiving. Don't you think?"

"Yes, I do." Sean drew her into his arms. He lowered his lips to hers, brushing them with the softest caress. The feel of her hands sliding up his chest threw a riot of tremors through his body. He wanted to ignore everyone and everything, but he needed to stop. He wanted to honor God and to honor Maggie and both required control he wasn't sure his body could manage. He rested his chin atop her mass of curly hair.

She smiled as he trailed his fingers up and down her back. "I think that might be my favorite." She whispered.

"I agree." He pressed his lips to her forehead. Taking a step back from her, he squeezed her shoulders. "But too much of even our favorites can be dangerous."

She nodded and turned away from him.

He shoved his hands in his pockets to avoid reaching for her. He loved her, but he trusted his mind more than his heart.

Maggie's hands shook as she slid the clear tureen in front of her. She methodically layered the final pieces of the custard and berry, a favorite the brothers had discussed the previous evening. She lifted the finished dessert, layers of rainbow fruit sandwiched between vanilla custard, whipped cream, and a mixture of coconut and ginger short-bread crumbles. "We should probably get back. Do you mind grabbing the coffee?"

A knowing grin stretched. "Is that Donovan's Delicacy?"

"I hope I got all of the pieces right. Everyone should have their favorites on Thanksgiving."

He lifted the coffee and pressed a light kiss to her temple. "I hope Joey and Mac haven't moved to the living room to sleep through football. We haven't had this since mom died."

She carried the heavy glass bowl into the dining room, assaulted with the rising volume of conversation. Her heart warmed at the delight she could see in satisfied customers.

"Maggie, these desserts are out of this world." Millie patted her barely burgeoning stomach. "Little Champ is doing somersaults in there over these raspberry shortbread numbers and these stupid good, lemon curd macaroons. Maybe he'll be a gymnast?"

Jason's face went pale. "No son of mine will be a gymnast. Wrestler, maybe. Hockey player, no doubt. Football player, could work? Lacrosse is a given. But gymnast . . . nope." He leaned back in his chair, crossed his arms and stared at Maggie with a glare that was intended to strike fear in the best goal-scorers in the NHL.

Maggie laughed. "Well, I don't think a dessert can dictate the athletic prowess of a baby. So, I think your son's future endeavors are safe from my malicious macaroons." She set the tureen in the center of the table. Taking a quick step back, she waited.

Mac dropped his spoon with a clink

against his plate. Joey slammed the front two legs of his chair on the ground with a thud.

But it was Bitsy who spoke first. "Is that what I think it is?" Her voice was a soft whisper.

"Donovan's Delicacy . . ." Joey said in a hushed, barely audible voice.

Mac squinted and tilted his head to the left, a mirror image of Gordie, who sat at his feet begging for scraps. "But I thought you'd never heard of it before last night?"

"I looked through a bunch of recipes on the internet and some of your mom's old cookbooks that Sean lent me. I think I pieced it together. You'll have to taste it and see."

Lindy draped his arm over Jane's chair and pulled her close to him. "What's Donovan's Delicacy?"

"The guys' mom used to make it every year for Thanksgiving. It was a big tradition. When Joe was really good, which wasn't very often, she would make it for his birthday. I haven't had it since a year before she got sick." She looked to Maggie. "Unbelievable," her voice dropped to a murmur.

Tears slid down Bitsy's cheeks.

Molly laid her head on Jake's shoulder.

Henry rubbed his eyes with the heel of his hand.

And both of Sean's brothers rubbed their necks.

Maggie could feel the blush burn to her cheeks as Sean pulled her tight to his side. "I don't think I've ever seen this group so quiet. You did good, kid."

"I didn't mean to upset everyone."

Bitsy stood and cupped Maggie's cheeks in her perfectly manicured hands. "Maggie, you didn't upset any of us. You have given us a great gift. It's as if Lorraine is here with us today. Thank you."

"But we don't even know if it is any good."

Joey swiped a plate from the sideboard. "No time like the present to find out." He drove the serving spoon down the side of the tureen and scooped out bits of each layer. He lifted a spoon and shoveled a man-size bite into his mouth.

Maggie's breath caught.

Joey's eyes fluttered open. "Well, we definitely made the right decision renting Mom's space. This is as good as hers. The only thing you are missing is actually being Lorraine Taylor. I think the woman had some sort of magic ingredient in her fingers. Other than that, it's perfect." He took another giant bite.

271

Maggie's heart flipped. She did it. She made another Taylor brother like her. She clasped her hands to stop from shoving a plate in front of Mac.

"Well, if Joey approves it must be terrific." Mac spooned some onto a plate. "No one liked Donovan's Delicacy as much as Sprout." He took a bite and nodded his head. "Pretty awesome, Maggie. Thank you."

She took a seat on the window ledge, but inside she was in a valley at the base of the Austrian Alps, singing a high C with her arms spread wide, twirling to her heart's content.

Sean handed her a cup of coffee that she sipped, watching the tureen dwindle to a few spoonfuls. Her heart swam as she listened to the mmm's and oh my's from the group. The lack of sleep and countless websites cross-referenced with a half-dozen cookbooks was all worth it for that sound. Better than fifteen curtain calls.

Mac leaned back in his chair and rubbed his belly. "I couldn't bear another bite seven bites ago, but it was too good to leave any." He chuckled. "So we know you are a master pastry chef and you clearly love my brother — not sure why — what other secret talents do you have hidden in that tiny frame of

272

yours, Miss McKitrick?"

"Nothing really. Just a baker."

Sean rested his arm across her lap. "Maggie, that's not entirely true. You've got a wicked set of pipes packed away in there."

"Yelling at you is not a talent," she said. The room collectively chuckled, but her stomach burned at the thought of singing. That was Mary Margaret, the girl she left behind in Maryland. The piece she kept buried deep inside. Singing couldn't be a part of who she was, not if she wanted to keep everyone she was coming to love safe.

"You are good at yelling, but I meant that angel voice trapped inside of that pint-sized body." He tapped her thigh, focusing his attention on the table. "A few weeks ago I was out for an early run and the light was on in the shop. I stopped and was treated to the most beautiful singing I've ever heard."

Joey shoved his plate to the middle of the table. "I brought my guitar."

Before she was able to utter a protest, he disappeared into the living room.

Maggie swallowed the fear rising in her throat. "I don't know . . ."

Millie snorted. "You might as well just sing one song. Once Joey starts playing, he'll make everyone join in. Someone told him when he was eight or nine that all girls love

273

guitar players, and he hasn't stopped playing since."

"He played in the praise band all through high school, the whole time trying to figure out how he could hook-up with the lead singer." Sean chuckled. "Not really sure if any of the Jesus message sank in, but the I'm-in-a-band mentality definitely translated to his baseball persona."

Joey ambled into the dining room with his acoustic guitar in one hand and a stool in the other. "Come on Mags, let's see what you've got in that teensy body of yours." He settled on the stool and tuned the guitar as both Chelsea and Lizzie began peppering him with questions, lobbying to sing songs of their own.

"Sean, I really don't want to sing," Maggie whispered as she leaned into Sean. "I haven't done it in front of people in a very long time."

He kissed her forehead. "I think you should try. Something . . . something, I hope you will tell me about someday, has kept you from sharing the gift God gave you. You can't let someone steal it from you. Your gifts and using them are directly attuned with the joy you have. It's like baking a cake. God gave you the ability to make people super happy with one bite of your

Chewy-Chocolate Turtle cake. Think of the joy you receive each time someone tastes that cake for the first time. You don't believe God wants your joy to diminish because you are afraid to share another precious gift, do you?"

She couldn't argue with him. For years, she'd buried her music. The time was here to start taking her life back. One step at a time. She moved to Joey.

He was patiently answering the girls' questions.

She leaned down and whispered in his ear.

He nodded and started strumming the opening.

Maggie closed her eyes, let out a deep breath and opened her mouth. The music flowed, starting at her toes and winding up and past her lips. She could feel God in the melody. And His smile warmed her soul. The words floated over her lips and she felt transported. She wasn't entertaining. She was worshipping.

Oh the love! The peace. The joy. All of it.

Here in this dining room. For the first time in years, she felt God's presence flow through her in a way that was only possible through complete and open worship. For Maggie, the only way to be fully open to the Spirit was through music, something

275

she'd denied herself for so long. The words to the song rang true in a way no other praise song ever had. She prayed as she sang. With the final bars, she opened her eyes and could feel the soppy wetness of tears splashing down her cheeks. Her breath came in spurts as she looked around the room.

Everyone had tears.

Even Joey.

"I want to clap, but . . . and don't be offended by this, Mags," Millie started. "Not for you. For God. That was amazing."

All of the adult heads nodded in unison.

Henry reached back and squeezed her hand. He nodded his head. "Your daddy would be proud of you, Maggie-girl. Beaming like a lighthouse. I just know it."

The tears flooded her eyes. She launched herself at Henry and received the fatherly hug she desperately needed. She kissed his cheek. "Thank you."

He patted her back. "Just speaking truth. Just speaking truth."

She swiped away the tears. "Sorry. I didn't mean to make everyone cry."

"Oh, don't worry about that." Bitsy waved her hands. "Tears are just the Holy Spirit spilling out. Cleanses the soul. Now let's start to clean this mess up. We can visit more over coffee in the living room. Jane. Molly. Help me get these dishes. Leave the Donovan's Delicacy for the boys to munch on."

The sisters stood and began clearing plates and cups with the ease of years of experience.

Maggie stacked her unused plate with Sean's.

Molly looked over her shoulder. "You better sit back down, missy. You've been working all day and I'm guessing non-stop the last few weeks to make this about as special a day as possible. You deserve to sit back and enjoy a little rest."

"Oh, but I can help. I like to stay busy."

Jane lifted the plates from Maggie's grasp. "You can help by taking that new carafe of coffee into the living room and entertain the men and Millie."

The men started to mosey into the living room with chatter about the OSU–Michigan football game the coming Saturday.

The little girls chased behind them, nipping at Joey to play more music.

The room tilted slightly and Maggie closed her eyes against a wave of nausea.

Football games. Thanksgiving. Loud kids. It was normal. Normal family. Normal chatter. Normal life. She longed for moments

277

just like this one for the last ten years. Times of laughing and simply enjoying the pleasure of company. She sucked in a deep breath and walked into the living room.

Starting today — tonight — she would take her whole life back.

She wanted this life. These moments. This family. These friends. Forever. And she wasn't going to let the devil — or anyone else — take anything precious from her. Not ever again. The last ten years of her life were enough.

Today she started fighting back.

17

Sean held the door open with his foot while Maggie swept in carrying a basket filled with leftovers in tidy to-go packages.

"I think Bitsy believes I don't know how to cook real food. Each one of these containers has heating instructions on it with how to create a new meal out of the leftovers." She dropped the basket on the counter with a thud.

Sean carried one of the coolers filled with dirty dishes she'd refused to allow Bitsy and company to scrub clean. "She was probably thinking that I would take at least half the leftovers and she knows I can't turn on the microwave without thinking twice. She's been my surrogate mother for a really long time." He set the cooler on the floor and rubbed his shoulder. "Explain to me again why we lugged all of those dishes that belong to the shop up three flights of stairs to your apartment so you could wash them?

And why you didn't just allow Bits to wash them for you?"

She dragged the container toward the dishwasher. "Number one, Jenna is working tomorrow and I don't want her to face a pile of dirty dishes before the doors are even unlocked. Number two, I didn't want to wait downstairs for the dishes to run through the commercial dishwasher. It takes forever for it to warm up. I'm not comfortable having it run without someone there, just in case. Number three, I thought it would be easier to just run the dishes through my dishwasher tonight while I slept. And number four, Bitsy, Jane, and Molly worked way too hard on creating a lovely dinner. They didn't need to do dishes that I would just have to wash again for health code reasons. At least if I run them through the first time up here I'm not wasting anyone's time."

"Woman's wisdom. Too hard to argue." He kissed her temple, and then took the two steps to plop on her loveseat. "You know, it's times like now when it would be a good to have a TV. I could mindlessly flip channels while my little woman slaves away in the kitchen."

She threw a dishtowel that wrapped around his head. "Watch it, Chief. I may be small, but I'm no one's little anything. Got it?"

He twisted and rested his chin on the back of the sofa, the tug of a grin at his lips. "Got it. Just don't throw anything heavy at me. You've got excellent aim."

"Deal." She loaded the dishwasher in minutes, filled the dispenser, set the washer to its highest heat setting, and closed the door. Her stomach rolled. She'd been preparing different speeches in her head all afternoon. Ways to explain to Sean who she was, why she'd lied. But every path she'd taken ended with him bolting out the door and never talking to her again. The worst version had him evicting her from the bakery and her apartment.

He loved her. But could he possibly love all of her? Could he love Mary Margaret, too?

Maggie loaded the dishwasher, her movements efficient and almost tight. Something had been weighing on her mind since dinner. The cop in him could feel her wheels turning from a mile away. Sean wasn't only a trained police investigator, he was a man in love. He didn't want her to have to carry this burden alone anymore. He wanted her to trust him. But he didn't want to do anything that would cause her to run.

He turned his back to the kitchen and picked up a cooking and lifestyle magazine from the trunk acting as her coffee table. Flipping through the pages, he didn't register the articles on planting the perfect winter box garden or the mother versus daughter outfits. He wanted to keep his hands busy. He started a simple repetitious prayer. *Help me help her. Help me help her.*

She slid onto the seat, setting a mug in front of him.

The clean aroma of peppermint tea filled his nostrils, driving a quick, crisp path through his body. He tossed the magazine on the trunk as he lifted the tea. "Just the pick-me-up I need."

She blew over the rim of her mug and sipped. "After that big meal, my stomach needed a little something to soothe it before I drop into bed tonight."

"You barely ate a thing. Joey could probably use a vat of this stuff."

"I'll pack a little thermos for when you go home tonight. But, it didn't sound like they would be back before you."

"Naw, they're going to catch up with some local buddies. Mac is dropping Joey at some place in Grandview, and then he's off to Clintonville to see the baby of one of his high school friends who teaches at Ohio State."

"That's kind of far to drive this late at night."

"They're big boys, Mom. They've both lived on their own for quite some time. But if you want, I can have them call or text you when they make it home safe."

Her cheeks flushed bright pink. She took a long drink from her mug.

His heart warmed. He could watch her for hours just like this, calm and relaxed after a day with friends and family. He could picture their life together in six months, six years . . . sixty years. He could see their wedding day, the birth of their first child, their first home, all of it. He just needed to convince her that all of the future planning he was doing meshed with her future. He knew there were holes in her story.

But he wasn't worried. He was a cop. He wasn't stupid. He had checked into her background when she first rented the space. Not much to tell. Her life seemed to start in the past few years, not much activity between her birth certificate in Baltimore and her culinary degree from the Culinary Institute of America in Napa Valley. More holes. But the holes didn't scare him. Holes could be patched, mended, and made to be like new. What scared him was why she kept putting off filling in those holes for him.

She rested her mug on top of her knees, pulled tight to her chest. She stared at nothing, her finger running the edge of the cup.

He reached for his own mug and sipped some of the nearing lukewarm tea. He lightly rubbed the top of her foot and she shifted her focus to him. "Are you ready to talk?"

She set her mug on the trunk and began pacing. Kneading her lower back as she moved, her bare feet were silent against the wooden floor.

Sean set his cup beside hers and reached out a hand, stopping her mid-stride. "Look at me, Maggie." He grasped her other hand. "Whatever it is, whatever is haunting you, it won't make me love you any less. I love you, regardless of what you do or what you did, or what was done to you." He tugged her to sit beside him. "I love you, Maggie McKitrick, and your past is not going to make me run scared. I promise." He kissed her cheek and drew her to his side.

She was trembling.

"You can tell me anything."

She exhaled a long breath, moved slightly away and looked up, her crystal blue eyes glistening with unshed tears. She laced her fingers with his and glided her thumb back and forth on his hand. "Sean, I know you love me. And I want your love more than I have ever wanted anything in my life. I love you, too."

He squeezed her hand.

She closed her eyes and leaned her head against the back of the sofa. Drawing her legs to her chest, she wrapped her free arm around her shins. Silence hung between them, an unseen, unknown weight that he wished he could carry for her.

Dear Lord, help her to find the strength to share this burden. Help her to know she is safe. To know it in her head and her heart.

"My parents died in a car accident when I was a senior in high school."

His eyes flittered open at the sound of her voice, soft but solid.

She didn't look at him. Her gaze focused toward the front window of her apartment. "They were protective. I was their only child. So they wouldn't think of letting me drive to a party on the other side of town. That night, they'd dropped me off and were planning on going to a movie, maybe dinner, too, and then pick me up around midnight. I felt like such a dork having my mommy and daddy drop me off at this cool kid's house. I refused to talk to them the whole way there. I didn't even say good-bye when I slammed the door. My mom rolled down her window and called out, 'I love you.' I remember my stomach clenching in embarrassment. Everyone would think I was such a little girl."

He gave a little snort as similar memories of his mom kissing him after a baseball game floated through his mind.

A faint smile brushed her lips, but she continued to stare into the dark distance. "By ten o'clock, I was ready to go. The party wasn't what I thought it would be. My best friend Cam hadn't been allowed to come. Her parents knew the kinds of parties these kids had. So I called her to come and pick me up. I didn't want to interrupt my parents' evening. I called my dad and got his voicemail. I told him I got a ride home and I would see them later. He didn't respond, but I never thought that was weird. I figured they were at the movies and he probably turned his phone off or something." She swallowed hard and wiped her cheek against her pant leg.

"At two-thirty-three in the morning, the doorbell to my house rang. I'd fallen asleep on the couch waiting for my parents. I wanted to apologize to them for being so rude and was kind of surprised they hadn't woken me up when they came home. I remember rubbing my eyes and yelling for my mom as I made my way to the front door. I looked out the side window and saw a State Highway patrolman and another man standing on the doorstep. I yelled again for my mom, but there wasn't any answer. The rest of the night was a blur. My parents had been hit by a drunk driver as they were turning into the movie theater. The police took me to the hospital. My dad was in surgery. My mom died on impact. I called my Uncle Jack and he got there just before my dad died." She gave him a sad smile. "I remember being super cold. I don't think I got warm again for months. I wore this scarf they'd given me everywhere."

His stomach dropped and his heart twisted at the pain of the loss she endured. The image of a petite, curly-headed teenager, frightened and alone, flashed through his mind and tears burned in his eyes. He'd lost his dad suddenly at twelve, but still had his mother. And when his mom became ill, they had nearly two years to prepare for her death. And even then, he had his brothers and the Greys, and this whole town to help grieve and move forward. How would he have felt if he'd been left alone at seventeen, without parents or any family to lean on for support?

He raised a hand to her wild hair and smoothed a strand behind her ear. "You must have been very brave. I'm sure your parents would be very proud of you."

She rested her cheek on her knee, her lips drawn in a tight line, tears dropping down her pant leg. "I never got to say good-bye." Her voice hiccupped and she drank in a deep breath. "It is my greatest regret. The last thing I did to my parents was ignore them. All they ever did was love me. And I treated them like . . . like they were nothing."

He stroked her hair and her eyes fluttered close. "I am sure they forgave you before you even crossed the threshold into that party."

She nodded her head and expelled a whisper of a sigh, opening her eyes. "My Uncle Jack wanted me to go to therapy to deal with their deaths, but I never felt right about discussing how I felt. They couldn't talk anymore so why should I get to? I knew they were in heaven, they were both so open about their faith. And that was enough. Eventually, many years later, when I finally made it to therapy, I forgave myself. They would've wanted it that way. And it was essentially as much a gift for them as it was for me." She tilted her head. "Therapy does really work. It's never too late." She sighed and rubbed her cheek. "I spent the rest of the school year with my friend Cam's family, and then moved to Washington with my Uncle Jack for the summer. I was already enrolled at the University of Maryland for the fall semester and decided I wanted to be a normal freshman." She stood and the pacing resumed.

He waited. He'd learned through years of interrogation that silence was the best way to keep a suspect talking. He figured the same rule applied when the love of your life was trying to share her life story.

She walked to the window, rested against the frame, and stared into the night. With a single finger, she began to trace a shape in the steam on the glass. He wished she would turn around and complain about the broken seal on the window. Yell at him that he was failing as a landlord. Anything — just so she didn't have to keep telling this story. Her pain weighed heavy in the room. He wanted to do whatever he could to ease her burden — to throw it through that window and watch it tumble down Main Street. But she needed to rip the bandage all of the way off. Tell her whole story.

The investigator in Sean wanted to prod

her with questions, get her to peel back another layer of the onion. But the boyfriend remained silent, waiting for her to give what she could.

She turned, leaning her back against the wall. "I was like any other freshman. Confused. Nervous. A little scared. My mom wanted me to major in musical theater. I didn't have her passion for it, but I also didn't have anything else I was good at so . . . I found myself with a theater-only course load and little time to breathe or think. Uncle Jack convinced me not to take extra classes so that I could try different activities, make friends. And that's what I did. I ended up in the chorus of the fall production and joined my roommate in a weekly Bible study. Tried to be normal."

Musical Theater major. That made sense. He imagined her mother recognized her gift and wanted her to be able to share it. Another piece to the Maggie McKitrick puzzle fell in place.

"The show was fun. I met a lot of new friends, but the Bible study was where I really felt comfortable. We met weekly on campus. There were about twenty of us, and our leader was a grad student. He was charming, handsome, a little mysterious, and knew the Bible better than anyone I'd ever met before.

"I'd been raised in the church, but it was through those weekly sessions — partly because of the teaching and partly because of the teacher — that I truly connected with Jesus. He seemed to sense I needed extra attention and would drop by my dorm room to chat, send me an email with reassurances, or leave little gifts in my mailbox. He was super supportive and I was grateful for the friendship.

"Fall turned to winter, and then spring semester started. I auditioned for the spring theater production. It was a long shot, but somehow I got the part. My Bible teacher wasn't thrilled, the part was racy. He thought I was somehow going against God's will by being in the play. But I didn't care. It was amazing. Being on stage. Being someone else. For two weeks of performances, I stopped being a pathetic little orphan and got to be a strong, powerful woman. And then, one night, after a show, I came back to my dressing room and there were flowers from Sam Riegle."

"Wait," Sean rubbed his face. "I know that name. He was a . . . he was a running back for the University of Maryland. He was touted to go in the top ten in the NFL draft. He bought you flowers?"

The corner of her mouth curled up and she laced her arms. "I've been known to attract some pretty amazing men."

Sean felt his face grow warm. He lifted his hand to his neck and worked the knot that seemed to perpetually have residence. "So, you got flowers from a football star . . ."

Her cheeks tinged a sweet pink, helping to stifle the irrational jealousy bubbling in his stomach.

"Sam waited for me that night and asked me out for coffee. After that, we were inseparable. Call it first love, call it youth, call it whatever you want, but for the first time in a year I was able to go a whole day without feeling pounding guilt over my parents' deaths. I laughed, truly laughed for the first time in months. All because of Sam." She closed the space between them. Perched on the trunk sitting just in front of him, she continued. "He was the sweetest boy-man I'd ever met. He was spontaneous and filled with such joy. He made time for me, even coming to Bible study. My teacher hated him. He kept trying to convince me that Sam was just a player who didn't really care about me. That Sam was keeping me from wholly devoting myself to God and The Mission." She shook her head. "Sorry, The Mission, was the organization Mitchell

— the leader of the group — represented on campus. They sponsored the Bible study."

Sean sat up straight. Mitchell . . . The Mission? A pretty little singer . . . a thousand questions started to race through his mind. Chuck's quick background check started to replay like the ticker on a news channel. He felt a twitch start in his left eye.

"Sam was pretty vocal about his distrust of Mitchell. He didn't like that Mitchell would drop by unannounced or send me notes in the mail. I guess I could see his point, but I didn't want to let Mitchell go. He'd been as much a part of my healing as Sam, and I was fearful to say goodbye to anyone, you know?"

Sean nodded. If he spoke his questions wouldn't stop.

She reached for his hand squeezing it tight. "After the Combine, Sam was high on everyone's draft board. He decided to forgo his senior year. We both knew that he'd be spending most of the summer at the facility of whatever NFL team drafted him in April, and I didn't want to waste my summer in a muggy apartment waiting for my Uncle Jack to return from one of his work trips. So, when Mitchell arranged for me to work at this summer retreat in the Catskills, I thought it was a perfect compromise. I would get some time to truly spend with the Lord and be able to make a little money teaching skits to the children of those attending the retreat." She sucked in a deep breath and dropped her gaze to their hands.

Sean knew his face reflected calm, years of training ensured a placid demeanor, but he could feel a burning swell in his stomach as the image of her, young and trusting, was etched into his mind. He had been trained not to anticipate, to let the evidence tell the story, but his logical brain was linking puzzle pieces together. Her thumb caressed the back of his hand and caused a wave of innocent yearning to wash over him, cooling the angry heat steadily growing.

Her eyes were without tears or a hint of emotion floating on the surface. "I left for New York a week after school let out. Uncle Jack wasn't thrilled with me being gone again, but when an assignment called him out of the country, he didn't have much ammunition to have me stay in D.C. alone. I was excited to spend the summer doing anything but more school work. I realize that it must seem that theater majors have it easy, but we have just as much studying and training as the hardest engineering major. It's just different. My classmates were spending their summers in workshops or performing at amusement parks, but I was grateful not to have to perform. I felt as if all I'd been doing for the past year was performing, on and off stage, and I was tired. And the bonus, Sam's rookie camp was only an hour away from the retreat at a local college. We made plans to see each other on the weekends. He even thought he might be able to come down for an occasional dinner."

An easy smile lifted her lips and softened her eyes. "The first few weeks at the retreat center were wonderful. We had chapel every morning and teachings every afternoon. I spent most days studying Scripture and The Mission guide. The whole thing was a little too group-sharing-commune-living for me to consider full time, but for the summer it worked. The kids were fun to teach, mostly songs we'd sung in Sunday school when I was little. But all and all it was restful, except for Mitchell. He seemed to think that since I'd chosen to come to the retreat that I'd come with him. He ate every meal with me. Sat beside me in chapel and afternoon teachings. It was as if he wanted everyone to think he owned me."

She swallowed deeply, pushing down

something he wasn't sure he was ready to hear.

"One morning, I got up super early to go for a run — way before anyone in the camp would be up. I locked the door to my cabin, turned around and he was sitting on a rock, just staring at me. He asked if he could run with me, but I told him that I needed to spend some time praying.

"That was two weeks into the summer and the first time all of Sam's and my room-mates' warnings started to sink in. We weren't allowed to have cell phones at the retreat, so I booked the five miles to the nearest gas station. My uncle was unreach-able, one of the consequences of his job, so I called Sam collect. By the time the call connected, I felt like I was overreacting. When I told Sam what happened, he flipped. He made me promise to stay at the gas station. Wait on the bench and not leave. He told me he would be there in under an hour." She dropped Sean's hands, scrubbed at her face, stood again, and went back to the window.

"Three hours went by, with me sitting on the little bench in front of the gas station, and no Sam." As she spoke, she laced her arms over her middle, hugging herself tight. "I was worried, but I wasn't sure what to do. Should I go back to the retreat, maybe he was there? What if he was lost? What if his car had broken down? The mile of 'what if's' that ran through my brain would've exhausted the most conditioned Olympic athlete. I kept feeling as if it was the night of my parents' accident all over again."

Sean slid up behind her, folding his arms over hers and easing her back to his chest. He rested his chin on her head.

"Thanks." She sighed, relaxing against him.

He brushed a light kiss on her temple. "Anytime. I'm a public servant."

"And I'm thankful to be a member of the public." She chuckled through her tears. "But I hope you aren't treating Sissy Jenkins to this kind of service."

"I reserve this for our special citizens. Sissy is special in an entirely different way."

Her faint smile reflected in the glass.

"Gotcha." She released a deep breath. "So, there I was. Sitting on this little bench outside of the gas station, a disaster in tears, and a local Sheriff pulled into the parking spot in front of me. He'd been called to look for me. When he started to put me in the car, I began screaming for Sam. People were watching me in horror." She opened her eyes and met his in the reflection. "I remember this mother yanked her little girl behind her, I guess to shield her from the crazy, but I didn't care. Something was wrong. I knew it."

With the first warm wet drop on his arm, Sean drew her in snug against him.

Sobs begin to wrack her tiny frame. "I k-kept yelling at the S-sh-sheriff to go look for Sam, but he wouldn't l-l-listen to me. He said they were w-w-worried about me at the retreat, and he needed to take me back. He said he d-didn't know anything about Sam. I remember crying and crying until I felt as if I was going to throw up."

Sean turned her in his arms. Tears chased after tears down her face. He hugged her wishing he could absorb the pain from the wound that was being reopened. He wanted to jump in, to tell her the pieces he had filled in on his own, but he kissed the top of her head, lightly caressed her back, and encouraged her to keep talking. Only she had the right to share her life.

"The Sheriff drove me back to the retreat compound. About two miles from the camp, we passed a cluster of emergency vehicles on the opposite side. I yelled at him to stop and thankfully, he did. I barely waited for him to put the car in park. I threw open the door and ran to the rim of the ravine where the crews were working. I remember firemen holding me back from the edge, the rocks slipping under my feet. When I saw the taillights of Sam's car, I started screaming again. I shouted, 'Save him, please save him.' I knew they had to hurry." She lifted her gaze to his. "They needed to hurry, to h-help him. To save him. But it was too late." Her voice lowered to a broken whisper. "They said his brakes were faulty. That he'd taken the turn to quickly. But I knew the truth. It was my fault he was gone. Just like my parents. It was all my fault." She broke away from Sean, went to the kitchen, lifted the teapot and lowered it under the tap. "You want some more tea?"

Sean closed the small space and gently placed his hand over hers. "Maggie . . . Maggie, look at me."

Her eyes were soggy with shed tears and make-up was smudged, but she was under control and so lovely she broke his heart. With his free hand he lightly caressed her cheek. "Maggie, none of this is your fault. None of it."

She yanked away and slammed the teapot onto the stove. "Don't you think I know that? Don't you think I know that it was a drunk driver who killed my parents and that Sam was the victim of horrible accident? I know it in my mind, but my heart won't let me rest." She pounded her chest with her fist. "If it wasn't for me they would all be alive. My rational mind understands that logically I didn't cause any of this to happen, but my heart continues to feed my guilt."

He dropped his hands to her shoulders. "But God doesn't want you to live with that guilt anymore."

"I know." She drew in a shaky breath. "I know. And most of the time I believe it. Like ninety percent of the time. But when I go through the whole thing, I have a hard time acquitting myself."

He tugged her into his arms. "Maggie, tell me the rest. Get it all out." He was sure there was more to the story. She needed to be free. And the only way to freedom was through truth.

"Do you mind if we sit?"

He led her back to the sofa, cradling her against his side as they sat.

Sean willed himself to remain silent. He stroked his hand up and down her arm; her head rested on his shoulder.

"I left the retreat that day." Her voice was low again. "Mitchell wanted to drive me home, back to D.C., but I insisted I'd be all right. One of the girls who shared my cabin helped me pack. She was pretty quiet most of the time, but that afternoon she asked me if the boy who'd fought Mitchell was the same one who'd died." She shook her head as if she could erase the memory from her mind. "I dropped on the bed, clothes still in my hands, and asked her to tell me everything that had happened earlier. She said that a young man she hadn't seen before was arguing with Mitchell and she heard my name."

She twisted to look at Sean. "It didn't make any sense to me. Sam knew I was at the gas station. Why would he go to the retreat center? I left the girl in my cabin and ran outside to find Mitchell. He was with this group of leaders talking in hushed tones, but I didn't care. I went straight up to him and started yelling. His eyes were filled with . . . with this cold fury. With a snap of his wrist, he backhanded me across the mouth, grabbed my arm and dragged me away from the group. I can remember the acid taste of the blood as it filled my mouth, but I think I was more shocked than anything. I didn't respond. I just let him haul me half way across the camp with no fight."

Sean felt the white heat of temper and he instinctively squeezed Maggie closer.

"When we got to my cabin, the girl who was helping me took one look at Mitchell and ran out the back door. He threw me on my bed and started pacing the room. He told me he had enough. He was tired of chasing after me. Of me pretending that God hadn't sent us to each other. He started quoting Scripture and interweaving it with parts of The Mission guide, parts about God's ordination of certain unions to be supreme unions, or something like that. He believed God spoke to him and meant for the two of us to be together. He grabbed my chin and looked me straight in the eye and said, 'Why else would Sam have died, if not for us to be together?'"

Sean smoothed a curl behind her ear. "He told you this on the day your boyfriend died?"

She nodded. "I didn't know what to do. He looked so . . . so . . . sane. I just knew I needed to get away from him, from the retreat center, from The Mission, from everything. And I needed to do it in a hurry. I pulled out every trick I'd learned in the last year of acting classes. I told him that it was a lot to think about and I needed to pray. I asked him to leave so I could be alone with God and his mouth twisted into this off-centered smile. He told me he could be patient, 'that was what love was all about,' he said. And then he kissed my forehead. I must have scrubbed that spot a hundred times, and it still didn't feel clean for months.

"I threw the rest of my stuff in my bag and raced out to my car. I'd locked my cellphone in my glove compartment and called my Uncle Jack's emergency line on the way back to D.C. It's almost an eight hour drive and I made it in seven flat. I didn't stop except to get gas. I locked myself in my uncle's apartment and didn't answer the door for three days, not until he got home."

"Maggie, what exactly does your uncle do?"

A faint grin touched her lips. "I'm not a hundred percent sure, but I think he might be a spy or some kind of law enforcement special agent. I know he works for the government in a classified division and he travels a lot."

More puzzle pieces. They were all fitting neatly together. And most of the picture made his stomach churn.

"Uncle Jack called a friend in the Justice Department and they arranged for a restraining order against Mitchell. I tried to put the whole incident — the whole year — in a box and forget about it. I let my uncle handle all of the legal hurdles and I went about trying to grieve and to start over . . . again. I didn't go back to Maryland. It was too hard to be at school. All of the memories and the possibility of Mitchell being around any corner. I told Uncle Jack I needed some time. Time to figure out what was next. I got a job at a coffee shop near his apartment. And that fall I auditioned for a regional theater production. I was the understudy for one of the main characters and sang in the chorus. I was thrilled to be working. To be able to set the past behind me, even for a little while. Each day that I was further away from that day, I started to imagine it hadn't happened. Maybe it had just been an accident."

"But it wasn't an accident, was it, Maggie?"

She shook her head. "A week into the play's run, I was called to understudy. I was excited, but also shocked. Understudies almost never get called the first week of the run, especially in regional theater. I went on and I was OK, not great, but OK."

"I highly doubt that. Remember, I've heard you sing."

"You might be a little biased. But when I left the theater, Mitchell was standing in the alley with a dozen white lilies. I've never been so frightened. He told me what a wonderful performance I had given and handed me the flowers. He leaned in to kiss me and I started to scream, but he grabbed my jaw, his hand was like a vise."

"I reminded him about the restraining order. He threw me into the alley wall and started to chuckle. He said, 'No piece of paper will stand in the way of God's will, my dearest.' He went on to talk about how God brought us together and nothing would ever separate us. He kept going on and on — long enough for me to dial 911 and the police to arrive. They took him away, but he was out in the morning."

"I left D.C. and moved to Miami the next day. Worked in a restaurant waiting tables and got in another show. Four shows into the run, I looked into the audience and he was sitting front row center. I almost threw up on stage. I made sure to leave with other cast mates and went straight to the airport. That was my last performance. The last time I sang in public before today.

"After the incident in D.C., Uncle Jack and I developed a plan to help me run. I spent the next six years hopping from New York to Chicago to Houston and everywhere in between. Uncle Jack had the restraining order registered in every state in the U.S., but no matter where I moved, within a few weeks or months Mitchell would track me down. His violence escalated with each incident, but nothing his parents' lawyers couldn't get him out of."

"So, I kept running. I'd become a great waitress, but when he kept showing up for dinner, I thought it would be safer, easier to run, if I worked in the back of the house. And that's how it started."

"How what started?"

"How I fell in love with cooking." She smiled and for the first time a twinkle sparkled in her eyes. "I was a sponge. I traipsed after every sous chef and line cook I could find. I asked smart and really stupid questions. It was all so amazing, how this tiny space behind the scene at a restaurant was filled with all of these different worlds. It was like being part of twenty great plays every night. I was hooked."

"After a year of kitchens, I talked my Uncle Jack into letting me apply to cooking school. At school, I was able to see how those backroom one act plays were developed and transported to a plate. As much as I loved cooking, I decided to specialize in pastry. Pastry is art in a bite — how could I resist? It was a wonderful time, the Napa Valley is so beautiful and the food is so special there. I was happy. For the first time in six years, I was happy. I accepted an apprenticeship under the executive pastry chef at a five star restaurant. Everything was perfect. Until June twenty-third three years ago."

"June twenty-third . . ." he whispered.

Scooting to the opposite side of the sofa, she drew her legs to her chest, enfolding them in her arms. "I was working early. Setting dough to proof. I was alone in the restaurant but I wasn't afraid. It had been over a year since he'd found me. Uncle Jack heard that The Mission had run into some trouble with the IRS, and we both assumed those legal issues put me on the backburner. I started to think that maybe he'd moved on, found a wife, started a new life. I thought Napa was my Promised Land.

"I remember I had this classic jazz album — one of my favorites — blaring in the back room. I used to love that CD." She gave her head a little shake. "Anyway, I was on my seventh batch of dough when I heard a click at the back door. I thought maybe one of the line cooks was coming in early to prep his station. I really didn't think much of it. And then crack, everything was black. The next thing I remember I was waking up in the trunk of a car. I was nauseous and dirty.

My hands were bound and so were my feet. I was bumping and banging. My head was swimming. I kept praying. I don't even think I was saying words, just praying, you know?"

He couldn't imagine.

"When the car stopped, I didn't know what to do. I thought we were still in California. But when the trunk popped open, I saw the University of Maryland football field in the distance. Somehow, he brought me back to Maryland. We were on campus. I was still bound as he dragged me into one of the dance studios. There were mirrors everywhere and I caught my first look at my face. It was awful. I had blood caked on my cheek from cuts on my forehead and my eye was swollen and purple. I thought I was going to die."

Sean's gut clenched, the anger from earlier pushing to explode. This man had laid a hand on his woman. No one had a right to do that. No one. Sean prayed to get past his anger.

"Most of that day is a blur. Mitchell kept spouting about God's will. How we were meant to be together. Shaking me. Calling me a sinner. A Jezebel. He hit me and I crashed into one of the dance mirrors, smashing it in hundreds of pieces." She pointed to a tiny scar at her hairline. "That's how I got this thing. I'm truly blessed that I wasn't more seriously injured, but that hit knocked me unconscious. When I woke up, my head was pounding and my face felt like it'd been ripped at the seams. "I was dressed in my costume from the play. White lilies were on the table beside me. We were in the theater. He'd set the stage with the sets from the play. It was eerie. Everything was exactly as it had been in the production six years earlier." She wiped at her tears and tugged her legs tighter to her chest. "He was sitting front row center staring at me. I was so afraid. I knew I was going to die." Shudders wracked her body.

Sean wanted to hold her close and never let her go. To infuse his strength into her. To protect her from a past she was forced to relive.

She continued describing the twisted wants and needs of her captor. Mitchell brought her back to the place where he felt he'd lost her, where Sam won. Where he was convinced she'd turned her back on God's will. He called her despicable names. He kept her trussed up on the stage for hours forcing her to relive the former part over and over again.

"It was a nightmare I desperately wanted to wake from. I kept trying to figure out how we'd gotten to Maryland. What day it was. Had anyone seen Mitchell bring me into the studio or to the theater? Would anyone find us? Why now? How could I get away? Would he hit me again? Would that hit kill me?

"He started to relax. I don't know what clicked in him, but he leaned back in his chair and started to rub his finger slowly across his lips. I'll never forget that . . . how he just sat there staring at me as if he were assessing the value of a piece of art. And I realized, he'd won. I wasn't resisting anymore. It had been hours and no one was coming to find us. I felt hollow. Empty. I didn't have any more tears or fight. I prayed for God to forgive me for quitting. And I prayed that Jesus would just take me home." Tears streamed down her cheeks. "Mitchell stood and walked toward me. He was slow, like a panther hunting his prey. I remember closing my eyes and waiting . . . I think I was waiting for him to give me the final blow, to kill me."

Sean reached for her.

"No, I'm OK. I'm OK. Mitchell was nearly to me, and then everything seemed to happen at the same time. Every entrance to the theater burst open simultaneously and dozens of police stormed into the room.

Mitchell lunged toward me, but this cop grabbed him by the waist and threw him to the ground. A tiny female cop unbound my hands and feet and wrapped me in a blanket. She looked at my face and started screaming for the EMT's.

"Uncle Jack came running to me, tears streaming down his cheeks. I'd never seen him cry before. He crushed me to him as they dragged Mitchell from the theater. He was kicking and screaming, yelling over and over, 'I'll never let you go. Never. You are mine.'

"All these years later, I can still smell the scent of fabric softener on my uncle's shirt and hear the muffled echo of screams and shouted orders. But I can't tell you what the cuts or bruises felt like. Or describe the face of the officer who was so kind to me. I can hear her voice as clear as a bell and feel the scratchy warmth of the blanket she gave me. The whole thing was surreal.

"From the moment I heard the click in the restaurant to the feel of my uncle's arms, I felt as if I were living someone else's life. The whole thing was like a movie. I didn't feel as if I was quite there, but rather watching the whole thing in slow motion. Sometimes, when I remember or have a dream, it feels as if all of it happened to

311

someone else. And, really, I guess it did." Maggie fell quiet; her eyes shuttered against Sean's gaze.

Sean wouldn't be satisfied unless the story had a clean, tight ending. He needed to know the rest of the story because without it, he wouldn't be able to protect her.

She stood as if every bone in her body ached and moved to the kitchen. Leaning against the counter, she looked at ease and casual, but the skin over her knuckles was pulled taut-white.

He closed the distance to the kitchen in three steps and laced his arms across her middle, pulling her back to his chest in a soft embrace. He kissed her temple and she leaned her head against his shoulder. "Maggie, I love you. And I wish I could change everything that has happened to you. But there's still a missing piece, isn't there? There's more to the story. What did you mean, 'it happened to someone else'?"

She turned to him, folding her arms around his waist, burying her face into his chest. "Because it did." Her words were muffled against his shirt and a new wave of tears dampened the heavy cotton fabric.

"What does that mean? Maggie, who did it happen to?"

"Mary Margaret Sloan. That's my real

name, or at least it was my real name."

"I'm going to need a little more help."

Sucking in a deep breath, she unlinked her arms and leaned against the counter. "My name was Mary Margaret Sloan. Mary Margaret, the girl who loved Sam, lost her parents too young, and lived in a constant state of panic for over six years. Mary Margaret, who fell in love with Jesus, with the help of a loony cult and a crazed stalker. I was Mary Margaret throughout the trial and my testimony against Mitchell. Through all of the running and the terror. Through the loss of a dream and the birth of a new one. I was her through it all. First, I was just fighting to survive, and then fighting to win. And we won, Mary Margaret and I, we won the day Mitchell was sentenced for kidnapping and attempted murder. The day he was dragged out of the courtroom, screaming and in handcuffs, I walked out and left Mary Margaret behind.

"He was right. Mary Margaret would never be free of Mitchell O'Donnell. So I walked out of that courtroom and down the hall to the county registrar. Uncle Jack helped me start a new life, new social security number, the whole nine yards, and I became Maggie McKitrick. Just like that. One new driver's license, a box of hair color, a one way ticket to Columbus, and Maggie McKitrick was born. Old life gone. New life started."

He lifted his hands and smoothed his fingers over her hair, cupping her cheeks. "It's wonderful to finally meet you, Miss McKitrick." He lowered his lips to hers, brushing them lightly. "Thank you for trusting me."

Rising on her toes, she draped her arms around his neck and kissed him with passion. A heady mixture of peace and hard-fought freedom infused each caress of her lips.

His arms tightened around to small of her back drawing her closer.

After a moment, she lifted her mouth from his. A soft sigh slipped out. Snuggling against him, her voice was low as she spoke. "I feel as if I could float away. I didn't realize how all of the dishonesty was weighing me down. I hated lying to you. From that first day in the shop, I had this strange desire to hand you a tub of popcorn and tell you my whole life story. I've just been afraid." She slid her hand up his chest, drawing a line of fiery heat in its wake and raked her fingers through his short hair. "I'm sorry, Sean. I want you to know just how sorry I am. I shouldn't have waited so long."

He lowered his lips to the base of her neck and sprinkled a few light kisses over her turtleneck. "I know. I'm just thankful for whatever clicked that made you able to tell me."

"Today, at the Greys, all I could think was how wonderfully loud and full of love everyone was and I got scared."

Scared?

"I know we're a lot to handle, but scared?"

"Not of you. Of what loving you, all of you, could mean. If Mitchell ever finds me . . . figures out where I am and who I love . . ." She closed her eyes. "He's been in prison a long time, Sean. Longer than he ever went before without finding me. And now that he's paroled, I'm afraid of what he's planning. He's had years to scheme. He has more money than I could ever imagine at his fingertips. It's part of the reason why he's always been able to find me. He has resources beyond all of our imaginations.

"He would use those resources to try and teach me a lesson — on behalf of God, of course. And he would start by going after anyone he thought I loved. He would relish the pain that would cause, hurting those

315

whom I've chosen over him. He would justify it by saying that we'd sinned by not following God's will. He would use all of you as a weapon against me. If he ever finds me, I am petrified of what he will do to all of your family because I love you."

O'Donnell had been here. Sean was sure of it. But he couldn't let Maggie know yet. He needed to have a strategy. He would tell her. Just not tonight. He kissed her forehead and squeezed her shoulders. "He can't hurt you anymore. I won't let him. I will protect you. I'm kind of good at the whole security detail thing."

"I guess you're OK for a small town cop."

"Hey . . . who are you calling small-town?"

"If the one traffic light fits . . ."

"We have two traffic lights."

"Well . . . I don't know if the blinking one entering town really counts."

He chuckled and hugged her. "I'll give you that." Smoothing his hand across her hair, he smiled. "So . . . this beautiful dark hair is from a box? I feel completely betrayed."

"Men."

18

The grring sound of the fax machine filled the empty police station. The clock on the wall flashed barely six o'clock. Thousands of people would be swarming the malls in Columbus to get Black Friday deals, making Sean once again thankful for the advent of gift cards and online shopping. He scanned the first three pages in the stack as the remaining twenty the machine promised crept out of the printer. The twenty-first century brought little advancement to Gibson's Run.

At Maggie's the evening before he'd tried to keep his questions at a minimum. She'd told him about her uncle, where he lived, his contact information, but she wasn't completely certain which branch of the government employed him.

She knew very little about O'Donnell since he'd been released from prison. She'd told him a few more details about Sam's accident, and although the evidence was circumstantial, Sean was convinced that O'Donnell caused the young man's death. But through all of the questions and her lengthy story, Maggie's faith was unshakeable.

She'd lost her parents, her first love, was manipulated by a cult, and abused by a trusted spiritual mentor. How could anyone endure all of those trials, give up her identity, and still be so in love with the Lord that one could feel her passion ooze off of her within minutes of being in her presence?

He'd only known her story for a few hours and he was struggling to keep his heart open to God's will and His grace. Maggie had been running for nearly a decade and still had the dewy freshness of a new believer when she spoke of God. Her voice held little blame or hatred toward the man who stole her life. And nothing negative crossed her lips in reference to the Lord.

He kneaded his shoulders and neck, closing his eyes as the final pages screeched through the ancient machine. *Father, I know you brought us, Maggie and me, together for a purpose. One that is probably bigger than I can even imagine. Help me to draw on her faith — allow it to inspire deeper love for You, in me. And Dear God, please keep her safe. I know I can't do it alone. I need You. She needs You. She's right. I'm just a small town cop, but You have used small town people before. Please use me, Lord. Please use me to keep her safe.*

He opened his eyes as silence filled the room. Pulling the stack of paper from the fax, he sipped his early morning, pre-Maggie, fast food restaurant coffee. Reviewing the front page, he walked back to his office. Skimming the top sheet in the stack, he discarded the cover page and began scrutinizing the details of page two: Mitchell O'Donnell's first arrest.

After he'd left Maggie's, he'd called Chuck and asked him to pull O'Donnell's whole file, tapping into the cooperative law enforcement database that the fine council of Gibson's Run denied needing. His old partner had volunteered for the midnight-to-eight shift Thanksgiving night into Friday morning and easily accessed O'Donnell's history.

Sean read through his various arrests beginning with D.C. and weaving through Miami, Chicago, Houston, and every other major city in the lower forty-eight. Maggie hadn't embellished. Each report detailed a pattern of escalating violence and skilled pursuit. The scum-bag was relentless in his

319

desire for Maggie.

But, she wasn't his first. O'Donnell had a run-in with the police when he was seventeen.

The bust should have been expunged from his record, but Chuck was a determined detective and a little thing like statute of limitations and sealed records rarely stood in his way.

O'Donnell had been charged with malicious assault and stalking. To this day, his victim remained in a vegetative state in upstate New York. Based on the charges and his actions, he should have been tried as an adult, but his father's expensive lawyers made certain he didn't suffer the consequences. The court sentenced him to time served, three hundred hours of community service, and mandatory therapy for six months. His therapist was Rich Falcon, founder of The Mission. From his old PO's records, O'Donnell displayed genuine remorse and seemed to have "turned over a new leaf."

Parole officers who reduced their parolees to clichés turned Sean's stomach. Nothing in life, especially criminal behavior, was that easily remedied.

But O'Donnell became a model citizen. He joined The Mission and started leading

Bible studies during his under-grad years at Georgetown. He became a graduate assistant at the University of Maryland a year before Maggie started school, but other than the occasional write up for noise violations due to a couple concerts The Mission group threw, he kept his nose clean. Or kept his tracks very well hidden.

Sean studied the rest of the file, absorbed in the details of his arrests and releases. He knew O'Donnell had been in town. But how long?

He compared some of the details with Sissy's in-depth journal and photos. Sissy catalogued O'Donnell's movements for two weeks. The thought that he had been watching Maggie made the acid rise in Sean's stomach.

The more he reviewed the arrest patterns, the frustrations that seeped through the various officers' detailed notes, the more Sean was convinced that O'Donnell already laid the ground work a month ago for whatever his next move would be.

Despite her diligent efforts to conceal her identity, he'd found her. The obsessed rarely found obstacles they couldn't overcome.

A single thud at the front door caused Sean to jump up reflexively, checking his weapon in his shoulder holster. Leaning across his desk, he angled to see who was at the door. A bright blue arm of what looked like a wool jacket was visible, but the owner was a mystery. His hand was twisting the lock open when a smile stretched across his cheeks. "Well, this is a good morning surprise." He leaned forward and pecked a kiss on Maggie's cold lips.

She swept into the station with a coffee carrier and a box that was filled with something cinnamon and spicy. Its warm aroma permeated the tiny space. "I saw your light on this morning when I set the first round of bagels to proof and was worried you cheated on me with fast food coffee." She peeped over his shoulder and shook her head. "I feel so betrayed. Maybe you don't want my coffee anymore?" She pivoted toward the front door.

He quickly clamped his hands on her shoulders. "Don't you even think about taking that wonderful smelling stuff you have back out that door. I may starve and my insides might stop working from trying to process old coffee. Then how would you feel? Me, all crumpled up at my desk with only a cup of stale coffee for nourishment." He lifted the box and carrier from her hands, nudging her toward his office.

She slid onto the seat opposite his desk,

causing a quick flash of their make-shift picnic to swipe through his mind, warming his heart.

"Now, what did you bring me?" He set the drink carrier and pastry box discreetly over the pile of fax papers and Sissy's notes. Plopping onto his chair, he popped open the box and inhaled. He couldn't suppress the corners of his mouth lifting. "Cinnamon pecan rolls? Do you want me to get fat?"

"You could stand to gain a few pounds." Her cheeks flared a subtle pink as she lifted one of the cups from the carrier.

"You'll have me chubbier than Alvin." He sank his teeth into the sticky sweetness of his favorite breakfast treat. The pecans were slightly salty and the cinnamon-sugar filling was still warm. He was in breakfast heaven.

"That would take a whole lot more than a couple cinnamon rolls." She paused. "So, what do you think?"

"I guess they're OK."

She slammed her hand on the table. "You guess they're OK? I got up a half-hour early to make those stupid things, in my own kitchen, mind you, and I all get is, 'they're OK'?"

He chuckled. "Man, you're easy, McKitrick." He couldn't resist leaning across the desk to kiss her. He was off balance and the kiss was a little awkward, but having her here, bantering with her, all of it was so right. And he wouldn't let anything or anyone threaten what they had. He had sworn to protect and serve. And that was just what he was going to do.

19

With another Thanksgiving weekend behind them, the bustling weeks of pre-Christmas shopping and parties barreled in like a train. Dozens of recommendations, based on Maggie's successful Thanksgiving desserts, swirled around town and even into Columbus. She was blissfully inundated with requests for cookies, cakes, pies, and the occasional yule log to celebrate the season. The increase in business allowed her to hire a couple college students, who were home over their long winter break, to run the café during the day. That gave Maggie free reign to play in the kitchen with minimal distractions.

Sean missed seeing her during the daylight, but he was able to focus more research on O'Donnell and set preparations for his eventual return to Gibson's Run. He contacted O'Donnell's parole officer, his halfway house, and the computer repair shop that hired him. All agreed that he was a model ex-con, whatever that meant.

His PO volunteered to share O'Donnell's work history and his notes on their weekly meetings. "But I'm not sure what help they will be," Officer Riddle offered in a brief phone conversation a week after Maggie shared her story. "I think you may be chasing a ghost who no longer exists. Mitchell's been great. Easiest parolee I've had and I've been doing this more years than I care to remember."

"Riddle, did O'Donnell leave the state recently?" Sean asked as their conversation drew to a close.

"Well, now that you mention it, Mitchell's grandmother passed away about a month ago, and he was out of town for the funeral. Gone a little over two weeks, but back before he was originally scheduled. Checked in every day, even volunteered to meet with a court-appointed officer while he was out of town, but I didn't think it was necessary."

Sean's belly burned with anger, but he kept his voice steady. "Why wasn't it? Necessary, I mean. The guy's a convicted felon, not the pope."

"Yep, I get all that, but the guy wears an ankle monitor, part of his early release protocol. I was able to track him every minute of the day if I wanted. Those things are impossible to break or remove. It's a wonder they don't just replace all of us parole officers with those things and save the government a chunk of change."

Sean thanked the PO for his notes and his time, but didn't bother to let the officer know that a simple home block created with aluminum foil and some ingenuity could break the best ankle bracelet's effectiveness. After the call, he was less convinced that O'Donnell was reformed than when he had picked up the phone.

No one with the well-documented history of violence and ego changed overnight or even in three years. And someone fitting his description had been camped out in Gibson's Run at the same time O'Donnell's grandmother was supposedly interred.

Sean didn't believe in coincidences. Through all of his research and digging, he'd developed a fairly rounded view of the man who had tortured and terrorized Maggie for over six years before his conviction and imprisonment. Based on their history, O'Donnell couldn't seem to resist taking quick and violent action each time he tracked Maggie. So why had he apparently watched her for weeks only to vanish? What was his ultimate game?

Sean knew he should warn Maggie about O'Donnell's "visit" to town, but some sense of doubt or fear held him back. Maggie loved him. She was wholly committed to him, to their relationship, and even to this town, but he couldn't be certain that she wouldn't run. And as wrong as it felt, he didn't want to give her the choice, at least not until he had a fully formed plan.

On Saturday, the week following Thanksgiving, Sean and his brothers drove into Columbus for dinner and what Maggie referred to as "brotherly bonding" before the Taylor boys went their separate ways until Christmas. The brothers settled into a backroom booth at a family-owned sports restaurant located in the South-end of Columbus bordering the Historic German Village.

The restaurant was third generation, had the best pizza for three counties and boasted fourteen televisions to watch one's favorite team. Ohio State football or basketball most days between September and March, baseball in the summer and a smattering of games throughout the winter. The walls of the old restaurant were jammed with photos of coaches, players and momentous events. Shoved onto the free space were pennants and mementoes from Ohio colleges and local high schools. The memorabilia included various programs, autographs, and pictures of famous people who had dined at the local establishment — including the three Taylor brothers, made famous by the youngest.

They placed their order: two large pizzas and a pitcher of soda. Then relaxed, chomping on popcorn from the complimentary basket. A basketball game played on the TV and the brothers watched a few minutes in companionable silence. Their drinks were slid wordlessly in front of them and they each filled a glass without breaking their invisible link to the game.

Joey swung his focus from the TV to Sean. "So, what's the full skinny between you and the baker? Anymore visits to Smoochtown?"

"Hey, that's the woman I love, Sprout." Sean kicked his brother in the shin. "Don't you even think about talking about her in any way, shape, or form, other than with the highest respect, got it?"

Mac rolled his eyes. "That doesn't even make sense. I'm not sure it would even qualify as English. When did you turn into a fourteen-year-old girl?"

"I know. Sorry, Joe. There's just a lot going on right now and my brain's a little fried."

"Whatever." Joey popped a kernel of popcorn in his mouth. "I think it's great that you've got someone since you're stuck in Gibson's Run and everything. At least you've got a woman to keep you company." His eyebrows lifted in a quick one-two causing both of his brothers to kick him in the shins. "Hey, I'm just saying, if Sean's happy with the cute little brunette, I'm happy for him."

"Then why didn't you just say that? Why do you always place your stink-foot into your mouth before you say something like a grown human being?" Mac slid the empty red plastic basket toward Joey. "Just for being an idiot, go fill up the popcorn."

Joey let out a sigh, but made his way around the bar to the popcorn machine.

Sean traced the rim of his glass with his finger, watching the slight beads of condensation chase each other down the outer edges. His mind wandered to Maggie. She was baking tonight, an elaborate Christmas cookie order for a party in Upper Arlington on Sunday afternoon.

Jenna was with her, staying after close to help with icing and final details.

He wasn't worried. He had it covered.

He'd spoken with the county sheriff and arranged for an hourly drive by of her shop. He couldn't count on Alvin to stay awake, let alone watch over Maggie. Chuck had been helping him, keeping abreast of flights, buses and trains coming into all parts of Ohio and the surrounding states.

He'd enlisted some contacts with the State Highway Patrol to watch for any suspicious activities on 70W, the most direct route from Maryland. And a contact he'd made years earlier at an NAPO event, who now served with the Baltimore police department, was passing him regular reports on O'Donnell's movements via his ankle monitor.

Sean had done everything he could do within legal limits. But he wanted to do more. If he could lock Maggie up in a safe house until O'Donnell slipped up and landed back in jail, he'd happily do so, but that wasn't the answer.

O'Donnell might not make a move for weeks, months or even years.

The waiting was making Sean edgy.

A well-worn cowboy boot kicked his shin.

"Hey, what was that for?" He stared at his older brother.

Mac leaned back into the booth, stretching his arms along the top of the bench.

"You want to tell me what rabbit is chasing circles in that brain of yours?"

Sean relied on Mac's advice in all areas of his life from applying to the Police Academy to buying his house to his final purchase of his prized drill, but this was different. Maggie trusted Sean with her deepest secrets and he didn't want to break Maggie's confidence just so he could get the advice of his big brother. "Just work stuff. I have a case that's weighing a little heavy, but nothing I can't handle."

"If you say so . . ."

"I do."

A bell clanged twice at the bar and all heads swiveled toward the owner in his bow tie and suspenders. "Hey all, we've got a local boy in here tonight whose been doing some pretty spectacular things up in Minnesota." He slapped Joey on the back. "Welcome our most famous customer of the evening, outfielder, Joe Taylor."

The restaurant erupted into applause and vocal chatter.

Sean looked at Mac and they simultaneously rolled their eyes.

Joey gave his goofy wide grin and took a small slip of paper and a pen from a woman in the sudden crowd surrounding him.

"Guess we won't get our popcorn anytime soon."

"That boy needs an ego setback." Mac stared at his brother. "He's got more talent in his pinky finger than you and I combined, and yet he's not working at his game or giving back in any meaningful way."

"He's still pretty young. He'll figure it out sooner or later."

"I just hope sooner comes before later or we'll have our hands full in about twenty years with a washed-up old ballplayer who talks about the good old days and doesn't have a penny or a meaningful relationship to show for it."

"When did you become a relationship expert?" Sean chuckled.

Mac lifted a single shoulder. "I don't know. In the past few weeks, I've watched Bent's two daughters, as different as a hockey puck and ballet shoes, try and deal with the death of their father and how they are supposed to move forward. Georgie, the one I've known forever, has been taking it all in a stride. Loved her dad. Knew he loved her. Loves the Lord. Sweet kid. But her sister, Charlie, excuse me, Charlotte, is another animal all together. Daddy abandonment issues. A mother who would drive St. Teresa insane. No faith in anything. And a real pain, too. I guess it's all made me appreciate what we had as kids. What we have as brothers, even as adults. I'm thankful for the foundation Mom and Dad gave us — in church, on the farm, in Gibson's Run. I just wish Joe could see that everything he's chasing after is going down a path of heartache and pain."

"I know. I worry about him. He could do so much for so many because he can hit a round ball with a round bat. I just wish he could see it, too." Sean glanced over his shoulder.

Joey was signing autographs, posing for pictures, being adored by dozens of people he didn't and would never know. He appeared happy, but only on the surface.

"Not a lot we can do for him tonight," Sean mused.

Their waitress appeared with two steaming pies and slid them on the table between Mac and Sean. "Here you go, boys. Is there anything else I can get you?"

Sean handed Mac a plate and gave a little head nod toward Joey. "You could whisper to our brother that his food is here."

Mac lifted two square pieces to his plate, the cheese stretching to remain attached to the balance of the pizza. "Or you could not tell him and we could eat all of this deliciousness ourselves."

She chuckled, sliding a pen behind her ear. "I've been serving you three boys since you were barely tall enough to see over the table. You've always made me laugh." She turned and made her way to Joey.

"Eat fast," Mac mumbled through a mouth filled with cheese and pepperoni.

Sean shoved a square slice into his mouth. The hot cheese nearly scalded the roof of his mouth, but the sweet, tender crust and subtle sauce made suffering worth it. "Mmm. I can't believe I forget how good this pizza is."

"Slingshots me back to childhood . . . sweaty baseball games . . . Dad."

". . . Dad . . ." An image, really just a smile, brushed across Sean's mind. His dad always seemed bigger than life, wise and happy. The one word to describe Frank Taylor was . . . wise. He missed his dad, even twenty plus years after his death. Sean wished he could draw on some of that famous Taylor insight now. He wished he could ask him what to do about Maggie.

Joey dropped onto the bench beside Sean with a thud, empty popcorn basket in hand, and shoved a piece of pizza into his mouth in one bite. "Oh, my good-wiss. Id's sooo . . . g-wood," he mumbled through his full mouth.

Mac threw a napkin at him. "Hey, mom taught us all better than that. I don't need to have your spray on my pizza."

Sean felt a wide grin stretch across his face. He loved his brothers. With all of their faults, his included, he wouldn't want to call anyone else on the planet siblings. He knew he could trust them with his life. And Maggie's. Maybe he could get a little Taylor wisdom after all.

"Guys, I need some advice."

20

"Just dot those reindeer with a single chocolate bit for an eye. You can use a toothpick or a long skewer." Maggie called out to Jenna from the back of the walk-in.

"Got it," Jenna yelled over the industrial mixer and the upbeat harmonies of the Broadway soundtrack they'd chosen for the evening. Both agreed that Christmas music was wonderful, but after twelve hours a day, even elves needed a palate cleanser.

Maggie balanced a tray loaded with eggs, butter, and milk as she walked out of the cooler, slamming the door shut with her foot. She weaved between various makeshift cooling stations and slippery smatterings of flour. Mopping tonight would be a chore, but Maggie couldn't remember the last time she was so happy.

Since Thanksgiving evening, she felt free and alive in ways she hadn't since before her parents' deaths. Even when she was

Mary Margaret Sloan — living all over the country — she never shared who she really was for fear of Mitchell finding her. But now that Sean knew everything, she was walking on clouds.

She had her music back, her joy, and she belted out the "la-la-la's" of the musical's upbeat song. She slid the heavy tray onto a side counter, grabbed Jenna's hands, and started to spin her around the messy kitchen as she sang.

Jenna put up a hand, giggling and out of breath. "Whew, I haven't moved that fast since the last time I took an exercise class."

"I just love this song. It's so peppy and ridiculous." She lifted the tray and glanced over her shoulder at the dozens of reindeer Jenna was decorating. "They look as if they'll come to life with a simple snap of a rein and the rolling belly of a chuckling Santa. You'll put me out of a job before you know it."

"I don't know about that, but it's so much fun." Jenna leaned forward and dotted the final eye on the last reindeer on the tray. "How long until these will be dry enough to pack, do you think?"

Maggie heaved the industrial mixing bowl filled with dough for the raspberry short-bread bars and waddled to the last clear counter space. The bowl landed on the table with a muffled thud. "Whew, that will give your arms a workout." She glanced at the cookies and looked at the clock. "Probably about an hour? Do you need to go? I'll be fine to finish up."

Jenna shook her head and wiped her hands against her flour- and butter-caked apron. "I just wanted to run a pizza home to Ty. He's been studying non-stop from the time he gets home until he can barely keep his eyes open. I'd like to take him some dinner, maybe a few cookies, and be back before we pack up all of these delectable goodies."

Maggie flipped the bowl over, tugging the heavy dough onto the stainless steel surface. "I think that sounds wonderful. I'm just going to bake this shortbread crust and mix up the chocolate-chocolate cookies Mr. Paul requested, and then we'll be in the home stretch. Maybe only another hour or two tonight. I can't thank you enough, Jenna. Between you, Cassie, and Robert helping, my stress level has been reduced from a hundred to a steady twenty-seven."

"It's my pleasure. What does it say about me when I am more excited about Christmas break than my students because I get to work at the coolest shop in town?" She yanked off her apron, tossed it in the laundry basket, and lifted her coat from the rack. "I should be back in less than an hour."

"Take your time. You barely get to see Ty. Tell him thank you, again, for me."

"You got it." Jenna flashed her a quick grin. Stopping, she leaned backwards, holding the door open and letting the cool air battle against the billowing heat filling the kitchen. "I almost forgot. Cass said that some guy came by today to see you. Left you an envelope at the front. Cassie said he was super cute in a Clark Kent kind of way. Should the good chief be worried?" Jenna lifted an eyebrow.

"Hardly. Thanks for letting me know. Now, go see your husband." She waved a dough encrusted hand to shoo Jenna out the back door.

"Roger that."

The door slammed shut and Maggie focused on spreading a quarter-inch layer of shortbread in prepped jelly roll pans. A fleeting thought about locking the door chased through her mind, but her hands were covered in sticky globs of butter, sugar, and flour.

She smoothed the surface with a wide off-set spatula, careful not to overwork the shortbread and make it tough. The ovens were pre-set and steaming hot as she slid the four trays in. She flipped the egg timer to ten minutes and washed her hands.

She lifted a clean dishtowel from the rack near the sink and then thrust the door open with her hip and scanned the café counters for an envelope. The space nearly sparkled. Hiring a couple of college kids was a genius plan. They were great. Maybe, they would be interested in working some Saturdays or for the summer? She tossed the dishcloth over her shoulder and shook her head. No need to get ahead of herself. *Get through Christmas, girl. One step at a time.*

She poked around the register, a couple of coffee sleeves, a few customer copies of credit card slips. She would have to remind the kids to throw those in the shredder. But no envelope.

Where could it be? Who would leave her an envelope? Clark Kent good-looking? Probably Marshall Smith. Maggie chuckled. "More Superman than Clark Kent, but whatever."

Poking out from under the register, she saw the tip of white and tugged the thick business envelope into her hand. Nothing was written on the front. The envelope was heavy. She tore off the end and slid a stack of photos into her hand.

Bile burned up her throat as her smiling face stared back at her, glossy and shiny. The picture was of her in her apartment. Not blurred through the window or choppy between blinds, but a clear, high resolution shot of Maggie in her kitchen laughing. She dropped the stack onto the counter and they scattered like leaves in the wind. Her breaths came in small shallow bursts. Every cell in her body was alert, burning. Blood beat in her head. Her heart pounded. Cold sweat beaded across her neck and forehead.

One picture peeked through from the bottom of the pile. She slid it out with two fingers, gently, as if it might burn to touch. Her profile was framed in a thick red heart. The other person in the photo was scratched out with hundreds of small scrapes, wiping the face until only white paper showed. She didn't need to see the face to know it was Sean. The picture was from the night of the Policeman's Ball, the night he'd first kissed her.

The back door. Dropping the photo, she shoved through the swinging door and ran to the heavy metal exit. Slamming the lock into its shaft she leaned against the door.

Run.

She ripped off her apron and threw it on

the counter. She crashed into the long table and barely noticed the tear in her cotton pants as she shot up the back stairs that connected to her apartment on the third floor. The keys in her hands clinked together as she shakily unlocked her door. With a forceful thrust, the warped entry door slammed against the living room wall. She skated through the walkway closet, yanking a full backpack from the shelf and skidded to a stop in her bedroom.

She ripped off her t-shirt and pants and yanked on jeans and a hoodie that were folded in the bag. Jerking the ponytail holder from her head, she wrapped her hair in a tight coil, fitting a tattered ball cap onto her head and grabbed a fleece jacket from the bottom of the bag. She checked the remaining contents quickly: two burn phones, a thousand dollars in cash, a new ID with a matching credit card, a box of auburn hair dye, and keys to a beat-up truck, registered in Indiana, purchased two weeks after Mitchell's release. Zipping the bag closed, she tossed the backpack over her shoulder and skidded to the open door.

"Hello Mary Margaret." The voice, slow, deep with a hint of New England on the edges, caused every hair to stand at attention on the back of her neck. Her body went rigid with the ice running through her veins. Wishing her mind was playing a horrible, awful trick on her, she turned. Her eyes locked on the face that had haunted her nightmares, both sleeping and awake, for a decade. She swallowed, her throat suddenly thick and dry.

He leaned casually against her kitchen island. His gray-and-black tweed jacket topped a crisp white button down shirt. His jeans were dark blue — stiff with the crease of the salesroom floor. He seemed broader, more muscular. His hair was nearly buzzed, not the slick coiffed mane she remembered. A light day's growth of beard shaded the slight pallor of his face, but did little to diminish the sharp angles of his cheekbones. But his eyes were the same. Cold, steely gray. Narrow and piercing from behind wide black framed glasses.

"Mitchell."

A slow sneer curled the corners of his lips. He uncrossed his arms and slithered across the living room until he stood steps from her. He drew a long finger down her cheek. His touch on her was only for a second, and yet she instantly felt the need for a scalding shower. But she didn't move. She knew he wanted her to run. Her running was part of his game, made him punishing her justified.

So she stood, rooted to the ground.

He stretched his arms wide revealing the hint of her tattered navy blue scarf lay loosely around his neck. She swallowed against the lump in her throat.

Leaning toward her, he lifted the strap of her backpack. "Going somewhere?"

She gritted her teeth, mentally coaching the burning acid back down her throat. *Oh, no, Jenna.* How much time did she have until her new friend returned to help her with the Pauls' order? Had she been gone fifteen minutes? Ten? Twenty? She had to get him out of her place. She had to get Mitchell away from her apartment. Away from the bakery. Away from Gibson's Run.

"You know, my dear, you can't run away from me." He leaned forward his breath warm on her cheek. Tobacco laced with his aftershave; the scent curdled in her stomach. "You know you will always be mine."

Yanking her arm away from his grasp, she spun to the door. His hand slammed against the frame. She tugged at the handle but it wouldn't budge. She felt tears pooling behind her lids. *Please God, keep Jenna safe. Let him do whatever he wants to me, but keep Jenna safe. Please don't let him find Sean.*

"Tsk, tsk, my dear . . . you know I hate it

when you run. You make me punish you."

He grabbed her head from behind.

Slam.

Her head bounced off the door frame, her hat dropping to her feet. The metallic flavor of blood filled her mouth, but she knew better than to let a sound escape her lips.

"I do hate to hurt you. But discipline is required when one sins."

Slam.

And the world went black.

21

Sean parked his truck in the rear of the bakery. He and his brothers tumbled out of the front seat.

Mac rubbed his shoulder. "We look like those clowns getting out of a car at the circus."

Sean chuckled and searched through his key ring for the back door's new lock. He slipped the key in and the door swung open.

At the same instant, the smoke alarm screeching assaulted his ears.

The bitter charcoal odor of burning cookies ripped through his senses. "MAGGIE! MAGGIE!"

His brothers were close behind him, their feet pounding.

He wrenched open the oven and smoke billowed out. He grabbed a dishcloth and started swatting at the air. "Can you get that thing off?" He hollered at Mac. He snatched the hot cookie trays from the oven and slammed each one into the sink. Flipping on the water, steam hissed against the hot pan as he yelled again for Maggie. No response.

Joey had run into the café and slipped back through the swinging door. "She's not in there. But these were." He handed Sean a mess of photos.

Each one was of Maggie. Maggie in her kitchen. In the shop. In her bedroom. And there were more, Maggie and Jane. Maggie and Jenna. Maggie and him, not that he saw his own face. It had been scratched out.

He raked a hand through his hair. "He's got her. I know it."

Mac jumped down from the counter with the front of the smoke detector in his hand. "O'Donnell?"

"The crazy dude?" Joey asked.

"Yep. Crazy dude." Sean pulled his phone from his jacket pocket and pressed the speed dial for Chuck Riley.

"Riley."

"Chuck. It's Sean. O'Donnell's got Maggie. I'm sure of it." He scrambled up the back stairs two at a time to Maggie's apartment as he talked. "I don't know how long, not too long, by the look of things. She was supposed to have her assistant working with her tonight. I don't know if she's with them, too."

"Calm down, Taylor. He can't have gotten too far. I'll call his PO and the Baltimore PD. We'll get an APB out for her. You call the Sheriff, yet? Aren't they doing drive-bys?"

"You're right. I'll call them next." He walked through the entry of her apartment. The door was jarred open. Inside he saw little that spoke of a struggle. He scanned the door frame and saw a stream of dried blood down the edge. His stomach clenched. *What did he do to you?*

Riley's voice interrupted his thoughts. "Don't worry about it. I'll take care of the Sheriff. Did you ever track down her god-father?"

Sean stepped over a backpack and a baseball cap, continuing through the closet into Maggie's bedroom. Her work clothes were in a pile on the floor. He dropped to her bed. "Nope. He's a ghost." He wiped his hand down his face.

"Well, based on what you've told me, I think we need to track him down. He could be the key."

"Call O'Donnell's PO and the BPD. They might know how to get in touch with her uncle. He was in on this last arrest." Sean kneaded his neck.

"Got it. Call me if you hear anything."

"Thanks, Chuck."

He slipped his phone back in his jacket pocket. Standing, he lifted her clothes from the floor with a pen from his pocket. The detective training never went away. Her pants were ripped, but no sign of blood or real struggle. She likely changed them in a hurry after she saw the pictures. Dropping the pants and t-shirt back to the floor, he slid open the drawer on her night stand with his pen. Inside lay a Bible and a notepad, but otherwise neat and tidy. He slammed the drawer shut. So much for clean detective work. He walked back into the living room and squatted by the bag. With a handkerchief from his back pocket, he slid open the zipper and stretched the bag wide.

Cash. Hair dye. Clothes.

She was going to run.

He swallowed the lump forming in his throat. She didn't trust him to keep her safe.

And she was right.

"Hey bro," Joey said from the doorway. "Jenna's downstairs, a little freaked out."

Sean shuffled down the stairs, the sound of wailing rushing his ears as they closed in on the kitchen.

"I don't know where she is! Where's

S-sean? H-h-he'll know w-w-what to do."
Jenna slumped on a work stool near the
prep-counter. Her shoulders shook and she
held a dishcloth to her face.

"Hey Jenna," Sean whispered. He patted
her shoulder and crouched to her eye level.
"When's the last time you saw Maggie?"

She lunged for him, wrapping her arms
around his neck. "Oh, Sean, I'm s-s-so
s-sorry. I shouldn't have l-l-left her alone.
But I d-d-didn't know."

"No one knew, Jen. It's not your fault.
But you can help. What do you know about
the pictures, the ones on the counter in the
shop?"

"Nothing." She swiped at the tears on her
cheeks. Sucking in a deep breath she continued, "Cassie, the new girl Maggie hired this
week, said that someone dropped off an
envelope for Maggie."

"Did she give you a description? Anything?"

"Not much. She said he was cute. That he
had a Clark Kent vibe, but Cassie's really
into comics so I didn't think much of it."

"Can you call her? Get her down here?
We can get someone in to do a sketch." But
Sean didn't need a sketch. Clark Kent, at
least an evil version of him, was a fairly ac-
curate description of the photos he'd seen

of O'Donnell.

"Sean." She reached out her hand and placed it on his shoulder. "How much danger is Maggie in? Will he hurt her?"

His phone buzzed in his jacket. He turned from Jenna. "Taylor."

"Hey, Sean." Chuck's gravel voice filled his ear.

"What you got for me?"

"BPD has a BOLO out on O'Donnell. His PO was found unconscious, hog-tied, and wearing the perp's ankle monitor. Clueless how he was able to transfer it. Maggie's uncle was notified. He's already en-route to Ohio. FBI's here. And we got direct calls from Homeland Security. It's like an action movie in the station."

"Can you get CSI down here to make a sweep of the place? Based on the photos he left her, he's got cameras everywhere. I want this by the black-and white book. When we find him, he's not going to slither away with only three years and good behavior."

"Already got a crew coming down from the county. Not Columbus jurisdiction. Like you said, black-and-white book. This guy's not getting off on some messy cop work. Which means you need to be hands off. I know it will be hard, but you've got too much personal interest in this case and any

352

lawyer worth his salt will scream prejudice."

"I hear you. Thanks, Chuck." His phone beeped with an incoming call. "Another call's coming through. I'll be in touch."

He swiped the bar on his phone. "Taylor."

"Well, Chief Taylor, we finally meet." The voice was smooth, cultured, and extremely arrogant.

"O'Donnell."

"I never liked the lack of formality used amongst men. Something has been lost in our culture. A respect for God. A respect for man and what belongs to him. What was endowed to him by God."

"OK, I'll play along, Mr. O'Donnell. Where's Maggie?"

"That vile name. She is Mary Margaret. Not Maggie. That's where all of these little hiccups started. She is mine. You never should have tried to lay claim to her."

"Her name is Maggie and she doesn't belong to anyone. Except God."

Mitchell's snicker sent chills racing down Sean's spine. "Oh, you small-minded, little cop. You don't know anything of God. You are merely a follower, but I am a leader. And Mary Margaret is intended to stand behind me as I lead."

Sean's stomach burned and twisted at the mention of Maggie. *Stay calm, Taylor. Calm.*

Psychos love rage. "Where are you leading her now?"

"Wouldn't you like to know?"

"Why are you calling me?"

"Because you are an obstacle I must overcome to fulfill my destiny. Our destiny."

I'll be an obstacle all right. Not for the first time, he wished he had the resources of his old detective gig. He could track this idiot in a heartbeat. "So, how do you plan to overcome me? The same way you overcame Sam Riegle? And your PO? Who else are you going to overcome, O'Donnell?"

Mitchell's voice dropped, low and steely. "That football player had no right to interfere with God's plan, turning her head from The Mission and all God had designed for us. He was a hindrance. A splinter in her eye. I was required to remove it."

"And I'm another splinter?"

"In a manner of speaking. It seems Mary Margaret is drawn to your type, lower bred, little intelligence, blind faith. But with time, she will see the light. She will return to the fold. She will have no choice but to submit to God's Will."

"How're you gonna remove this splinter, O'Donnell? Why didn't you stick around and wait for me? Seems like you prefer to beat up a little lady, and then run away like a scared dog. You only like to hit those who can't hit back?"

"Discipline is a necessary requirement of faith. Sometimes discipline is painful."

Sean's gut twisted and rolled. He dropped a wall in his mind to keep his burning anger from overtaking him. He needed to remain clear headed. He needed to stay calm for Maggie. "Discipline, huh? Is that what you have waiting for me?"

"We all must make sacrifices for the Lord."

God had nothing to do with this man's sick, twisted obsession. But, Sean would play along. He would do just about anything to keep Maggie safe. "Is Mag . . . Mary Margaret, is she OK?"

"Of course she is safe. She's my intended bride. I am the only one who can truly keep her safe."

"Can I talk to her?"

"Why would I let someone like you, a sinner, someone who is trying to thwart God's Will, talk to my sweet Mary Margaret? Haven't you swayed her enough? Haven't you tried to keep her from God?"

"You're right, O'Donnell. I'm a sinner. And I could definitely use discipline. Why don't you let me talk to Mary Margaret, and then I will do whatever you want. You have my word."

Mitchell let out sigh. "Fine."

There was rustling and a slight clanging through the phone. Sean tried to isolate the noises. Anything to distinguish their setting.

"Sean?" Her voice sounded as if she was talking through a wall.

Relief swelled through his body. "Maggie . . . Maggie, are you OK?"

"I'll be OK. Mitchell will take care of me. Just like always." She coughed and he heard rustling against the phone.

"There, you've talked with her. She's fine."

"You're right. You held up your end, now I'll hold up mine. What do you want?"

"Just you, Chief." He cackled. "Just you."

22

Sean drove the nearly forty-five minute drive to downtown Columbus in under thirty. He'd fought with Mac and Joey about going to O'Donnell alone. They threw the brother card on the table, wanting to fight alongside him. But this wasn't the playground. They weren't going up against the bully who stole Joey's lunch money in the first grade.

O'Donnell was a psychopath. He was unstable and smart. One misstep and he would take Maggie away forever. This was the only way to keep Maggie safe.

He put his car in park, near the corner of 4th and Main streets, following O'Donnell's directions. O'Donnell had instructed Sean to come alone and unarmed. Sean didn't have a gun on him, but he wasn't unarmed.

The city was quiet at this early hour on Sunday morning, not even a bus or a cab running the streets.

Sean made his way up Main Street to the Southern Theatre. The building was over a hundred years old and a landmark in Columbus. Sean walked around the corner, his eyes needing time to adjust to the sudden darkness. He looked up to his left. The security light was broken. The crush of glass under a foot drew his attention.

Smack.

Stars filled his vision as he dropped to his knees. And as if a curtain dropped, the world was draped in black.

His breath was slow as awareness seeped into his body. His jaw felt as if he'd gone three rounds with the heavyweight champ. His eyelids lids were weighed down with invisible rocks and a thousand needles were sticking his hands.

Blinking against the weight, he tried to lift his head but the room tilted. Nausea rolled and he sucked in a deep breath to suppress his precious pizza from performing an Act Two. The ramrod-straight chairback burrowed into his shoulder blades. He willed his fingers to move, but his whole arm was immobile. He couldn't see them, but he guessed his arms and hands were bound. His ankles were tied, each to a separate leg. Not surprising.

"Well, Chief Taylor, you've finally decided to join us." The voice echoed in the old theatre, but it sounded as if it was coming from behind him.

Sean lifted his head slightly and felt the rough burning of a rope around his neck. No sudden movements, Taylor. "Thanks for having me." His voice sounded sandy and strained to his own ears.

"Wouldn't have it any other way. My love needs to close the chapter on that horrid little town of yours. Can't put the nail in the coffin without the body in the box, so to speak."

"So to speak," Sean mumbled. "Where's Maggie?"

"Oh, I am sorry. You can't see her where you're sitting, can you? What an awful host I am. You must have a good view for the performance."

O'Donnell was beside him in seconds. He tilted Sean's chair backward, dragging him to the center stage. The chair scraped the century old wood planks and jerked to a stop, throwing him forward. His neck thrust against the rope. He gasped for air and tried to lean back to relieve the tension.

O'Donnell's hands tightened around his windpipe, his cheek pressed against Sean's. "Isn't she beautiful? My Mary Margaret."

His voice was low; his breath was steamy and laced with the acrid aroma of tobacco and nicotine.

Sean remained silent. His gaze shifted to the wrought-iron bed set in the middle of the stage; a vase of white lilies rested on a small table just to the right. Maggie was dressed in a white slip, a blond wig hiding her beautiful hair. Her arms and legs were tied to the bed posts. He couldn't tell if she was conscious. She wasn't moving but he could see the shallow rise and fall of her chest. *She's breathing. That's good. Need the breathing. Helps with the living.*

O'Donnell walked to the bed and drew his hand slowly down her body.

"Get your hands off of her!" Rage exploded through Sean.

O'Donnell spun, his eyes dancing with anger. "You dare to tell me not to touch her? You, who had your filthy sinner hands all over my gift." Closing the distance between them in a step, he grabbed Sean's jaw in his hand and squeezed, shooting bullets of pain ricocheting through Sean's body. "You have no right to her, and yet you presume to think you can warn me not to touch what is mine." He shoved Sean and the chair over with a flick of his wrist.

Sean's head slammed against the stage

and he felt the crack of wood near his back. With a wiggle he felt his ankles move freely.

Sean crashed to the floor and Maggie's heart dropped. "Don't hurt him, Mitchell, please." Her voice was barely a whisper as she tried to yell.

Mitchell's footsteps were quick and heavy, closing the distance to the bed. "Why would you care about him?" He screeched, his spit hitting her face with each word. "He's nothing. Nobody. You are more than he'll ever be. Don't let yourself be swayed into sin, not again, Mary Margaret. There may be no saving you from it." He sat on the edge of the bed; the frame creaked from the added weight. He reached out to touch her cheek.

Maggie jerked, tugging at the ropes binding her wrists and ankles, jostling the bed.

Mitchell clamped a hand on either shoulder.

She clenched her eyes shut as he lowered his face to hers.

"Stop," his voice was low and controlled. "Mary Margaret, you must stop resisting your calling. You've turned your back on me for the last time. You will give up this life. Return to me. Return to God."

Her eyelids fluttered open. She prayed to God for strength. "I never turned my back on God. And He never turned His back on me. You are the one who can't hear God anymore, Mitchell."

He swung quickly, backhanding her.

Blood pooled in her mouth, tasting like sea water and metal. Reflexive tears raced down her cheeks. She shut her eyes as he raised his hand to strike her again.

Whack! Thud.

But nothing. No slap. No burning sensation on her cheek. The sound was there, but she didn't feel anything. She opened her eyes.

Sean towered over a crumpled Mitchell, a rail from the chair clutched in his hands. His wrists were still bound, but his feet were free. He dropped the spindle to the stage with a clatter. Sitting on the bed, his hands reached to Maggie's wrist to unbind it. "Are you OK?"

Tears cascaded down her cheeks. The moment both her arms were free, she lunged, wrapping her arm around Sean's middle and sinking into his protective warmth.

"Do you mind helping me out?" He chuckled and shrugged his bound arms trapped between their bodies.

She swiped at her tears and smiled. "Of course." She quickly undid the duct tape around his wrists.

"Oww." He rubbed his skin before reaching to untie her ankles.

"You complain about that?" She rested her chin on his back.

He moved to her second leg. "Well, if you hadn't been so rough yanking on that tape."

With both her legs free, she slid her knees under her and knelt in front of Sean. Her fingers brushed his temple where blood had clotted. Drawing her hand down his cheek, she barely brushed the forming angry red and blue bruise from Mitchell's blow. Fresh tears streamed down her face. "I'm so sorry. This is all my fault."

He drew her gently into his embrace. "It's no one's fault, Maggie."

"She's right." The voice was deep and groaning. "It *is* her fault."

Sean was ripped from her arms and tossed across the stage like a pillow.

Maggie scurried off the bed toward Sean. Her body screamed from the pain shooting through her head and down her back. "Don't hurt him, Mitchell. You want me, not him!"

Mitchell continued to stalk his prey.

She looked around the room for a weapon, anything she could use to stop him from hurting Sean. *Father, please help me. Please help us. I know You are here. Please help us.*

Something glittered. Lying just steps from her feet was a camping knife. Mitchell's knife. She recognized it from previous experience.

He once bragged that he never left home without the multi-faceted tool — always prepared.

She reached for it and popped the blade. "Mitchell. . . ." she yelled, her voice reverberating off the high ceilings. "Mitchell, you don't want Sean. You want to punish me. I've been a very bad student. Haven't followed any of your rules. Come and get me." Ignoring the tremors of pain rolling through her body, she forced herself to stand — feet apart — her hands clasped behind her back, clutching the hidden knife.

Mitchell pivoted. His steps wobbled as he closed the gap between them.

Maggie slid back two steps, her bare heels grazing the edge of the stage to the orchestra pit, a dark chasm behind her.

"Why do you always have to make everything so difficult, Mary Margaret?" He tilted his head to the side. "Hmm . . . first with that football player, and then forcing me to chase you all over the country. And then prison?" He stopped just in front of her. "Prison is not a place for someone like me." He grabbed her jaw in one hand, dragging her to him. "And you sent me there." He pressed his cheek to hers. "But I've forgiven you. I've thought of myself as Paul, a great leader who was falsely imprisoned for his cause."

The wretched smell of tobacco burned a path through her nostrils. His breath ran hot against her cheek. A wave of nausea rippled through her belly. The knife in her hand was cool in her grasp.

Sean stood and staggered as he began to move toward them.

"No . . ." She shouted through clenched teeth.

Mitchell's hand gripped tighter and she feared her jaw would break, but she held still.

He lifted her to her tiptoes.

If she moved, even a fraction of an inch, her feet would dangle over the edge.

His eyes, nearly black, bored into hers. "You dare to tell me no? When will you learn? I am the leader. You are the follower. You do what I tell you. Only God can tell me what to do."

"Well, God told me to listen to Him." She flipped the knife into her right hand. "And just say NO!" She thrust her hand forward, the knife grazed the side of his waist.

His face flashed shock as his hands released her and went to his belly.

She stumbled out of his reach.

Mitchell staggered forward, reaching for her. He tripped into the pit, crashing against cymbals and other instruments.

The main door slammed open and police poured into the great auditorium.

She let out a scream as hands reached from behind.

"Whoa," Sean whispered in her ear. "Just me Maggie-girl. It's just me."

She turned to him and clasped her arms around his waist. The real tears started. Her body shook with the release. She cried for Sean. For Sam. For the years of running. For Mary Margaret. And she cried for Mitchell, for the man she'd once known.

Heavy footsteps tromped onto the stage, shaking the floor beneath her feet, but she didn't release her hold on Sean.

"He's down here. He's still breathing. Get the medic." The shout echoed off the walls.

She sucked in a quick breath and stepped back from Sean. "He's alive?"

"Seems like."

"Good. Good. That's good . . ."

"Sweet girl?" She turned and saw her Uncle Jack running across the stage.

"Uncle Jack!" Maggie nearly leaped into his arms. "Uncle Jack, I am so sorry. I thought it would be OK. I really thought I would finally be safe."

He tugged the wig off her head and stroked her hair, lightly patting her back. "You did everything right. Including, unless I missed my guess, falling in love with a pretty good investigator."

"I don't know what you mean."

"Your young man, that Chief Taylor." He pointed to Sean who was talking with a policeman. "He orchestrated this whole bust."

Sean winked with a quick grin. Her champion.

Shaking her head she turned back to her uncle. "But I don't understand. He didn't even know about Mitchell until a week ago. Didn't know I was taken until he called him."

"Sweet girl, that young man of yours has been moving heaven and earth to protect you since you finally shared your story with him. He had every local law enforcement agency alerted to the potential danger. Even hired some private security firm to stake out the local theatres for the past week. He's been trying to track me down, not that he ever could, much to the chagrin of my superiors. He covered every base to keep you safe. He loves you that much. I think

God finally heard your prayer."

"Which prayer is that?"

He tweaked her nose with his finger. "Your prayer to find pure love, love with no strings attached, I recall you praying for that one thing all those years ago . . . when you didn't think I was listening at your door."

"But I haven't prayed for love for years."

"Doesn't mean God wasn't listening the first time you asked. He just works in His own time."

With a soft grin on her lips, she wrapped her arms tighter around her uncle, and whispered, "Thank you."

"No need to thank me."

"Oh, I wasn't thanking you, Uncle Jack. I was thanking Him."

The EMT's loaded O'Donnell onto a stretcher.

Part of Sean wished they were zipping him into a bag instead of tightening safety straps across his body, but he was actually grateful the psychopath survived.

Maggie would gain justice without having to endure the guilt that would likely have buried her. God would have forgiven her, but he knew his sweet Maggie may have never found peace in forgiving herself.

He kneaded the knot at his neck, twisting

his head toward Maggie and her uncle. Her arm was looped around his waist and her head rested on his broad shoulder. He couldn't hear what they were saying to each other, but Sean's heart steadied at seeing her in the safety of her Uncle Jack's arms.

Pain radiated through his body as a large palm thumped his back. He pivoted on his heel and felt a grin stretch his cheeks. "Man," he smacked Chuck on the shoulder. "I can't thank you enough. Your timing was perfect."

"Of course it was. Always is."

"And so modest." Sean chuckled.

"You know it, brother." Riley shoved his hands in his front pockets. "Couple of D's are going to need to talk to your girl." He looked over his shoulder. "You think she'll be up for it tonight?"

Sean raised his focus to Maggie and her uncle as they meandered across the stage in his direction. "You can ask her yourself."

"She's a pretty tough woman. Caught a look at the slice she put in O'Donnell." He let out a low whistle. "You definitely don't want to rile her up."

Maggie closed the distance between them. Stepping out of her uncle's protective grip, she didn't hesitate as she walked into his waiting embrace. He hugged her tightly, ignoring his bruised body. His chin rested on her head.

"I don't know," he said lifting his eyes to Chuck with a wink. "It's worked out pretty well for me, so far. Wouldn't want to spoil my average." Lifting her chin with a touch of his finger, he locked his gaze with Maggie's. "And besides, making her mad keeps my life pretty interesting."

23

Three days before Christmas, Maggie was hustling between boxing cookies and the final touches on a cake for Sissy Jenkins. The cake was a thank-you-and-sorry-I-brought-a-psycho-stalker-to-town gesture. In a thousand lifetimes, she couldn't have imagined being grateful to Sissy and her binocular-snooping behavior. But without her, Maggie would likely be dead or worse. Instead, she only had minor traces of her final encounter with Mitchell. Her stiffness was gone within a week. Her bruises had nearly all faded. Sleeping without nightmares would come. She just needed to be patient.

She closed the lid of the fourth box of cookies for the Smith brothers' office Christmas party and glanced at the clock. Fifteen minutes to spare. She loaded a carrier and lugged the container through the swinging door.

The chatter of happy customers in varying states of eating and drinking warmed Maggie's heart. Everyone in town had heard the story within a week of Mitchell's arrest, but not one person had come to gawk or ask questions. They'd shown concern, but life returned to normal in Gibson's Run.

Maggie shoved the carrier on the back counter.

Jenna was ringing up a sale. "Thank you Mrs. Henderson. Merry Christmas. Now that you know what you like, I hope you stop by again in the New Year." As the bell jingled with Mrs. Henderson's exit, Jenna turned to Maggie. "That woman can't make up her mind. She asked to sample four different cookies, two coffees, and a brownie before she decided all she wanted was a hot tea . . . to go."

"She pretty much does that once a month and always on a Wednesday. I think she believes if she wears a different hat, I won't recognize her. But I figure, I'll take a few freebies if we get afternoons like this one." She swept her hands toward the café.

Every table was full and most had more than empty coffee cups.

"I know. You are right."

Maggie squeezed her shoulders. "I think we're doing just fine. Are you sure you're able to close up tonight? I need to get ready for the Greys's Christmas party."

"Not a problem. Shop closes at five on Wednesdays. Ty and I are doing our own little Christmas tonight before the swirl of family Christmas over the weekend."

"Thanks. I really appreciate it." She glanced at her watch. "Marshall should be here any minute for the cookies. He's already paid. I'll be upstairs if you need anything. Just leave the dishes for me. I will get them in the morning."

"Leave it to me. Your trusty assistant." She kissed Maggie on the cheek. "I'm just so happy you are safe."

"Thanks Jen."

Two hours later, Maggie tied a navy blue grosgrain ribbon around a small box papered in solid white. The package held her great-grandfather's pocket watch, one of her only remnants from her childhood. She wanted to give the treasure to Sean tonight as a pre-Christmas gift. She dropped the box in her tiny shoulder purse and laid the bag on her island. She walked to the bathroom for one last look.

Draped in a full-skirted, midnight blue cocktail dress, she finally looked more woman than baker. The dress was covered with a gauzy layer of matching dyed lace and accented with a velvet belt encrusted with petite rhinestones. She smoothed the front of her dress and patted the top of her wild hair twisted into a side ponytail. A knock on her front door caused a flock of butterflies to fill her belly. She shuffled to the door, her heels threatening to cause a stumble. She opened the door and her breath caught in her chest.

Sean was leaning against the doorframe dressed in a dark navy suit with a crisp white shirt, his navy overcoat folded over his arm. Only a faint yellow stain remained on his cheek, the final physical reminder of that awful night. A slow grin stretched across his face. "You clean up well, McKitrick."

She stepped forward and brushed her lips across his. Running her fingers under his lapels, she settled back. "You don't look half bad yourself, Taylor." She turned. "Let me just grab my coat and purse. I'm so excited. I haven't been to a Christmas party since my parents were alive. Their friends used to have one every year." She slipped on her coat, wrapped her blue scarf around her neck, and slid her bag on her shoulder. Glancing down at her dress, she laughed. "But certainly nothing this fancy."

"Well, Bits likes to go overboard." He extended his arm to her. "Shall we?"

Linking her arm through his, she shut the door behind them. "Let's do it."

His brows drew together. "No lock?"

She squeezed his arms. "Not tonight. I think tonight we will be free of all locks."

The party was smaller than she thought. She lifted sparkling water to her lips and glanced around the room. Less than a dozen people were in attendance, Jane and Lindy, Millie and Jason, Bitsy and Henry, Molly and Jake, all tight within her group. Her group. Who would have thought that Maggie McKitrick, formerly Mary Margaret Sloan, would ever have a group? She wished her Uncle Jack could be here.

Mitchell was in custody, his injuries were not life-threatening, so he was able to be moved to a prison hospital.

There was no reason to hide.

But Jack was working on some top secret project, which was pretty much the story of her life, and said he didn't think he could make it in for the holidays.

Despite the missing people, the evening had been delightful. Bitsy and her daughters created a feast. Maggie wasn't sure she would be able to eat again for a week, or at least until she baked the ham for Sean and his brothers on Saturday.

At the moment, the group was passing around Millie's first ultrasound photos.

Life was pretty perfect.

Sean slipped his arm around her waist and whispered in her ear. "Having fun?"

Nodding, she laid her head on his shoulder. "It's been a wonderful evening."

He kissed her temple. "I think it might get just a little bit better."

As she lifted her head to ask, why, the lights shut off. A door opened. Cold breeze blew in and shuffling and whispering could be heard. What was happening?

The room slowly grew brighter. One by one, candles filled the space held by dozens of friends from town, from church, from her new life.

Maggie stepped from Sean's embrace as she watched his brothers, Jenna, Ty and her Uncle Jack round out the assembly. She looked over her shoulder. "I don't understand."

"It's for you." Sean kissed her on the cheek. "Everyone wanted to join in the celebration."

Her brows drew together as she felt a light hand on her shoulder. She turned to a smiling Jane who handed her a candle. "I was talking with Sean after . . . well, after everything that happened and we realized you've never had a celebration of your new you. And we thought there couldn't be a better time than Christmas, a time when the whole world celebrates the start of the Savior's life."

The tears flowed down her cheeks as she clutched the candle in her hand. Swallowing deeply, the butterflies from earlier started a new dance, but not from nerves or excitement, they were dancing a waltz of love.

"OK, everyone," Bitsy yelled from the back of the crowd. "We are moving this little shindig outside before you burn down this lovely house."

People began to pour out of the French doors and onto the patio toward the back lawn.

"Here," Sean said from behind her. "It's a little chilly out there. You might need this."

He held open her coat. She slid her arms into the sleeves, gently transferring the candle from hand to hand. He secured the belt at her waist and knotted the scarf at her neck, before picking up his own candle. "Shall we?"

They followed the crowd into the backyard. Dozens of Chinese sky lanterns peppered the yard. Each person selected a lantern and lit a small fuel source at the base with their candle.

Jane handed Maggie and Sean the final two. Jane beamed as she lit her lantern and released it into the air. "Maggie, I met you just a year ago, but I feel as if we have known each other a lifetime. I am amazed by your spirit and your grace. God has granted you love," she said, looking at Sean and back to Maggie. "And He has granted you new life. Tonight we celebrate both."

One at a time, the lanterns were released, trailing each other in an exquisite parade across the sky.

Sean lit his lantern and turned to her as he waited for the heat to build. "Maggie-girl, I wasn't the nicest to you when you first moved to town."

The group rolled in a chuckle and the mayor hollered from the back. "Well, that's certainly an understatement."

"True enough. But even from that first meeting I knew you were someone special. That somehow, in the midst of all of your nagging, there was a gift from God wrapped tight by a beautiful bow." He released his lantern and turned back to face her. "So tonight, when we celebrate the gift of Maggie McKitrick in our lives, I would like you to grant me the great honor of changing your name one last time." Drawing a small box from his jacket, he knelt on one knee. "Maggie, will you marry me?" He cracked the lid on the velvet box and revealed an antique-set diamond in white gold.

She wrapped her arms around him, the candle and the lantern forgotten.

"Well, don't burn him, Maggie," Millie yelled. "A simple yes or no will do."

Maggie laughed and nodded her head. "Yes."

Sean stood straight up, Maggie's arms still linked around his neck, her toes barely touching the ground. He leaned down and kissed her with an aching tenderness that rolled a wave of heat through her body.

Her feet slid to the ground when he released her, candle and lantern still in hand. The tears that started earlier grew in abundance, chilling her cheeks as they chased frosty paths down her face. She lit her lantern and spoke surprisingly solid and steady. "This town, all of you, have been my refuge. A place to call home. You've given me the freedom to be me again. A gift I wasn't sure would ever be mine. Thank you for loving me enough that I could fall in love. Both with Sean —" she said with a smile over her shoulder, "— and with Maggie." She glanced around the backyard, taking in the people who had transformed her life in a few short months. "Ten years ago, this was a life I never would have dreamed of having. But now, I can't imagine anywhere else I would rather be. Thank you." She released her lantern and watched it trail behind the others.

Sean wrapped his arms around her, sliding the ring on her finger with subtle ease. "It looks like they could go all the way to heaven."

"They might make it there, but I've already had a glimpse tonight. A small peek of the love that must be rooted in the grace of the Father." She turned in his arms and brushed a light kiss on his lips. Her champion.

"I love you, Mr. Taylor."

"I love you, Miss McKitrick."

She closed her eyes and rested her head against his shoulder. *I love you, Lord. Thank You for loving me more.*

ABOUT THE AUTHOR

C.E. Hilbert lives in Columbus, Ohio and works in the fashion industry by day and writes romantic fiction by night.